the BROKEN HEART of ARELIUM

WAR OF THE TWELVE
BOOK ONE

· ALEX ROBINS ·

Cover and Interior Design by Damonza
Maps by Alex Robins

ISBN 978-2-9576580-0-8 (e-book)
ISBN 978-2-9576580-1-5 (paperback)

Published by Bradypus Publishing
4 rue du vigneau - 49380 Bellevigne en Layon
Dépôt légal : mars 2021

www.warofthetwelve.com

For Mum & Dad

Life is a journey of highs and lows, of mountain peaks and sunken valleys

Thank you for always helping me find that winding road back to the top

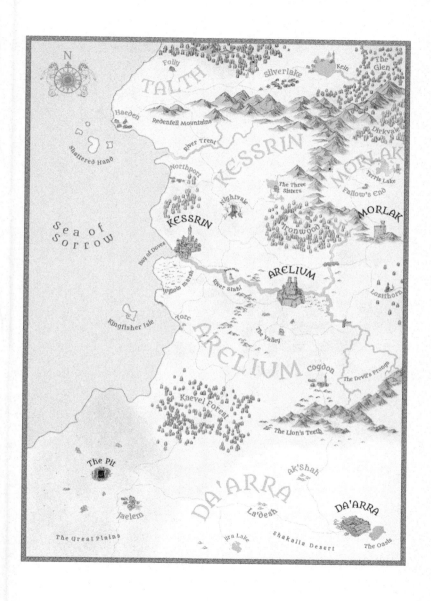

TABLE OF CONTENTS

CHAPTER 1
THE PIT

"Fear. Insidious and tenacious. It worms its way into the body of a man and wraps its cold tendrils around his slowly-beating heart. And what do we fear above all else? Is it the shadow by the door? The cry for help we hear in the night? The whispered echoes that keep us from sleep? No, our greatest fear is what we cannot comprehend, what we do not understand. The fear of the unknown."

BRACHYURA, FOURTH OF THE TWELVE, 12 AT

⤜

THE WIND CAME screaming up from the Pit like a demon, rolling in chilling waves over the crumbling stone battlements and down into the plains below. Flames flickered in wrought-iron lanterns hanging from metal poles at intervals along the wall, casting strange shadows across the faces of the Old Guard manning their posts. With a resounding crack, one of the poles was torn free and fell spinning into the Pit, the light from the lantern dwindling to a spark before disappearing from sight.

"Damn," mumbled Reed.

He had been standing only a few feet away and a small chip of stone had hit his cheek when the metal rod fell. He wiped away the trickle of blood with a gloved hand and pulled his threadbare vermilion cloak closer to his body in an effort to keep warm. His leather mask had been knocked down from his nose and the wind was not only cold but stank of sulphur and death, a nauseous mixture of rotten eggs and decaying flesh that crawled its way into his mouth and nostrils, making him gag. Eyes watering, Reed pulled the mask tightly around his bearded lower face and stared out over the Pit.

The Pit. An enormous circular crater in the earth, as deep as it was wide. It stretched out from the base of the wall to the horizon like a lake of smooth, slick tar. The sun had set many hours ago, and murky clouds obscured all but the brightest stars, making it impossible to discern where the Pit ended and the night sky began. No lights, no movement, only an endless gaping maw of crushing blackness.

Men of the Old Guard became surly and irritable staring into the inky depths day after day, night after night. It sapped the light and energy from even the sturdiest of watchmen and left them pale-faced, hollow-eyed, and shivering from the cold.

The chasm was surrounded on all sides by a twelve-foot-high ancient stone wall. Squat towers sprouted like forest mushrooms along the ramparts, topped with signal fires and filled with stacked faggots of dry wood to keep the lanterns burning day and night. On one of the towers, the tattered remains of a flag depicting a red sun on a field of gold flapped limply in the wind. A paved pathway, wide enough for two or three men, ran the entire length of the wall: miles and miles of mouldy, slippery slabs of weathered stone. And Reed had walked along it all.

The Old Guard existed for one immutable duty: to maintain and defend the wall. Once several hundred strong, it had been looked upon with honour and respect, a regiment of veteran soldiers resplendent in their uniforms of red and grey. But the years passed, and the Pit remained dark and silent. Vigilance gave way to monotony. Their numbers dwindled. Some retired, others left to carry out menial tasks and never returned, or chose family over celibacy. Those who remained were not nearly enough to keep the wall intact and, much like their faded cloaks and rusting spears, the Old Guard was becoming a dull echo of its former glory.

Attempts were made to recruit new members from the several dozen or so villages eking out a meagre living on the windswept plains close to the Pit. Most of the hamlets were nothing more than a haphazard jumble of wattle huts, huddled close together to offer some comfort from the howling gales that raced across the flatlands and raked the walls with grit and dirt. Only the largest of the villages, Jaelem, had a few stone buildings and a wooden palisade to keep out the worst of the dust.

Reed remembered the day the recruiter had come to Jaelem, the memory forever etched in his mind despite the years that had passed since. He had been helping his ailing mother gut and clean silvery fish from the nearby lake when the goatskin drum had sounded loudly over the whistling wind, calling villagers to the public square.

The recruiter was a large, barrel-chested brute of a man with a bushy black beard and two rotten front teeth. He had been dressed in a frayed leather surcoat emblazoned with a stylised red sun, and his discoloured vermilion cloak had billowed out behind him like the sputtering embers of a dying flame.

He had spoken at length in a booming voice about the Old Guard; the watchers, the protectors, the guardians of the wall. "The Old Guard is the light against the darkness," he had intoned. "The burning sun against the cold of night, the mighty shield against the unknown."

Reed had been enraptured and had left with the recruiter the next day, promising his mother to return soon. It was the last time he had seen her alive; she had died from a severe case of winter fever a few years later, tired and alone. And Merad Reed had spent the rest of his youth and a large portion of his middle years walking the wall.

A buzzard screeched somewhere out over the Pit, startling Reed out of his melancholy thoughts. He looked up to see Hode, his fellow watchman, slowly approaching along the ramparts, a mug of something hot and steaming in each hand, a spear slung across his back. Hode edged carefully around a mound of fallen rubble and proffered one of the tin mugs to Reed, who accepted it gratefully.

"By the Twelve, it's cold tonight!" said Hode, the steam from the mug obscuring his pudgy face and thinning fair hair. "I can barely feel my toes after an hour standing around out here."

Reed grunted noncommittally and eyed the contents of the mug warily. It looked palatable enough: some sort of stringy meat stew and the odd carrot. As he watched, a morsel of gristle rose to the surface and floated there forlornly.

"It's like this every night, Hode," he replied irritably. "We haul ourselves up the one hundred and twenty steps from the barracks an hour before sunset, freeze our members off for eight hours straight, then shamble back down and drink ourselves to sleep until we do it all again. It's always cold, it's always windy, and nothing ever happens." Reed's scraggly beard was beginning to itch terribly under his mask.

"Now that's wrong for a start," said Hode cheerfully. "Remember last autumn? When the second Southern Tower split apart and we lost two men to the Pit? It took us weeks to clear the debris and consolidate the tower again. Captain Yusifel said he would send a request to the Council, petitioning for a team of engineers to come down here and shore up some of the other dangerous parts of the wall."

"That was months ago, no one has come, nothing has changed," said Reed, gesturing with one gloved hand at the heap of rubble Hode had skirted around just moments before. He lowered his mask, took a mouthful of stew and grimaced. It was still piping hot despite the cold and tasted awful. He swallowed with difficulty, then shrugged and took another swig.

The buzzard screeched again over the wind, more insistent this time, and both men looked up, scanning the horizon for some sign of the bird.

"You're wrong again, you know," continued Hode, returning to his stew. "Someone *has* come to see us, I heard it from one of the men up on the third Northern Tower; a visitor rode down directly from Arelium."

Arelium was the provincial capital, a week's ride away for someone on a fast horse. Reed looked at Hode sceptically.

"You heard this from who exactly? Not Kohl I hope, that peg-legged old miser is missing more than just his leg!" He tapped a finger on his forehead emphatically.

"No, not Kohl." Hode frowned. "One of the younger recruits, the lad who helped me fix my boot when I tore it open on a loose stone last week, remember? Anyway, he said that it was some kind of knight, maybe even a Knight of the Twelve, sent to help us guard the wall and maybe—"

Reed cut him off. "Guard the wall? Do you really still believe that? After all this time? Guard against what exactly? Old age? Nigh on twenty years I've been up here. I've seen the twenty towers a thousand times. I've seen the Pit from every conceivable angle. I've maintained the signal fires and the lanterns, washed my cloak and polished my spear, scrubbed my leathers and brushed my boots. And guess what? The only thing I've got to show for it is a handful of stray grey hairs. Do you know how many times I've used my spear for anything more than stabbing a few straw bales in the practice yard? Never! Not once! None of us has seen anything other than wild animals up here, even Kohl who is older than the two of us put together! And a Knight of the Twelve? Why would any of them come down here where all there is to do is look out into nothing but the DAMNED PIT?"

Reed paused for breath, realising he had shouted the last few words. He shook his head and smiled sadly, then looked up at Hode who was staring at him wide-eyed, small drops of stew escaping his open mouth and running down his chin to pool in the leather mask hanging around his neck.

"Sorry, Hode," said Reed slowly. "You're right. It is cold,

and cloudy too. Damn Pit is messing with my head again, didn't mean to raise my voice like that. Thanks for the stew, by the way. Where did you manage to get hold of fresh meat? Storemaster said we were on dry rations 'til next full moon!"

Hode sipped his stew thoughtfully.

"So, you know I was on resupply duty yesterday for the third Southern Tower? Well, I was restocking the wood for the beacon and I found a couple of big black rats hiding in a corner. Got 'em both with the butt of my spear and took them to the storemaster who offered to stew them for a couple of pennies and a mug or two of ale for his men. Pretty good deal I thought!"

Reed scratched his itching beard and looked down at the stew. What he had thought was a carrot turned out to be a small spindly rat's tail, bobbing merrily among the bone and gristle.

He opened his mouth to reply but, before he could say anything, something fell from the sky and slammed into the rampart with a wet smack. It was the buzzard, its headless body rent by two large gashes oozing blood, its wings reduced to a tangled mess of feather and bone.

A strangled cry echoed further down the wall and, for the first and last time in his life, Reed saw the signal fire atop a distant tower roar to life in an explosive burst of smoke and flame.

❧

The beacon burned brightly in the night sky and was soon joined by another, then another, until a half-dozen fires lit up the horizon to the east like a colony of faraway fireflies.

Reed turned to Hode who had dropped his mug and unslung his spear from behind his back. He stood shivering, breathing fast, eyes darting left and right along the ramparts, stopping briefly to linger on the broken body of the buzzard.

"What now?" asked the stocky watchman, pointing at the pinpricks of light in the distance. "How far away do you think they are? You reckon we should do something?"

Both men knew what the beacons meant: that section of the wall was in danger and needed help. The Old Guard may only be a faint shadow of its past self but one thing would never change: the unspoken bond between guardsmen, ties that linked these men together as strong as any family. A family that could count on one another and protected its own.

"We can't be more than a half-hour away at most," replied Reed, pulling up his leather mask and grabbing his spear. "We have to go."

Another far-off cry echoed through the night, a wail of pain and anger that left little to the imagination.

His choice made, Reed started moving in the direction of the sound, not waiting to see if Hode followed. He could feel his heart beating wildly in his chest, a dull thumping rising up towards his throat, threatening to smother him. He forced himself to breathe out slowly and gripped the haft of his spear, its weight giving him some small comfort. Hode came up on his left, protecting Reed's weaker side with his own weapon.

For several minutes they crept slowly forwards, spears out, cloaks flapping in the wind. They reached the closest tower and found three other guardsmen milling around its base, lanky young recruits new to the wall. One had a surcoat several sizes too big that fell nearly to his ankles, another had lost his spear and was left with a dagger, which he brandished at Reed and Hode.

"W-w-who goes there?" stammered the youth, barely out of puberty, his voice wavering up and down like a poorly-tuned harp.

Reed battered the knife away hard enough to knock it out of the young recruit's hand and the man scurried to retrieve it, cursing profusely.

"Reed?" said the youth with the oversized surcoat. Reed vaguely remembered his name was Kellen. The recruit had removed his mask, revealing a few tufts of hair clumped around a spotty chin in a poor attempt at a beard.

Reed sighed. This was all some sort of karmic joke. After years of complaining, he had finally got what he wanted: danger on the wall and a chance to lead men into battle as a proud member of the Old Guard. He realised now that he had never been more wrong in his life. Repetition and boredom were terrible things, but safe and comforting. And in an instant, all that had been taken away from him.

What to do now? Fight or flight? Hode wouldn't be much help, the man might be good at restocking the wood and braining rats, but using his spear against anything bigger probably wouldn't end well.

Reed glanced over to where the fair-haired guardsman was leaning against the inner face of the tower, fiddling with the straps of his mask in an attempt to wrap it back around his nose and mouth. Hode felt Reed's gaze on him and looked up with a small smile and a shrug before returning to the task at hand.

"Reed? What now?" repeated Kellen.

"Give me a minute!" Reed snapped back and squinted down the ramparts towards where the signal fires still burned brightly. Silence had returned to the wall, a quiet and calm so absolute it made Reed wonder if those two painful screams had been a trick of the wind. But then who had lit the beacons, and why? He ran a hand through his greying hair and made a decision.

"Looks like the beacons are spread among the Eastern Towers," he said. "The eastern barracks will be close by, with Captain Yusifel and the night reserve. We'll proceed along this stretch of wall here till we get to the barracks and inform Yusifel of the situation. Either some idiot has been playing with a tinder block or there's something more serious going on. Either way, Yusifel will want to know. Hode and I will lead, Kellen you're behind me with your friend who doesn't know how to hold a knife—"

"Iden, Sir," piped up the young guardsman with the dagger.

"Right you are, Iden," said Reed. "You stay close to Kellen and Freckles here." He gestured to the third man, as tall and thin as his friends with a shock of ginger hair and a smattering of freckles over his wide nose.

Freckles gave him a sour look but said nothing and took up position behind the others. Reed set them moving with a curt nod and they advanced briskly down the ramparts, scanning the way ahead with wary eyes. The towers drew closer and closer, the beacons no longer pinpricks of light in the distance but the cone-shaped flickering of large bonfires, smoke curling up from the apex to mingle with the dark grey clouds hanging heavily in the night sky.

Reed reckoned they couldn't be more than four or

five hundred yards away from the stone steps that would lead them down off the wall towards the eastern barracks, Captain Yusifel, and the reserve guard. His confidence grew and he picked up the pace, his booted feet pounding heavily on the paving stones accompanied by the rhythmic tapping of the spear's wooden butt.

A few minutes more and something appeared out of the night, a dark shape lying motionless across the width of the wall. A flurry of wind tugged at the shape and Reed saw a flash of vermilion. A cloak of the Old Guard, still attached to its owner. Reed heard a gasp from behind him as one of the young recruits realised what they had discovered.

"Hode, with me, mask on and tight. The rest of you, stay here," he said, pulling his mask tighter around his face and moving closer to examine the body. The guardsman had died face down, one arm folded under him, the other stretching out for his spear that lay just out of reach. The back of his head was crusted with blood and more had seeped down into his cloak, turning it an even darker shade of red.

Reed used his spear to flip the body over onto its back and his eyes widened as he took in the damage done to the man's face. Two deep gashes had opened the skin diagonally from eyebrow to lower lip, pulping the man's left eye and mutilating the nose. The remains of the bottom lip were hanging by a thin thread of flesh, exposing his lower jaw and teeth. No wild animal could have done this; it was something much, much worse.

Reed turned to confer with Hode and something flitted across his vision as he did so, a dark shadow there and gone again like a cloud passing across the sun. Hode stood looking at him, mask dangling around his chin, jaw half-open as if to say something.

"Is everything all right?" asked Reed haltingly, trying hard to keep the tremor out of his voice.

Hode made a small choking sound and a thin rivulet of blood trickled down from his mouth. He took one half-step forwards, eyes searching for something, then coughed violently, spattering Reed's face and hair with bright crimson droplets and remains of stew. Reed recoiled with a shout, scrambling away from Hode in shock until his back hit the parapet of the wall and he could go no further.

Hode fell spluttering to his knees, fighting to draw breath as he drowned in his own blood. And Reed saw what had been hiding behind his fellow guardsman, a hunched shadow given form.

The creature was short, no more than five feet tall, and covered in grey, wrinkled skin. It had bulbous yellow eyes set in a cadaverous face, cheekbones and jawline starkly visible. Spindly arms ended in three clawed fingers; one claw shorter and wider than the others, viciously hooked like a sickle. It was naked apart from a piece of mouldy leather strapped around its groin. Reed met the creature's eyes and thought he could discern some dark intelligence there, a seething malice scorched deep into the thing's core.

The creature cocked its head and gave Reed a wide smile, revealing dozens of dirty, triangular teeth. It sauntered over to where Hode rested on his knees and, never taking its eyes off Reed, drew one of its dagger-length claws across the dying man's throat. Fresh blood sprayed from the wound. Hode pitched forwards onto his face with a muffled gurgle. His legs thrashed briefly one final time, then he was still. The thing brought a wet claw up to its maw and a black tongue darted out from between dry lips, licking it clean.

On seeing the creature taste his friend's blood, something broke inside Reed. An angry scream exploded from his lungs. Pushing himself up with his spear, he bounded forwards, jabbing his weapon at the grey-skinned apparition with a strength born of desperation. The creature gave a screech of surprise and dodged backwards, avoiding a blade through the chest but taking a ragged slash across its navel, deep enough to draw blood. Reed pivoted and sent the butt of his spear hurtling forwards, hammering into the thing's head just behind the ear with a crack that echoed off the sides of the Pit.

Black ichor oozed from the creature's skull and it cried out in pain. Dazed, it floundered backwards, tripping over Hode's lifeless body and landing heavily on the stone walkway. Reed moved in quickly and stabbed down with his spear as hard as he could. The sharp tip pierced the thing's chest and, with a rattling cry, the light left its eyes.

Reed staggered over to the parapet and fumbled with the straps of his mask, his stomach clenching uncontrollably. He managed to release the straps just in time, turning to retch violently over the wall and into the Pit. He heard the sound of running feet as Kellen and the others caught up with him. He looked up at them, angry words forming on his lips.

"Where the HELL were you?" he shouted. "Hode, my friend, a man I have known for ten years, is dead! Killed by that … grey-skinned monstrosity and you all just stood there, you just STOOD there!" He stopped to catch his breath and looked again at the soldiers standing before him.

Three skinny, inexperienced, scared young men; barely old enough to handle a spear, let alone use one in combat. They shifted uneasily on their feet, eyes downcast, weapons held loosely in trembling hands.

Reed exhaled slowly. What shame could he bring to them that they did not already feel themselves? It was courage they needed now, courage and hope, enough to get them through the night alive. He felt his anger drain away, only to be replaced by a feeling of dread. They needed to move.

"Sorry," he said quietly. "I apologise, I am not myself." He turned and scanned the way ahead. They were close to the towers now, no more than a few minutes march.

"You have seen terrible things here. Things that are difficult for us to comprehend, things that make it hard to think rationally, to keep calm. We will come back for our fallen comrades and we will find out what is happening here but for now, we must keep moving forwards, we must get to the barracks. Once we arrive there it—"

He was interrupted by a screech that cut through the night air close by, somewhere in the darkness back the way they had come. An answering shriek came from in front of them, resonating out over the Pit.

They were surrounded.

CHAPTER 2

THE SECOND LAW

"No, I have no idea what we are guarding the wall against, but does it really matter? We have been given a task and we will see it through. It is not for us to question why."

ORLEUS YUSIFEL, CAPTAIN OF THE OLD GUARD, 424 AT

❧

"MOVE!" REED YELLED, and without checking to see if the others were following, he sprinted towards the signal fires. A long-clawed hand appeared over the battlements on his left and he slashed at it with his spear as he ran, sending the emerging creature tumbling back into the Pit. He heard a cry of pain and risked a glance behind him.

One of the creatures had reached the battlements and leapt from the parapet onto Freckles' fleeing back, sending him crashing to the ground. More creatures skittered up onto the ramparts and fell upon the hapless youth, claws slashing down through his cloak into his unprotected back. His cries were soon smothered by the inhuman screeches of his assailants as they tore him apart.

There was nothing they could do but run, each step bringing them ever closer to safety. The paved walkway started to widen as the towers drew nearer, the thick smog from the fires filling the air and obscuring the path ahead. Reed could hear the faint clash of steel on claw. With a burst of effort, he pushed through the last few yards of curling smoke and soot to arrive at his destination, and what was left of the reserve guard.

The walkway opened out into a flagged square, wide enough for twenty men to stand shoulder to shoulder. The front of the square was bordered on either side by round signal towers, their bonfires lit. At the opposite end, a modest two-storey gatehouse supporting an iron portcullis protected the entrance to a set of stairs.

These were the only way off the eastern part of the wall, slabs of granite that zigzagged down from the ramparts to the barracks and outbuildings below. The gatehouse was the last obstacle blocking access to the plains and scattered villages beyond the wall, and where the reserve guard were making their final stand.

Bodies from both sides were strewn across the square, crimson blood and black ichor spattering the cold stone. A dozen or so corpses grouped together near the furthermost signal tower bore claw marks along their backs and legs; in all probability the guardsmen patrolling the wall who, like Reed, had tried to get back to the barracks before being cut down from behind by the creatures of the Pit.

A trail of blood dotted with discarded cloaks and broken spears led from the tower to the gatehouse at the end of the square. More bodies littered the ground before the portcullis, men of the Old Guard but a good number of the enemy too. It was here that the fleeing watchmen had turned to fight, and it was here that the last surviving members of the reserve guard were keeping the creatures at bay.

They were spread out before the gatehouse in a convex half-circle formation, two ranks deep. The first rank was down on one knee, spear butts braced firmly on the ground behind them, steel tips pointing towards the enemy. The second rank was standing a pace behind the first, their spears resting lightly on the shoulders of the kneeling men in front of them.

Inside the half-circle of spears, Reed could just make out the red-cloaked officer who had recruited him all those years before, his bushy black beard streaked with grey, his rotten teeth clearly visible as he bellowed orders to the defenders. Captain Yusifel, commander of the reserve guard.

Before the defensive ring, just out of reach of the bristling spears, a score of the grey-skinned creatures paced back and forth, baring their needle-sharp teeth and shrieking obscenities at the defenders. As Reed watched, two of them suddenly surged forwards, claws raised, eyes fixed on a small gap in the circle where two guardsmen stood slightly too far apart. Reed started to shout out a warning, but there was no need. As the creatures reached the defensive line, the guardsmen moved smoothly to close the gap and lowered their weapons, impaling the surprised attackers before they could react.

Reed realised Yusifel was baiting the enemy into attacking the spearwall. Tactically it made sense, as it allowed him to whittle down their numbers slowly without risking the lives of his own men, but Reed knew that more of the enemy were on the way, and that the guards would end up being overwhelmed. They had to retreat.

A figure lurched out of the smoke behind him and nearly bowled him over. It was Kellen, face and leather mask spattered with blood, hair covered in a thin layer of ash from the fires. His wide eyes focused with some difficulty on Reed.

"Iden's down!" he yelled over the wind. "Two of them got over the wall on his right and took his leg off at the knee. I couldn't save him!" He gave a short laugh that turned into a sob. "He managed to make it a few more yards on one foot, but then another one jumped him and ..."

Reed grabbed his arm and forced the man to look at him. "From the right? Are you sure?" he asked.

"Right you are, Reed, as right as right can be!" said Kellen with a manic cackle, shrugging off Reed's hand and wiping his bloodshot eyes with his sleeve.

"By the Twelve!" swore Reed. If the enemy had really attacked from the right then they had managed to climb over the wall and down the other side. They were surrounded. And Yusifel's spearwall would be rendered useless if the creatures could circle round to attack the exposed flank or rear of the defensive line. He had to warn them.

"With me!" he shouted at Kellen, who just stared at him blankly. Reed gave him a sharp slap across the face and pulled him close. "Come on, Kellen, we've got to get to Yusifel!"

A shriek from behind spurred him into action and he started running towards the reserve guard, pulling Kellen with him.

"Yusifel! Yusifel, listen to me, you bastard!" he screamed.

He had lost his mask and acrid smoke filled his lungs, making him cough and splutter.

Yusifel caught sight of the approaching men and, sensing something was amiss, drew his officer's sabre and looked around wildly. And he was not alone. Three of the creatures, alerted by Reed's shouts, broke off the attack on the spearwall and turned to meet this new threat head-on.

Reed didn't slow for a second, charging full tilt into the attackers. His spear punched through the torso of the closest creature, the blade erupting from its back in a spray of dark ichor and bone. Its hands scrabbled weakly for a moment at the spear haft protruding from its chest before it crumpled to the ground.

Reed barely had time to pull his weapon free before a second creature leapt towards him, dirty nails slicing towards his chest. He managed to raise his spear to parry the attack and both sets of claws thudded into the dry wood with a crack, splitting the haft in two and sending splinters spinning in all directions. Reed fell heavily, the broken spear rolling from his grasp. The creature fell with him, scratching at his surcoat, its teeth bared in a snarl. Reed balled his hand into a fist and punched his aggressor hard in the mouth, breaking two teeth and shattering its jaw.

It screeched and rolled off him. Reed's groping hand closed around the broken shaft of his spear and, with a grunt of effort, he swung his arm round and buried the shattered wood deep into the creature's neck. It gave a throaty groan and lay still.

Reed laughed in disbelief and pushed himself up onto his elbows, just in time to see a horde of creatures flow over the gatehouse walls like a tidal wave and crash down onto the unsuspecting reserve guard below.

Men screamed as the sharp talons pierced their flesh, and the ordered wall of spears dissolved into chaos. With no more wood to fuel the flames, the signal fires were going out, making it even harder to distinguish friend from foe through the smoke and ash that covered the square. Dark shapes shimmered in and out of focus amid the sounds of spears clashing against claws, shouts of anger, and screams of pain. Reed could hear Yusifel close by yelling and cursing, his curses turning to pleas for help before stopping altogether.

Reed stumbled onwards, tripped over a body and fell back hard onto the stone. The body belonged to Kellen. The last of Reed's group would not make it off the wall. He had died face up and his glassy-eyed stare fixed Reed accusingly. Reed sighed and closed the young man's eyes, before prying Kellen's spear from his dead hands and pulling himself to his feet. Gripping the spear tightly, he started moving towards where he had last heard Yusifel.

He found the captain moments later in the shadow of the gatehouse, holding his own against two of the creatures, pushing them back with wide sweeps of his sword. Reed joined him and together they cornered them against the gatehouse wall and cut them down.

Yusifel turned to him, breathing heavily. "Reed! Glad you could make it! What took you so long? We set the beacons alight an age ago!" He wiped his sword on his cloak then hawked and spat a wad of something dark and nasty.

Reed looked at him incredulously. "Oh, I'm sorry. I would have been here sooner but I had to run half the length of the wall with a bunch of green recruits, dodging dozens of these grey bastards along the way, then fight across the square, while trying not to die, to save you from getting cut to pieces ... Sir," he added belatedly.

Yusifel frowned and seemed to see Reed for the first time. Reed's salt-and-pepper hair and beard were encrusted with dried blood and stew, his surcoat torn and ripped, his cloak hanging in tatters from his shoulders. A large bruise the size of a hen's egg coloured his left temple, while his eyes were bloody and tear-stained from the constant smoke.

"How many men did you bring with you, lad?" asked Yusifel softly, eyes scanning the smog behind Reed as if expecting a full patrol of guardsmen to come running into view.

"Four with me when we set off, Sir," Reed replied despondently. "I'm the only one left now."

The wind howled across the square, thinning the veil of smoke and revealing the massacre of the last few remaining Old Guard. Grey-skinned creatures were everywhere, shrieking to each other in their strange guttural language, crawling along the walls and up the towers like grotesque flies, bickering loudly over their spoils of war: the severed limbs and ears of the fallen.

Even more were climbing up from the Pit, sickle-like claws hammering into the crumbling mortar to aid their ascent. There were too many, far too many. And with no more smoke to hide their presence, it would only be a matter of time before Reed and Yusifel were discovered.

"This is the end, then," said Reed. He'd always thought that someday he'd leave the wall and go back to Jaelem to start a new life, maybe as a thatcher or a fisherman like his father. Spending his days out on the lake with only his rod and tackle for company, watching the way the sunlight reflected off the water's surface. Maybe even take some time to visit his mother's grave. He owed her that much. But things never happen the way you want them to, do they? Instead, he was going to die here on the wall, unremembered, his body divided up between these Pit-spawned creatures.

"Reed, my boy. Remember all those years ago, your first day in the training yard, standing to attention in the wind and rain?" said Yusifel absently. "What was the first thing I taught you, the first law of the Old Guard?" He wasn't looking at Reed, nor even at the host of creatures behind him, but at the portcullis and some huge shape approaching rapidly from the other side.

"I pledge my life to the defence of the wall," replied Reed automatically.

"Indeed, and the second?"

"I trust my life to the will of the Twelve," said Reed in a halting voice. For he could see the figure clearly now. A single tear of relief rolled down his cheek. Hode had been right. On the other side of the portcullis stood a Knight of the Twelve.

The knight was well over seven feet tall, dressed in magnificent burnished plate armour that gleamed despite the poor light. He wore a barbute-style helmet, visor-less with a T-shaped opening for his eyes and mouth. Two horns fixed on either side of the helmet curved outwards then back towards the centre, like some enormous steel crab's pincers. Slung across his back was a massive double-bladed battle-axe, at least five feet long, made from black hardwood topped with twin crescent-shaped blades as big as a man's head.

The knight's weapon and armour were impressive, but the man who wore them was even more so. Power and confidence radiated from him in waves, every move he made was precise and economical. Piercing ocean-blue eyes burned deep in the shadows of his horned helmet.

Then the knight spoke in a calm, firm voice at odds with his imposing frame.

"Good morrow, Sir Guardsmen," he said politely to the two men, nodding briefly to them both. "I must apologise for my tardiness. I ran into some trouble on my way to assist you that needed to be dealt with before I could proceed." He eyed the portcullis pensively.

"Sir Aldarin!" shouted Yusifel ecstatically. "I was beginning to lose hope! The gate chain has slipped from its gears, I'm afraid, but if you can find some way to get through to us, we would be most grateful!"

Aldarin placed both gauntleted hands on the portcullis. "You would do well to take a few steps back," he cautioned. "I believe this will be of no great impediment." He braced himself hard against the gate and heaved. For a moment, nothing happened. Then, with a plaintive screech of tortured metal and rusty chains, the portcullis moved slowly upwards, one, two, three feet off the ground. Aldarin gave a grunt of effort, stooped under the gate and let go. The portcullis slammed back into place with a deafening clang that resonated around the square. Dozens of small grey heads turned towards the sound.

The knight's gaze roamed the battlefield, lingering on

the bodies of the fallen guardsmen and the grisly trophies. His eyes grew cold.

"These men did not deserve this fate," he said quietly. Reaching over his shoulder with one hand, he smoothly drew forth the vicious-looking double-bladed axe from the metal rings that bound it to his armoured back. He held the weapon lightly in one hand as if it was a toy.

"Greylings!" he intoned, his deep voice carrying easily across the square. "You have desecrated the bodies of these fine men and made a mockery of the Treaty of Peace written in stone by the Twelve themselves. This treachery cannot stand. I have no other choice but to return you to the Pit. Stand ready!" Raising the axe, he touched the haft lightly to his open helm in a duellist's salute. Reed could just make out the words 'Brachyura' etched in silver on the wood.

The two guardsmen moved wearily to stand beside the knight, but he waved them back and strode out to meet the enemy alone.

Five of the creatures skittered closer, fanning out left and right to pounce on him from all sides. Aldarin, barely breaking his stride, calmly swung his axe in a low, wide arc. The razor-sharp blades decapitated the first attacker, scythed through the chests of three more and clipped the arm of the fifth, sending its clawed hand spinning from its body.

Reed stared open-mouthed at the carnage, unable to comprehend what had just happened. In a few seconds, the knight had killed more of the creatures than he had managed himself over the last hour.

He had heard the many rumours surrounding the Knights of the Twelve. It was told they lived in seclusion, far from prying eyes, building and maintaining great temples on lonely mountain peaks, scorched desert sands or windswept island cliffs. Supposedly, they spent all their waking hours locked in isolation, honing their bodies and minds in defence of the realm, only called upon by the ruling Baronies in times of need.

Much like the Old Guard, knights could once be found in every major province, serving the Barons and their vassals; but that was long ago. Reed knew no one who had ever seen a Knight of the Twelve in the flesh, not even the oldest members of the Guard. Until now.

Aldarin had reached the centre of the square, surrounded by the creatures. His axe rose and fell in sharp, practised movements. Each swing was perfectly timed, aimed at inflicting heavy damage with minimal effort. The greylings wore no armour and had no shields or weapons to parry the blows. Packed tightly into the square, they had nowhere to fall back to, no line of retreat. They were getting butchered.

Reed saw some of them try to fight back, their claws scraping across the knight's armour looking for an opening, but there was none. The segmented overlapping plates adjusted position as Aldarin fought, his armpits and the back of his knees protected by interlocking coils of silver mail.

As Reed looked on, one attacker jumped high onto the knight's back and plunged its talons fiercely into his neck, only to shatter them completely, finger joints twisting and cracking. The creature fell screeching and was lost in the crush of bodies.

The dead were piling up around the knight, restricting his movements and forcing him to make tighter swings. More of the creatures leapt onto his arms and back, pulling him forwards and for a moment he fell to one knee before throwing them off with a shout.

Suddenly, an unearthly shriek echoed up from the Pit, a primordial roar of anger and malice multiplied tenfold by the acoustics of the chasm. It hit Reed like a physical wave of pain, making him yell and cover his ears. A quick glance sideways told him Yusifel was doing the same.

The sound had an immediate effect on the remaining creatures who replied with shrieks and cries of their own, pulling away from Aldarin and scampering back towards the ramparts and over them into the Pit.

Aldarin stood leaning on his axe and scowling, but he made no move to pursue them. With a small shrug, he flicked the blades to remove some of the blood and gore stuck to their tips, then carefully holstered the weapon on his back, threading the haft through the three metal rings evenly spaced from shoulder to hip.

He turned and flashed a smile at the guardsmen, his white teeth stark against the darkness of his pronged helmet.

"Praise the Twelve!" he said reverently. "For justice has been wrought this day!"

"Indeed it has!" replied Yusifel, returning the smile. "What would you have us do now, Sir Knight?"

"Aldarin will suffice. I fear the enemy will not give up; this may be but a short reprieve. The greylings are weaker after dawn; after so many years in the dark, the light of our sun hurts their eyes and burns their dry skin. They will not venture further afield this day unless they must."

Reed saw the knight was right, there was a slight bluish tinge to the horizon. Dawn must not be far off. Thank the Twelve.

"The temple did well to send me here," continued Aldarin, "as it seems their fears are well-founded — the greylings have broken the Pact of the Twelve and returned to the surface."

"Greylings?" asked Reed. He had never heard the word before.

"That is correct," replied Aldarin. "For that is the name that was given to these creatures hundreds of years ago. You must have questions, but we cannot linger here, I need to return to Arelium post-haste. I would suggest we descend from the wall and proceed to the stables."

Grunting, he lifted the portcullis again, muscular arms and legs straining against the heavy metal. The two surviving guardsmen made their way through the gatehouse and down the hundred or so winding steps leading to the barracks, a rectangular structure built against the base of the wall.

As they approached, they could see that even though the thick wooden door was still closed and intact, there were several ragged holes in the thatching. Reed entered the building warily, his eyes scouring the room. It was unoccupied but everything of use had been stolen or destroyed. The weapon rack stood empty while the many tables and chairs were smashed to pieces against the wall. In one corner lay a pile of urine-soaked linen, in another the military canvas camp beds slashed and broken. A banner depicting the red and gold of the Old Guard had been torn down the middle, bisecting the crimson sun like a split orange. Wooden shutters ripped off their hinges allowed the soft dawn light to filter in through open windows, bathing the room in a muted glow.

"Damn them to the Pit!" swore Yusifel. He shuffled into

the room, up-righted one of the chairs and sat down heavily. The old captain was suffering from a limp since reaching the bottom of the stairs.

Aldarin's large shape appeared in the doorway, frowning at the ransacked interior. "We will find nothing here," he said, and turned towards the only other building in the yard, a ramshackle structure housing the stables, kitchens, washhouse, and smithy.

Reed leant his spear against the door and reached mechanically to untie his mask before realising he was no longer wearing it. He remembered how they had been told again and again during training to always wear masks on patrol to protect against the noxious fumes of the Pit. He gave a short laugh. None of that seemed to matter now. The Pit had become far more perilous than that.

"What are you laughing at, boy?" grumbled Yusifel tiredly. He had stripped off his oiled leather breastplate and was probing a long cut under his lower left rib with a grimy finger.

Reed found another battered chair and sank gratefully down onto it. "I suppose at the absurdity of the situation, Sir," he replied.

"Aye, you're right there, lad." Yusifel patted the pockets of his trousers and pulled out a scuffed tobacco pouch, miraculously still intact. He struck a match on his boot heel and, shortly afterwards, a sweet smoky smell spread through the barracks, masking the sour stench of urine and faeces.

"What happened?" asked Reed. "They came out of nowhere! Why now?"

"Can't really tell you much," Yusifel replied. "'Bout two days ago that big knight showed up here, horse lathered in sweat. Strode into my quarters asking about the Pit, had anything strange been going on ... was a bit of a shock, to be honest. I remember my mam telling me about the Parades held in Arelium for the Knights of the Twelve when she was a lass, but they haven't been seen 'round here for a good fifty years, then this one turns up."

He paused and inhaled a lungful of smoke. "Told him everything was same-old same-old, didn't seem to please him much, muttered something about 'a bad feeling' and 'she has never been wrong before', whatever that means. Ended up telling me he'd be staying on for a few days. Slept in the stables. Talked to a lot of the patrols coming down from the wall, even went up there himself once or twice, but kept to himself for the most part. Then last night, old Kohl was shaking me awake yelling 'The fires are lit, the fires are lit!' Got the lads out and kitted up, headed up to the wall and did what we could, but it was too late, far too late." His gaze shifted. "I lost all of them ... all of them. They were my responsibility and I failed."

Yusifel coughed sharply and stared down at his boots. An uncomfortable silence filled the room. Reed didn't know what to say. He looked across at the captain. The large, boisterous recruiter who had convinced him to join the Guard was gone, replaced by a haggard old man hunched over his smoke. Reed opened his mouth to speak, but was cut off by a loud voice from outside.

"Fellow guardsman!" Aldarin's baritone echoed round the yard. "I am in dire straits indeed. The greylings have befouled the kitchens and I fear my horse is dead. I cannot reach Arelium without transportation or supplies. I would implore your assistance."

Reed glanced at Yusifel, but the old man only shrugged and nodded towards the doorway. Reed got up with a sigh and went out into the yard, which was nothing more than a scruffy patch of dirt, empty but for a small grated well and a couple of practice bales of hay, swinging forlornly from their posts. Aldarin approached from the stables, a steely glint in his eyes.

"What do you propose, guardsman?" he asked.

Reed scratched his beard thoughtfully. "My hometown of Jaelem is a couple of days' ride from here," he replied. "Don't think you'll find anything closer. They'll have horses and provisions. It's all flat ground from here to there, only plains and the odd cluster of trees. If we set out now, we could make good time before night sets in again." He paused, trying to frame his next thought correctly. "Thing is, Sir Knight, I'm not sure it's right just to leave the Old Guard here. There are miles of wall up there and dozens of men like me still not accounted for. Some of them might still be alive, might need our help. They are my friends. We can't just go and leave them to their fate."

Aldarin stared at him intently from deep within his ornate helm. "What is your name, guardsman?"

"Merad Reed, Sir Knight."

"Reed. Do you know why the Old Guard exists?"

"When I signed up, people kept telling me that we are the light against the darkness, the shield against the unknown," said Reed, struggling to keep the sarcasm from his voice.

"Exactly," said Aldarin. "Your role is just as crucial as that of a soldier of Arelium, or a Knight of the Twelve, or a loving father. You are here to watch, to guard and, above all, to protect those who cannot protect themselves. Did you know the first Captain of the Old Guard was sworn in by one of the Twelve themselves? That the torn banner from your barracks was a gift to honour your loyalty and devotion? How many villages surround the Pit? How many lives have been saved tonight through the actions of the Guard?"

"But we didn't stop them!" said Reed, hands clenched in exasperation. "We fought and died."

"No, you didn't stop them," said Aldarin. "But you did *slow* them. You did stem the tide. You did give us time to prepare, give others time to flee. But that will only mean something if we can warn them, if we can tell them what we have seen here. Arelium can call upon others like me. Together, if we act fast, and the Twelve willing, we can drive them back."

"I understand if you wish to stay," he continued mildly, "and, if you ask it of me, I will assist you here at the wall. You must decide what is more important: to help those few still here or to help countless others."

"Why not both?" said Yusifel. He was leaning against the barracks wall and had been listening silently. "I am in no fit state to travel, got more scrapes and bruises on me than I can count, and that cut on my ribs don't feel too good. You two head to Jaelem. I'll rest for a while then head back up to the wall, relight the signal fires and have a look round, see what and who I can find." He coughed again, then hawked and spat. "Anyways, need some time to bury my men."

"And afterwards?" said Reed. "When you've found a few survivors and patched them up? What will you do when night falls and those things come back?"

Yusifel stood up straight and looked him in the eye.

"We'll buy you some time, my lad," he said. "Not much, I reckon, but maybe it'll be enough."

"No way!" replied Reed angrily. "I'm not leaving you here."

"'Fraid you are. See, I'm still your captain, right, and I'm ordering you to go with this knight and assist him as best you can. You'll be the emissary of the Old Guard to Arelium."

"And if I refuse?"

"'Seems to me the punishment for refusing an order is exile, ain't that right, Sir Knight?" said Yusifel, and he favoured Reed with a yellow-toothed grin. "C'mon, lad, do this one last thing for me, it's important."

There was nothing more to say. Reed clasped wrists with the old recruiter, raw emotion clear on his face. "I will do what I can," he said, and turned to join Aldarin waiting patiently at the end of the yard, a burlap sack at his side.

"Reed!" Yusifel called after him. "Don't waste this, Reed. Don't forget what was done here!"

Reed didn't look back.

CHAPTER 3

THE JUGGLER'S DAGGERS

"Of the nine Baronies, Arelium is without a shadow of a doubt the richest of them all. Its location, perched like a swan's nest on the banks of the River Stahl, enables it to profit from a myriad of superb trade opportunities. Marble, iron, and precious stones from the mountains of Morlak. Fish, glass, and silks from the estuary of Kessrin. All must pass through Arelium. And beyond its fortified walls, a hundred fields of bountiful crops and livestock! I am, of course, but a minor cog in this great mercantile machine, but I would hope that my small contribution will help make our Barony greater still."

PRAXIS, STEWARD TO BARON LISTUS DEL ARELIUM, 419 AT

⤜

J ELAÏA DEL ARELIUM, first and only daughter of Baron del Arelium, heiress to his innumerable titles and considerable fortune, was bored.

She removed her wire-framed reading glasses and tossed
them onto the table in front of her, narrowly missing a stack
of scrolls that teetered precariously on one corner. Maps of
all shapes and sizes, rolls of paper, illustrated books, pencils,
and burnt-out candles covered the entire table surface, as if
someone had set out to fill up every available free space until
there was nothing left.

Her education, as her mother frequently reminded her,
was of paramount importance if she wished to understand
fully the intricate workings of the Barony and its place in
the greater scheme of things. Arelium was one of the nine
Baronies, nine regions stretching from the snowy plains
in the North to the scorching deserts of the South. Each
region functioned more or less autonomously, governed by
a ruler who had complete control over military, judiciary,
and economic policies. The Baron, her father, was aided by
his vassals, a dozen or so nobles each with their own lands
and subjects, who swore fealty to their lord in exchange for
protection and a share of the region's income.

The alliance between Baronies was consolidated by the
Council, a yearly summit created in the hope of strengthen-
ing the union of the nine regions. The Council could also be
convened during times of great strife at the behest of one of
the Barons, an extremely rare occurrence that had never happened in the twenty-one years since Jelaïa's birth. In fact, her
father hated attending the summit. It would put him in the
foulest of moods, and even weeks after his return she would
catch him muttering irritably about stolen trade routes or
exorbitant export taxes.

Jelaïa remembered a few years ago when a travelling
troupe of entertainers had set up camp near the town gates

and regaled the local populace with plays, tricks, mysteries, and other feats of skill. She had been fascinated by one of the jugglers, a young man barely older than herself, towering above the crowds on seven-foot-high stilts. He could send six or seven coloured balls spinning into the air with little effort. When his audience tired of the balls, he switched to clubs or to a set of throwing daggers. It was the daggers that had impressed Jelaïa the most. She had been transfixed by the glittering flashes of circling steel, knowing that one mistake would cost the juggler a finger.

Her father had found her hours later. "I see you have come upon my comrade in arms!" he had said with a smile, bowing to the stilted man. "Good Sir! We are much alike, you and I. I too spend my days juggling the political daggers of my nobles. And I too try to keep them spinning round and round, hoping I won't trip up or make a mistake that leads to one of them stabbing me in the back! I commend you, Sir, for it is not an easy thing." And tossing a gold coin to the startled juggler, he had led Jelaïa back to the keep.

And of course, he was right. A well-informed, well-educated governor could use that knowledge to negotiate, anticipate and, if the situation deemed it necessary, retaliate.

Nevertheless, that did not make the hours and hours of daily study any less boring.

Jelaïa pushed her chair back from the cluttered chaos and absentmindedly tucked a stray lock of chestnut-brown hair back into the coiled, braided bun pinned into place every morning by her long-suffering chambermaid. She stretched out her legs, twisting her knees to relieve some of the stiffness in her joints before wandering over to peer out of one of the windows.

Her bedroom and study were located on the topmost floor of the keep, six storeys high. Glass windows offered a breath-taking view of the town of Arelium and the lands beyond. Jelaïa gazed out over the Barony that carried her name and that would one day be hers.

Arelium lay in the centre of a wide valley on the banks of the River Stahl, bordered on all sides by rolling green hills. The fortified town was home to thousands, dwelling in several hundred half-timbered houses encircling the formidable stone keep that was the seat of the Baron's power. The keep itself was topped with four square turrets, each one flying the flag of Arelium: a white wolf on a field of crimson.

A winding curtain wall enclosed the town, built in the same style as the central keep and perforated with arrow slits and bretèches. The only way to get through the wall was via a single barbican, its gatehouse fitted with a heavy door and a series of portcullises that could be raised or lowered by the garrison stationed on the second floor. Jelaïa could see a slow, steady flow of merchants and travellers filtering through the gate, a flash of red or a glint of metal enabling her to pinpoint the halberdiers of the Baron's guard.

A shantytown of sorts had sprung up outside the town, a tangled web of tents, caravans, and ramshackle wooden structures. Jetties stretched out into the river, while tiny distant figures swarmed over barges, flatboats, and other smaller craft, unloading or loading freight like ants attacking a bowl of sugar.

The cloudless sunny day made it possible to see even further down into the valley where the land was given over to farming: wheat, maize, barley, hops, sunflowers, vineyards, and much more; a vibrant patchwork of agriculture. Walled

mansions, complete with ornamental gardens and outbuildings, lorded over the smaller villages and farmsteads. These
were the homes of the noble houses of Arelium, vassals to
the Baron himself.

Beyond the valley lay three neighbouring Baronies that
shared borders with Arelium: Da'arra far to the south beyond
the plains and villages of the Pit, Kessrin to the north-west
where the river met the sea, and Morlak to the east where the
hills became treacherous mountains.

For Jelaïa, the many hours spent staring out over the
valley always led to mixed emotions. Pride in what her father
and his ancestors had accomplished. Fear and doubt about
not being worthy of the family name. Responsibility for the
people far below her. Frustration and guilt that she knew
little to nothing of their way of life.

This last failing was one she was trying to remedy, bor-
rowing and stealing whatever books and papers she could
find in the town archives or the Baron's extensive personal
collection. Blueprints and floorplans of the keep, balance
sheets for the local businesses, crop yields, soil samples, bills
for raw materials, labour costs, road and structural mainte-
nance; the list went on and on.

And the books, so many books. A plethora of subjects,
each one more detailed than the last: farming, mining, trad-
ing, masonry, carpentry, weaving, sewing, baking — all the
things her tutor refused to educate her in as he deemed them
irrelevant for a person of noble standing. She read vora-
ciously, scribbling notes in the margins, adding thoughts
and comments of her own, leafing through page after page
with a moist index finger.

Would it be enough? One day, sooner or later, she was going to find out.

Three firm knocks on the door made her jump and nearly trip over the hem of her emerald skirt. She managed to catch herself on the corner of the table, spilling scrolls over the floor.

"Jelaïa, I hope you are decent because, ready or not, I'm coming in," came a muffled voice and the door was thrown open. A tall, immaculately groomed man with slicked-back hair and a slight five o'clock shadow walked briskly into the room with a mischievous smile on his face. He wore a high-necked black leather coat over a belted brown tunic and pants. A silver medallion hung from a chain around his neck, and a stiletto-like dagger was sheathed in a jewelled scabbard on his right thigh.

"I thought I'd find you here, holed up with your books when it's a glorious sunny day outside," he said teasingly. "Your skin needs a bit of sun occasionally, you know. If you get any whiter, we'll lose you in the snow come winter."

Jelaïa threw a scroll case at him, missing by a foot and a half.

"I would love to go outside, my dear steward Praxis, but my father doesn't let me wander around unaccompanied and my favourite chaperone hasn't come to see me in days!"

"Ah. Yes. Sorry about that," replied Praxis, fingering his medallion. The silver disk was engraved with the sign of his office: two bowls hanging equidistant from a fulcrum. "Your father is keeping me very busy. The harvest has been exceptional this year and we are rather overwhelmed, to be honest. The worst is the wheat: I'm trading it nearly as fast as the carts are offloading it and we're still running out of storage.

I should have argued harder last year when the Baron turned
down my proposal for a bigger granary."

"Why don't you just mill the grain?" asked Jelaïa. "Flour
takes up less space than seed."

"Because it's more difficult to—" Praxis cut himself
off. "By the Pit, I nearly fell for it again! I'm not going to
get drawn into another discussion about how to run your
father's estate, Jelaïa. If I am still steward when you become
Baroness, I will be happy to spend weeks debating agricultural policy, but for now you'll have to let me do my job as
I see fit. And speaking of doing my job, I came to fetch you
to see the Baron; he wants to talk to you about something."

"Fine," said Jelaïa petulantly. "But next time I go for a
walk in the gardens, I'll be asking someone else."

"No you won't," said Praxis with a smirk.

They descended the spiral staircase leading from Jelaïa's
study to the Great Hall on the first floor where the Baron
held council, granted audiences to his vassals, and received
important guests. Multi-coloured banners displaying the
heraldry of the nobles who had pledged an oath of fealty
to the Baron covered the walls. At the far end of the hall, a
polished oak table spanned the width of the room, its surface
covered with a detailed parchment map of the Barony. Small
carved figures dotted the map, representing farmsteads,
country houses, merchant caravans, boats, and groups of
soldiers. Behind the table were three simple chairs beneath a
banner depicting the white wolf of Arelium.

Jelaïa barely had time to catch her breath before her
father strode into the room, a gaggle of nobles, guards, and
servants trailing behind him. Baron Listus del Arelium was
a stern-faced, grizzled veteran with eyes the colour of cold

steel and a neatly trimmed grey beard. He was in his early sixties, although most would guess he was at least ten years younger. He was only betrayed by faded wrinkles around his eyes and mouth; and his thinning hair. Dressed in a red doublet decorated with white lace, and high doeskin boots, he walked with the confident pace of a soldier.

When he saw his daughter, the old man's frown disappeared, replaced by an indulgent smile. "Jeli! I see Praxis managed to coax you out of your little hidey-hole! Welcome back to the land of the living!" He collapsed into one of the chairs, ushering away the approaching sycophants with a wave of his hand. Two halberdiers in red livery and coats of chainmail took up position on either side of the Baron, leaving the remaining members of his court to mill aimlessly around the oak table.

"Approach, child, I won't bite!"

Jelaïa gave a quick curtsy and moved to stand before him, feeling like she was on trial for something, but she wasn't quite sure what.

"Praxis!" thundered the Baron. "How goes the harvest, will my subjects be well fed this coming winter?"

"Yes, my Lord, in fact the stores are overflowing, maybe we should—"

"Overflowing, eh? Excellent, excellent. You should have listened to me and built that granary last year like I told you to, it would have saved you a lot of hassle."

"Yes, my Lord," replied Praxis with a resigned sigh.

"Right. Now then, Jelaïa—" Before the Baron could continue, a door opened on the other side of the hall and the Baroness bustled in, her ladies-in-waiting not far behind.

She was the opposite of her husband in every way, a

round-faced mouse of a woman with curly greying hair and a friendly smile. She was easy-going, sociable, and talkative, well-liked by the Baron's vassals and their wives. Many of them made the mistake of thinking her hedonistic and a little simple-minded, telling her things in confidence they would never dream of revealing to the Baron himself.

This misconception suited the Baroness perfectly, and her husband was always well-informed of the shadier dealings and secret alliances that simmered and bubbled amongst his nobles. She also had a good head for numbers, meeting several times a week with Praxis to discuss the Barony's finances.

The Baroness gave Jelaïa a swift smile and sat down next to her husband. "I beg your pardons, my lords and ladies," she said brightly. "The tax ledgers got the better of me."

Her husband rolled his eyes and cleared his throat. "Ahem. Indeed. Back to the matter at hand. Now then, how to begin? Right. Jelaïa, you are now a young woman, in the prime of your life, as it were, and your mother and I have been talking—"

Oh no, thought Jelaïa.

"—And we think it's time we moved forwards with our plan to consolidate our alliances with the neighbouring Baronies—"

Oh no no no.

"—there seem to be several eligible suitors from Morlak and a delegation from Kessrin will be arriving here tomorrow so—"

"No, Father, no!" Jelaïa blurted out. The Baron, not used to being interrupted, frowned.

"I'm sorry, I need some air," she said, distraught, and bolted from the room, pushing past a surprised Praxis, feeling her father's eyes boring into her fleeing back as she escaped from the stifling confines of the keep and out into the town.

CHAPTER 4
RETURN TO JAELEM

"I do not refute the importance of soldiers. There will come a time when every kingdom will require a means to defend itself. I would simply postulate that fighters, however numerous or well-trained, are but a small part of the equation. For what would happen if the wall they are standing on is too brittle? If it collapses under its own weight? If the lack of proper foundations causes it to sink into the mud or sand? You may do as you wish, they are your temples and your initiates. But I believe the world already has plenty of soldiers. I will train builders."

BRACHYURA, FOURTH OF THE TWELVE, 39 AT

REED AND ALDARIN made good time crossing the flat terrain between the Pit and Jaelem, following the twisting animal trails that wound through scratchy thorn bushes and stubby acacia trees. The vast, sprawling plains stretched out before them for miles in every direction like a sea of amber and green, empty and lifeless save for the occasional herd of wild goats or soaring bird of prey.

They said little during their first day together, each lost in his own thoughts. When they did need to speak, they had to shout to be heard over the incessant gusts of wind that peppered them with sand and loose topsoil. Reed was constantly rubbing his eyes, nose, and mouth, cursing himself for leaving his leather mask back at the wall. After a few hours, he begrudgingly tore a strip of fabric off his cloak and tied it firmly around his lower face to keep out the worst of the dirt.

Aldarin didn't seem troubled by the wind, any more than he was by his plate armour. His long strides ate up the miles at a steady pace, only slowing when he saw Reed was lagging behind or to check they were heading in the right direction.

The day drew on, the sun rising high in the sky then dipping down towards the horizon, cooling the air and lengthening the shadows of the trees and shrubs. When they came to a small copse providing some shelter from the wind, Reed, exhausted, suggested they stop for the night.

Aldarin agreed and set about removing his armour. The horned helmet came off first. Reed saw that he twisted it sharply to the left before removing it as if disengaging some locking system. Then came gauntlets, greaves, vambraces, cuisses, and breastplate, each piece stacked carefully on the ground beside him. And at last, a day after they had first met, Reed could observe the face of Sir Aldarin, Knight of the Twelve.

He had lightly tanned skin and short black hair, cropped

close to his skull. Penetrating ocean-blue eyes stared out of
a hard, angular face. His square chin was clean-shaven, with
a small scar cutting through his lower lip, zigzagging down
towards his neck. A second scar crossed the bridge of a flat
nose that looked like it had been broken once or twice, and
healed badly.

The removal of his armour had done nothing to dimin-
ish the knight's physical presence. In fact, he was even more
remarkable when clad in a simple padded gambeson. His
wide shoulders and massive barrel chest were complemented
by toned muscular arms that gleamed with sweat from walking for hours in full plate.

He was different, very different, from what Reed had
imagined. In his mind's eye, the Knights of the Twelve were
always fair-skinned, long-haired nobles, with aquiline features
and perfect smiles. Aldarin was something else. He had the
physique of a warrior, a bruiser even, someone more used to
spending his time in a fighting ring than chasing after giggling
courtesans or discussing the politics of the nine Baronies, a
glass of white wine in one hand and a cigar in the other.

And yet, in their short time together, Aldarin had always
expressed himself eloquently, thoughtfully, and courteously.
Reed felt sure that the knight had far more knowledge and
insight than he himself had amassed during his many years
patrolling the wall but despite this, Aldarin always listened
to what he had to say, fixing Reed intently with his piercing
gaze. A myriad of emotions flickered like stars in those deep
blue irises: melancholy, sadness, anger, determination, and
a shrewd intellect. When Aldarin looked at Reed, he felt his
mind laid bare, his thoughts unhidden. It was both calming
and unnerving; and not always easy to look away.

Aldarin rolled his neck and shoulders, massaging some life back into his tired muscles. Squatting down beside his armour, he unknotted the drawstring of the burlap sack he had been carrying and emptied out its contents: a couple of bread loaves, strips of salted rabbit meat, three shrivelled carrots, a canteen of water, and a varnished wooden box. The box, it turned out, contained not only a leather money pouch but also paper, ink, and a whetstone; and even a fire striker, which Aldarin used to get the campfire going in a matter of minutes.

Reed removed his gloves and makeshift mask. Daylight was fading fast, leaching the warmth from the air and soil as it departed. He held his arms out over the fire and felt the heat seep up through his numb fingers. Aldarin shared out what little food they had and the two men ate their meagre supplies in companionable silence, exchanging a few words over the spitting and crackling of the flames.

"We have done well today, friend Reed," said Aldarin, chewing a chunk of dried meat. "Nothing to bother us out here apart from the wind and dust, methinks." He popped a carrot into his mouth.

"We've made good time," Reed agreed, shifting his aching legs. "It's been a while since I've travelled this far. Come to think of it, I don't think I've travelled this close to home since my mother died nearly ten years ago. Strange, really. It's a lot closer than I remember. If memory serves, we must already be about halfway there. Cutting along the game trails helped a fair bit, too."

"Indeed. However, I believe we are heading in a south-easterly direction? It is most unfortunate there is no better route. Arelium is due north of the Pit. Once we are resupplied, our journey north will be far longer, and if the greylings have taken the wall they will be on our trail." Aldarin added more dry wood to the fire, feeding the hungry blaze.

"If they have taken the wall, then Yusifel and the last of my fellow guardsmen will be dead," said Reed testily. He could feel his temper starting to fray as the strain and anxiety of recent events began to catch up with him. "I can read the sun as well as any of the Old Guard, I know which way we are heading. You saw how desolate our surroundings are. Jaelem is the best and closest place I know. You will have to trust me on this, Aldarin, just as I trust you, despite not knowing who you are, who sent you here — and how they knew those things would come crawling out of the Pit last night to claw my friends to pieces."

Aldarin looked at him silently for a moment, his face unreadable. "You are right, friend Reed, you deserve to know these things." He took a deep breath. "What can you tell me of the Knights of the Twelve?"

"Not much," admitted Reed. "I know your order spans the ages. Hundreds and hundreds of years. Some say that the first of you walked beside the Twelve themselves, benefitting from their wisdom and guidance. You are sworn to the Council and its members, including the Baron of Arelium, if I am not mistaken."

"There is some truth in what you say," Aldarin replied. "We are not one order, but Twelve. Each of the Twelve founded his or her own temple, a place of learning and meditation where they could train their own initiates in the philosophies and beliefs that defined them." He stood, retrieved his axe from where it lay next to the stacked plates of armour and held the haft up to the fire. The flickering

glow caught the engraving and the word 'Brachyura' sparkled silver in the firelight. "I am a Knight of the Order of
Brachyura, Fourth of the Twelve."

Reed stared at the cursive script, mesmerised. So
Brachyura was one of the Twelve, the founders and protectors of the realms of men, the first to scour the land of evil
and build the great towns and cities, including the wall of
the Old Guard! Their names had been lost to history, or
at least so Reed had thought. He swallowed a mouthful of
water and nodded for Aldarin to proceed.

"As I said, each of the Twelve had their own beliefs,
their own strengths and weaknesses. Some were skilled in
conversation and diplomacy, some in the art of war, others
in sculpture or poetry. Brachyura was first and foremost a
builder, an engineer of stone, wood, mortar, and steel. Our
temple is built into the side of an enormous cliff. Towers
and walkways, battlements, galleries, and balconies all hewn
from the rock itself. It is said that Brachyura raised our
temple with nothing but his bare hands for tools, working
for a year and a day without pause. One day I will show it to
you, friend Reed, if our fates are still intertwined."

Aldarin stared into the fire, thinking back to the place
he had called home. "And it was Brachyura who built the
wall around the Southern Pit," he continued. "Twenty
towers perfectly equidistant with a system of signal fires to
warn against the greylings. There was no stone nearby, so he
had thousands of barges and carts bring immense quantities
from the quarries of Morlak, far beyond Arelium. 'Twould
have been a magnificent sight!" His eyes twinkled.

"Now Brachyura was known for his skill not only in
raising great bastions of wood and stone but also in the art of

war and, more specifically, tactical defence. He would show others how to build a wall and then train them to guard it with sword, axe, shield, and spear. His preferred weapon was always the double-bladed axe. It is believed that this is because the axe, like the man, is both a tool and a weapon. Used as a tool, it can cut wood for a wall or a house, a door or a gate. Used as a weapon, it can sweep the battlements clear of the enemy, keep attackers from climbing the wall, or push away ladders and grappling hooks. Both uses are equally important."

Aldarin effortlessly balanced the haft of his massive axe on the palm of one hand, admiring how the two curved blades caught the light. "As a Knight of the Order of Brachyura, I am trained to build and I am trained to fight. It would seem the second part of my training will be of more use to us than the first. You asked me why I was sent here. It is because the founder of my Order built the wall, and we have always felt a responsibility towards the men he chose to defend it, the men now known as the Old Guard."

Night had fallen and Reed could feel his sore body telling him it was time to rest. "But why come now?" he asked, stifling a yawn. "Where have the Knights of the Twelve been all this time? Who sent you? Where are the others of your Order?"

"Some things are best left unsaid for now," Aldarin replied. "There will be time enough to talk of such matters on the way to Arelium." He suddenly stood up. "I will take first watch, friend Reed, you may sleep safely."

Reed nodded gratefully and spread his cloak down close to the fire. Closing his eyes, he reflected on all Aldarin had told him, thoughts and questions spinning round and round like a swarm of angry wasps in his head. Something was bothering him, but he wasn't sure what, something Aldarin had said. He was drifting off when it came to him.

"Aldarin," he murmured, "why did you call it the Southern Pit?"

There was no reply, only the crackling of the flames.

Sleep took him soon after.

Reed awoke the next morning feeling well-rested and refreshed. He realised rather guiltily that Aldarin had let him sleep and stood watch alone all night. He used his spear to heave himself up from the makeshift bedroll and went to relieve his full bladder. Aldarin was sitting on a fallen log close by, hunched over his axe, his arm running the whet-stone along the blades with smooth, methodical strokes. He was already fully armoured, humming some song or psalm quietly as he worked.

"A good morning to you, Sir Knight," said Reed. "Many thanks for letting me sleep, I will do the same for you tomor-row night if you wish to get some rest." He rubbed his stiff limbs. The ground had been hard beneath his cloak.

Aldarin looked up, smiling broadly. "Good morrow, friend Reed! Do not worry yourself over such trivial matters. During my time at the temple, I spent many a sleepless night training with my fellow initiates; for an enemy does not care if we do wake or sleep, be it day or night they will attack when they are ready, and when they think we are not." He threaded the haft of his axe carefully through the wide rings along his back and heaved the burlap sack over one shoulder.

"I would propose we break camp," he said. "The grey-lings will not have been idle last night. The sooner we are resupplied, the faster we can reach Arelium."

The second day of travel was as unexciting as the first: the same flat, monotonous terrain; the same cold, biting wind. Reed tried several times to engage the knight in conversation, but Aldarin remained tight-lipped, repeating that he would explain further once they were well on their way north.

They finished the remains of the meat and bread just after noon, sitting close together for shelter. After trudging a few miles further, wisps of smoke appeared on the horizon.

"Jaelem," Reed said with a relieved smile.

As they drew closer, the vague shapes became thatched huts protected by a ten-foot-high palisade. A single gate allowed entrance to the village, flanked on either side by flat-roofed watchtowers. On the southern side, a large grove of trees pushed up against the palisade. Not the scrubby aca-cias they had seen so many of for the last few days, but tall, venerable oaks, their wide branches sheltering a small lake. Reed thought he could just make out a couple of cowhide fishing boats rocking in the water.

Seeing Jaelem again released a flood of suppressed mem-ories: catching and filleting fish with his mother, climbing and hiding in the oak trees when a gang of older children were looking for someone to pick on, chasing the smith's daughter round the village square and, when he was older, stealing a kiss from her one night as they lay together by the lake watching the stars. And one, vague, blurred image of a bearded man with crinkly eyes and an easy smile showing him how to thread a line on a fishing pole; one of the only memories of his father he had left.

For the second time in as many days, he wondered if he had made the right choice to leave with the recruiter of the Old Guard, wondered what his life would have been if he had chosen to stay. Maybe he would have found his courage and asked the old blacksmith for his daughter's hand, invited his mother to come stay with them both. Raised a family.

He felt a heavy hand on his shoulder. "'Tis a fine-looking place," said Aldarin, seemingly guessing what Reed was thinking. "I'm sure we will find what we seek here. Forward!" He strode confidently up to the palisade, arms extended, palms raised above his head in the universal language of peace.

"Good men and women of Jaelem," he called out, his powerful voice carrying easily over the wind. "I am Sir Aldarin, Knight of the Twelve, and I am in need of your assistance." He looked up at the guard towers, which were unoccupied, with a slight frown. Moments later a young man came running hastily towards them, attempting to simultaneously button up his padded tunic and attach the flailing chin-strap of his rusty conical helm. He managed neither, tripping over his own boot-lace and tumbling to the ground in front of the two travellers with a muffled yelp.

Reed attempted unsuccessfully to smother a chuckle, which bordered dangerously on a laugh, before exploding from his mouth as a deep-throated guffaw. Aldarin raised a stern eyebrow, but Reed could see his eyes were twinkling. They both waited politely for the young man to disentangle himself.

"Good day to you both," he said, readjusting his lop-sided helmet. "You are most welcome. If you would please come with me, I will escort you to our mayor. He is eager to meet with you."

They passed through the gates, out of the wind and into the village proper. The rough dirt path opened out into a huge open space bustling with activity. Reed saw basket weavers, thatchers, carpenters, tanners, and fishermen going about their business. A wide assortment of wagons and cara- vans lined one side of the square: traders from other villages looking to return with fish from the lake or some of the hard wood from the oak trees. In the far corner, two dark- skinned Da'arran nomads were offloading reams of coloured silk from a mangy-looking camel.

Aldarin received a few cursory glances, but nothing more, almost as if the presence of a Knight of the Twelve was an everyday occurrence here. After days of relative silence, the cacophony of sound was overwhelming; the overlapping babble of merchants haggling, workers shouting orders, and children running left and right shrieking with laughter. It made Reed realise just how much he missed civilisation.

The watchman led them through the hubbub and up a half-dozen steps to the village hall, an imposing stone struc- ture on a raised platform dominating the square. At the top of the steps, a thick door of oak and metal strapwork was shut tight, halting any further progress.

"If you would just leave your weapons with me, I'll send you on in," said the guard, glancing nervously at Aldarin. Reed handed the man his spear without hesitation. Aldarin didn't move, only sighed and slowly shook his head. "I know what you ask of me, Sir Guardsman, but I cannot accept. I forged this axe alone and unaided, a final trial to prove my worth to my elders, a culmination of many years of sweat, blood, and hardship. Since the ceremony of restitution, no other hands but mine have held it. It has never left my side come day or night. It is as much a part of me as my arm or my leg … 'Twould perhaps be even more painful for me to lose my axe than my arm, for without it I am no longer a Knight of the Twelve."

The guardsman didn't seem to know quite how to respond to this. He licked his lips and his eyes flickered to the door behind him. "That may be so, Sir Knight, but you know how it is. I can't let any weapons into the village hall, you see? Mayor'll have my hide if you go in there with that big thing."

Aldarin stared blankly at the man for a few moments, then spun on his heel and started heading back the way they had come. "Come, friend Reed! It seems we must look else-where for help getting to Arelium." Reed gave the startled guardsman an apologetic shrug and turned to follow.

They were halfway across the square when the door burst open and a pockmarked, greasy-haired man staggered out, squinting into the fading sunlight. He wore a stained purple doublet, beige hose, and black buckled shoes. A dark crimson beret was balanced precariously on his head. The garish mix of colours made him look like some annoyed tropical bird. He shouted down the steps to them in a loud, somewhat slurred voice.

"Reed!" His voice was lost in the dense wall of sound. The man drew a deep breath and tried again.

"REED!" he screamed. The square fell silent.

"Merad Reed, by the Pit! I knew it was you! I'd recognise that scruffy beard and those bandy legs anywhere! It's been an age since we last saw you 'round here. What've you been up to, hiding out there on the wall?"

Reed stared at the man, trying to imagine him a few years younger and in plainer clothes. "Fernshaw, is that you?" he said, incredulously. "Last time I was here you were apprenticed to old Terrin the stablemaster! You were talking about leaving, even going up to Arelium if I remember rightly? And now you're what, Mayor of Jaelem? You've got to be joking!"

"Don't sound so surprised, Reed! Was never really for me, grooming and feeding horses. Met a nice girl, shrewd little minx persuaded me to stay here, run for mayor. Worked out all right, it did! Come on in, we'll find you and your friend a glass of wine and you can bore me with tales of what you've been up to on that Pit-forsaken wall for the last ten years! Oh, and we can tell your big scary bodyguard how I used to beat the living snot out of you when we were children."

"That's not quite how I remember it, Fern," said Reed as he made his way back up the stairs, Aldarin close behind. "We'd love to join you, but we do have a slight problem, I'm afraid. Seems no weapons are allowed inside and my friend is loath to part with his." He gestured at the massive axe-head visible over the knight's left shoulder.

Fernshaw took in the burnished plate armour and pincer-like helm. "Knight of the Twelve, are you?" he said. "You must be. Don't look like any of the nine Barons and they are the only ones that have the means to purchase such a lavish set of full plate. If you are indeed a Knight of the Twelve, your oath of conduct is as binding as the strongest steel. So swear to me on your honour that you will not draw that weapon in anger while you are in my village hall and you may keep it."

"An excellent decision!" replied Aldarin happily. "I give you my word as a knight, no weapon of mine will be drawn in your home."

This seemed to satisfy the mayor, as he turned back towards the entranceway and motioned for them to follow him inside. The interior of the hall was plain but spacious. Wooden tables took up much of the central area with seating enough for several dozen men and women. At the far end, a simple, high-backed leather chair stood upon a raised dais, giving whoever sat there a good view of the hall. Behind the chair, a large banner dyed with the colours of Jaelem hung down from the rafters: a silver fish on a field of forest green. Openings to the left and right led to kitchens, guest rooms, and Fernshaw's private chambers.

Light and heat came from a fireplace built into the wall, smoke escaping up a chimney and out through a hole in the roof. In front of the fire, a servant was roasting a goat on a spit, the smell of fatty juices and cooked meat making Reed's mouth water.

The hall's only other occupant was seated by the fire, a young, handsome-faced man with long blond hair tied back in a neat ponytail. He was dressed in a flowing white silk shirt and tight black leather trousers. One hand clutched a half-empty decanter, the other a pair of wine glasses. His face lit up as they entered the room and he rose to greet them, smiling.

"Uncle, you have guests! Excellent! I had feared I would have to spend the entire evening alone with you again." He leant forwards and whispered conspiratorially. "If I have to hear another story about how he met my aunt, or how his valorous electoral campaign won him the position of mayor, I may have to throw myself into the Pit!"

Visible anger clouded Reed's face and the man took a surprised step backwards, his palms raised in a placating gesture. "Apologies if I have offended you in some way, Sir," he said. "My mouth has a tendency to work faster than my brain, and by the time the latter catches up it's often too late. My name is Nidore." — he pronounced it Nee-door-ray — "Nidore del Conte. I am, as you may have surmised, the mayor's nephew, visiting from Arelium."

Mentioning the Pit had shaken Reed. The feeling of hot blood on his face, the guttering squeal of the greyling as he pushed the shaft of broken wood into its neck. The images were still there, but washed-out, as if they had not happened to him but to someone else. And as the memories began to fade, so too did the sense of urgency that had forced them to leave Yusifel behind and travel with all haste to Jaelem.

Aldarin broke the uncomfortable silence. "Well met, Nidore," he said, offering the man a large gauntleted hand. "I fear we will not be staying long, for we bring grave news. The wall has fallen, the Pit lies undefended, and the people of Jaelem are in great danger."

There was a loud clatter as Fernshaw half-fell against one of the tables. He steadied himself with one hand and grabbed the half-empty decanter from his nephew with the other, pouring himself a generous measure of thick red wine. There was barely enough to fill the glass. He set the empty jug aside with a frown, brought the liquid to his lips and downed the contents in a single gulp.

"I think we are going to need some more wine," he said grimly.

CHAPTER 5

SKIPPING STONES

"Baron Derello del Kessrin? Do not talk to me about that insufferable lout. He wears more make-up and jewellery than my wife and daughter combined, and enough perfume to knock out a horse! There is something about him though. When we were last in Kessrin, he challenged some of my nobles to a friendly wrestling match, had them all on their backs in less than five minutes! One of them couldn't walk for a week! He has a hidden strength in that wiry body of his. More than meets the eye. You'll want to be careful around that one."

BARON LISTUS DEL ARELIUM, 423 AT

୵

JELAÏA WALKED FOR hours through the twisting cobbled streets of Arelium. Confused thoughts buzzed round and round in her head making it throb painfully. She was angry. Angry at her father, angry at her mother and, most of all, angry at herself for behaving like a spoilt child. How in the Pit was she going to govern the entire valley one day if she wasn't even capable of controlling herself for a few minutes?

It was all her father's fault; it was from him she had inherited her short temper and impulsiveness. Of course, the Baron had long since mastered this facet of his personality, keeping his anger in check when it suited him and letting it loose only when the time was right.

The last time Jelaïa had seen her father truly angry was last summer. A band of men had pillaged one of the farmsteads nearby, beating the farmer senseless and raping his wife. The poor couple had been found the next day by a worried neighbour and the local noble had swiftly brought the news to the Baron's court.

It had taken the Baron half a day to find the culprits, hiding in an old abandoned mill. After a brief skirmish, all but one of the men were killed, and the only survivor had been dragged back to Arelium to receive a public lashing.

The Baron had carried out the sentence himself, his face emotionless but for his eyes that burned with a cold flame. Each crack of the whip had echoed around the square, mingling with the screams of the prisoner as the flesh was slowly stripped from his back. At fifty lashes, the man had lost consciousness. The Baron had wordlessly handed the whip to a member of his household guard and returned to the keep.

This was one of the reasons Listus del Arelium was so well-respected by his subjects: his justice was swift, ruthless and, above all, dealt by his own hand. There was a delicate balance to be struck between respect and fear, but her father managed to walk the line between the two exceedingly well.

"Never ask of another what you would not do yourself," he had told her. "If you decide to exact justice on a man, then you must be prepared to carry the sword."

Jelaïa's wandering steps had brought her out of the alleyways and onto the crowded main street leading down to the barbican. The half-timbered houses lining the road were multi-storeyed, with shopfronts built directly into the ground floor and living quarters above. In some cases, the exposed woodwork was carved or engraved, the wealthier owners covering their homes with decorative figures and motifs.

Jelaïa took a deep breath and filled her nose with the smells of freshly-baked bread, fish from the river, herbs and spices brought north from Da'arra, honey from the hives up in the mountains of Morlak, and much more besides, a regional concoction of odours.

Everywhere she looked, Jelaïa could see a frenzy of activity. A group of men from Kessrin with their wide baggy trousers and flowing silk shirts were haggling hard with a butcher over the price of veal. Two Morlakians, sweating in their fur-lined coats and felt caps, were manoeuvring heavy crates of goat's milk down from a nearby cart. A couple from Da'arra sat on stools at one of the open-topped bars, laughing as they shared puffs from a hookah, colourful turbans hiding their weathered ebony skin. And hundreds of Arelians, flowing steadily up towards the keep or down towards the gatehouse and the plains beyond.

Jelaïa stepped out into the street, her green skirt trailing through the muck. She was not quite ready to go back to the keep just yet. The other path took her down the slope to the barbican where she was briefly detained by two halberdiers in steel morion-style pot helms and chainmail vests. Both knew Jelaïa well and, although initially surprised that she was unaccompanied, they soon ushered her through the gatehouse, pushing travellers aside so she could slip by. She passed under two wrought-iron portcullises and out into the shantytown surrounding Arelium.

The crowds were thinner here, splitting between the jetties packed with merchant boats to the far west and the wide paved road cutting south across the valley floor towards the many fields and holdings.

She avoided both and turned east, following the curtain wall as it curved away from the clutter of ramshackle dwellings and down towards the river. The ground was wet and muddy here, a marshland too shallow to navigate by boat and too damp for planting crops. Tall reeds, some over eight feet high, soon surrounded her on all sides. The perfect place for someone who didn't want to be found.

A few years ago, she had discovered a pleasant spot away from prying eyes on the north-eastern bank near where the town wall met the water. She went there now, settling down in the shade of the cool stone. A quick search of the area turned up a fair number of flat, rounded pebbles and she sent them skimming across the water of the lake, aiming to get each one closer to the opposite bank than the last.

She didn't know how long she had been away, but the sun was low over the horizon when she decided it was time to head back. As she turned, a figure detached itself from the shadow of the wall a few yards ahead, making her yelp. It was Praxis, his black leather coat and hair allowing him to blend seamlessly with the darkness.

"Good evening, my Lady," he said, giving her one of his mischievous smiles. "That was a most impressive cry for help."

"Praxis, I nearly threw a rock at you. How long have you been standing there watching me? And, for that matter, how did you find me?"

"Must have arrived about an hour or so ago," he replied sardonically. "Didn't want to interrupt anything. Besides, you were getting awfully close to the opposite bank with those last few throws."

"And how did you find me?"

"Ah, well that was easy. I bribe the guards at the barbican to report any strange travellers entering or leaving Arelium. They told me you had turned east out of the gate so I correctly surmised that you were heading for your secret place. A basket weaver saw you down here a couple of months ago, by the way."

"I suppose my father was not too pleased with my little tantrum earlier."

"I'm not sure it bothered him that much, to be honest. He seemed to be expecting it. He grumbled a bit after you left, then we moved on to other things."

"It's just—" Jelaïa stopped herself, realising she was going to complain again. She needed to do better.

"It's just he caught me by surprise, that's all. I knew this day would come. It has always been this way. Mother was from Morlak, after all. An arranged marriage, just like so many others. They seem to have worked it out."

"I'd even go as far as to say they're quite fond of each other," said the steward. He was no longer smiling, but looking at Jelaïa with a strange expression on his face. "You do know, I hope, that it is not because something has always

been done a certain way that it is the right way. Despite
the pressure of traditions, history, or your parents' wishes.
In the end, it is for each and every one of us to do what we
believe in." He absentmindedly fingered his silver medallion,
tracing the engraving of scales. "I do have one small piece of
advice, if you would like to hear it?"

"I imagine if I say no, you'll tell me anyway?"

"You know me so well. My advice is this: meeting with
a delegation from Kessrin or having dinner with a young
nobleman from Morlak costs you nothing and gains you
something: time. Time to think and plan ahead. Something
for nothing is often a pretty good deal." He winked.

"I hate you right now, Praxis," said Jelaïa tiredly, massaging her temples with her index fingers. "Could you please
stop being so insufferably good at everything and escort me
back to my chambers. I need to rest."

"Of course, my Lady," Praxis replied with a short bow.

"And Praxis?"

"Yes, my Lady?"

"Please inform my father I would be happy to meet with
the Kessrin delegation when they arrive tomorrow to discuss
what can be done to strengthen our alliance."

◆

Jelaïa awoke the next morning to a blurred image of her
chambermaid hovering at the foot of her bed, a steaming hot
towel in one hand and a stiff bristle hairbrush in the other.
Light streamed in through the bedroom windows. The sun
was already high in the sky. She groaned and rubbed the last

vestiges of sleep from her eyes, throwing back the covers of her impressive four-poster bed.

"Morning, M'lady!" said her maid cheerfully. Her name was Mava, a chubby-faced, big-boned woman with bushy eyebrows and a hairy upper lip. Jelaïa suspected she was some sort of witch as she never seemed to sleep and yet managed to be annoyingly chirpy and full of energy at all times.

"Plenty to do before the delegation arrives!" Mava continued, thrusting the warm towel into Jelaïa's hands. "Let's start with that unruly haystack you call your hair, then we can get you dressed up all good and proper."

Jelaïa grunted and allowed herself to be manoeuvred from the bed to her dressing table. The table was one of the most expensive pieces of furniture in the entire keep, with clawed feet and intricately decorated drawers. The varnished surface was topped by a polished glass mirror worth a fortune. It had been gifted to her by her parents on her eighteenth birthday, much to the envy of the other ladies of the Baron's court.

Mava pulled the brush through Jelaïa's chestnut-brown hair, tut-tutting occasionally when she came across a particularly resistant knot. Once combed and tressed, her hair was wound into a stiff bun and pinned in place at the back of her head.

Dresses arrived, accompanied by their dreaded corsets. Jelaïa spent an hour trying to choose one that would both enhance her rather modest physique and not make her faint from lack of air. She finally decided on a long, flowing red dress and a creamy-white under-corset that left her shoulders and neck bare. Mava helped her apply a light coat of make-up to soften her features, and a dab of red lipstick.

The last thing she added was another present from the
Baron: a silver wolf's head brooch — the symbol of the
house of Arelium — its eyes small glittering rubies.

Jelaïa gave herself a quick critical once-over in the
mirror, thanked Mava with a peck on the cheek and carefully
navigated the narrow stairs down to the Great Hall. She was
late. Her parents had already arrived and were seated at the
head of the table. Her father was resplendent in his red and
white doublet, her mother just as radiant in a dark purple
felt dress, hair braided into a bun like her daughter. Praxis
stood beside the Baron, the two conversing in hushed tones.

Jelaïa quickly settled herself in the last empty chair and
rearranged her corset, drawing an approving glance from
Praxis. She smirked and batted her eyelashes at him. The
Baron turned his steely gaze towards her.

"Daughter."

"Father."

"I am … pleased you have decided to join us here,
Daughter," said the Baron stiffly. "I was maybe a bit too
hasty with my words yesterday. I didn't mean to press you or
offend you in any way."

"Oh stop, Father!" replied Jelaïa. "It was me who was
acting like an idiot. It's time I came down from my ivory
tower — both figuratively and literally — and started acting
like the heir to Arelium instead of a spoilt courtesan."

"Ah, excellent, excellent!" said the Baron, smiling
broadly and slapping her on the back. "Then let us see what
these men from Kessrin have to say before we take the horses
out for a canter, what do you say? Both my horse and I could
do with a bit of fresh air and a good run!"

"I would like that very much, Father," said Jelaïa, finding his calloused hand and giving it a squeeze.

The double doors at the end of the hall were pushed open and the Kessrin delegation entered the room. They wore steel ridged breastplates, striped puffed sleeves, baggy trousers, and white stockings. Four of the men were carrying a hefty mahogany chest, biceps taut under the strain. The fifth man, tall and wiry with a pointed chin-beard, wore a wide-brimmed feather hat and appeared to be their leader. All were unarmed save for the fifth man who wore an exotic curved sword in a scabbard on his belt.

Reaching the Baron, he swept the plumed hat off his head and went down on one knee, speaking in the lightly-accented marine drawl of Kessrin, rolling the 'r's' and elongating the vowels.

"Baron del Arelium, Baroness, Lady del Arelium. I give you my thanks for receiving me so gracefully in your home. My name is Diacrosa and I have travelled far to meet you." His eyes flickered to Jelaïa. "Lady, I am pleased to see that the tales of your beauty have not been exaggerated." He smiled openly, revealing two rows of immaculate teeth. "My liege, we have many things to discuss but first, if it would please you, I would be honoured to present you with this gift from Baron del Kessrin, Lord of the Western Coasts." He gestured at the men behind him and they set the chest down with a clunk.

"Welcome, men of Kessrin," said the Baron, rising from his seat and circling the table to grasp forearms with Diacrosa. "Let us see what that perfumed dandy of a Baron has sent me this time."

He walked over to the chest and undid the clasps,

throwing the lid back to reveal its contents. A bright-red gilded flag filled the width of the interior, embroidered with the snarling form of a white wolf and the word 'Arelium' in gold stitching.

"Exquisite!" murmured the Baron, lifting the flag out to admire it in the light.

"I do hope it pleases you," said Diacrosa and with one fluid motion he drew his sword and sent it darting towards the Baron's exposed neck.

Reflexes honed by years of duelling saved the Baron's life. He swayed backwards, angling his head away from the blow so that instead of opening his jugular, it scored a thin red line just below his Adam's apple.

"To arms!" he yelled, and punched Diacrosa hard in the face. The man's nose broke in a spray of blood and he stumbled back with a cry, dropping his weapon.

The hall erupted in pandemonium. The few noble-men present stood rooted to the spot, unsure if they should intervene. Only the two halberdiers, who had been stand-ing guard, ran forwards to protect their Lord. Jelaïa dived beneath the table, pulling her mother down beside her. The four remaining members of the Kessrin delegation surged towards the chest, drawing forth swords and crossbows that had been hidden under the flag.

Once armed, they split into two groups of two. The first duo ran to the large double doors at the end of the hall, cutting down any of the nobles who got in their way. They heaved the doors closed and barred the entrance with a metal shaft, trapping the Baron's men and destroying all hope of any immediate help from the outside.

The second pair of men turned to face the Baron and

his halberdiers. A crossbow bolt struck the closest guard in the chest, his chainmail offering little resistance to the steel-tipped point at such close range. The surviving guard barrelled into one of the Kessrin, jabbing his halberd wildly in an effort to pin him to the ground.

The other men returned to the fray and three grim-faced Kessrin closed on the Baron, curved swords flashing. The Lord of Arelium dived to his left, scooping up Diacrosa's abandoned weapon. He lunged, his sword taking the closest Kessrin through the shoulder and pushing the other two back.

A scream of pain echoed throughout the hall as the last of the Baron's halberdiers was cut down by his opponent. Diacrosa hauled himself to his feet and joined his four accomplices as they advanced once more upon the Baron, spreading out in a rough semi-circle.

"I've never been very good at counting," said Diacrosa with a smile. "But I'm fairly sure that five men are better than one." He looked hungrily at Jelaïa and her mother, clasped in each other's arms under the table. "However, our employer only wants your head, we have no specific instructions for the rest of your family. Come with us peacefully and we will leave your family alone. Refuse and, once we have dealt with you, I will give your wife to my men and keep your daughter for myself. She looks like she needs some instruction in the ways of the world."

"You dare speak to the Lord of Arelium in such a manner?" snarled the Baron, eyes ablaze. "When I have finished carving you to pieces, I will send whatever is left of you back to Kessrin in a box! Now come, let us finish this."

"With great pleasure, Lord Baron," replied Diacrosa

mockingly, pausing by the chest and choosing a particularly vicious curved scimitar from the pile of weapons. "In fact, I think I will—" he gasped suddenly, then spasmed, his face contorted in agony.

Praxis withdrew his stiletto-like dagger from the Kessrin's side, pivoted smoothly and cut the man's throat. Diacrosa fell, hands scrabbling at his neck. The Baron's steward launched himself at the four remaining men, dodging a cut to the face, his return stroke opening his opponent from thigh to groin. He sidestepped a clumsy overhead thrust and retaliated, the tip of his dagger taking his opponent through the eye.

The two remaining men surged forwards, but Praxis was ready for them. Shrugging off his long leather coat, he threw it at his closest attacker, blinding him. The second Kessrin brought his sword up, but Praxis gave him no time to react, slipping under the man's guard like an eel and stabbing his knife up under the breastplate deep into his ribs. With a savage twist, the knife cracked the assailant's rib and punctured his lung.

The last surviving Kessrin disentangled himself from the steward's cloak but it was far too late. The Baron impaled the man on Diacrosa's sword, his steel armour shattering under the power of the blow.

The ambush was over in a matter of minutes. The five attackers were down, four of them dead, the fifth bleeding heavily from his groin and leg. Praxis carefully wiped his bloody dagger on one of the bodies and returned it to its sheath.

"My Lord, are you hurt?"

The Baron touched his neck and looked at the bright red

blood staining his hands. "'Tis but a scratch, Praxis, nothing that a tight bandage and a glass of wine can't cure." He approached the wounded Kessrin who was dragging himself on his hands and knees towards the exit. "What we need to know now is who wanted me dead, and why?" He grabbed the man by the scruff of the neck and pulled him to his feet. "I want nothing more than to feed your body to the crows," he said coldly. "But I suppose information is more important than petty vengeance. Here is my offer: tell me who you are, and who hired you, and I give my word as Baron of Arelium that you will not be harmed."

The Kessrin tore himself from the Baron's grasp with a snarl, grabbed an unused quarrel from a fallen comrade and plunged the bolt into his eye. He dropped to the ground without a sound, his remaining eye staring sightlessly at the rafters.

"By the Pit!" swore the Baron with feeling. "You there!" he pointed to a trembling noble. "Unbar the door and get me the healer. Praxis! Search the bodies, find me something that'll help us determine who they are or who sent them." He clapped the steward heartily on the shoulder. "And Praxis, you've been hiding your sword skills from me, you devil! That reverse pivot and counterthrust was a thing of beauty. No holding back in the practice yard next time, you hear? You've been going easy on me!"

Jelaïa crawled out from under the table and patted down her unruly hair. She was surprised at her own reaction to the attack: adrenaline coursed through her body but she could detect no undercurrent of fear or doubt. She held her hand out flat in front of her and examined it critically: no visible tremors. Maybe she wasn't as useless as she thought.

She looked up to see her father striding towards her, hand pressed to his neck.

"Jeli! Thank the Twelve you are not hurt! I apologise, but I fear we will have to take the horses out another time. There is much work to be done!"

Jelaïa smiled ruefully. "I think that may be for the best, Father. On the bright side, it looks like I will have to wait a while longer to find a suitable suitor."

The Baron laughed so hard he nearly choked.

CHAPTER 6

THE CARVED FISH

"At first, we believed the greylings to be primal, animalistic beings. Strong in numbers, certainly, but predictable and easily contained. And we were right, for a time. Then something changed. Supply trains vanished without a trace. Our forces stationed in the mountain passes waited for reinforcements that never came. I cannot explain it. Either the greylings were adapting to our presence, or they were being guided by another unknown hand."

MAKARA, TENTH OF THE TWELVE, 8 AT

IT TOOK A couple of hours for Aldarin and Reed to recount the events of the last few days. The goat roasted slowly on the spit as they talked until the cook deemed it ready, smearing it with acacia honey and serving it to the hungry guests with hard-boiled potatoes. The decanter was refilled several times, Fernshaw's blotchy complexion becoming redder and his eyes more bloodshot as the evening wore on. Aldarin looked on disapprovingly, drinking only a little water from his flask.

Once the tale was told, the four men quickly decided on the best course of action. If — or rather when — the greylings broke through the paltry defences left on the wall, Jaelem would be a tempting target. The villagers had no real means of protecting themselves. The palisade would be useless against the enemy, they could simply climb over it as they had done at the Pit. They would have to abandon their homes and flee north towards Arelium.

Fernshaw was reluctant to relinquish any horses or supplies, but was forced to agree that the Baron needed to be warned as soon as possible. Reed, adamant about keeping his promise to Yusifel, chose to leave the next morning with Aldarin. Nidore announced he would be accompanying them, citing his skill with the rapier and his good standing with the Baron as undeniable qualities they would need on the journey.

Guest rooms next to the kitchens were arranged for Aldarin and Reed and they staggered tiredly to their beds, the fire reduced to a scattering of smouldering embers. Darkness reclaimed the village hall.

The greyling entered Jaelem easily, clawed hands and feet hammering into the wooden palisade. In moments it was up and over, moving silently towards the village hall. The open chimney was still warm from the fire, but the heat did nothing to bother

it after years of living in the hot, snaking tunnels of the Pit.
It landed silently in the fireplace and edged towards the guest
rooms, feet clicking on the stone floor. It entered the first bed-
room and fixed its bulbous yellow eyes on the figure in the bed,
a slim, middle-aged man with careworn features and a scraggly
beard. A leather surcoat and faded red cloak lay on a chair next
to the bed above a dusty pair of boots.

With a shriek, the greyling leapt at its prey, claws plunging
into the sleeping man's chest, puncturing the lungs and heart,
bright red blood gushing from the wound, soaking the bed and
sheets. The man opened his mouth and—

Reed screamed himself awake, the dream still vivid and
real in his mind. He could feel the thing's talons raking his
chest, feel its malevolent gaze as it watched him contort in
agony. Never had his nightmares been this visceral, and he
feared it was only the beginning.

Suppressing a shudder, he sat up. His undergarments
were soaked in sweat. Light spilled into the room through a
small window over the bed, and he could hear low voices and
sounds of clinking cutlery coming from the hall. Someone
had attempted to clean the dirt and grime from his clothes
and boots, leaving a washbasin and cloth on the floor by the
door.

Reed spent a few minutes washing his body and face,
trimming his beard the best he could with a sharp dagger.
He ran a hand through his hair, then buckled on the leather
surcoat and cloak. Entering the hall, he saw Aldarin alone at
the table, focused on stripping the remains of the meat from
the goat carcass. He was, as always, wearing his armour save
for the horned visor-less helm. Further down the table, two

empty wine glasses and a half-eaten loaf of bread were all that remained of breakfast.

"Friend Reed!" said Aldarin, saluting him with the remnant of a goat leg. "I must confess I was beginning to think we would have to leave without you. Nidore was ready at dawn and was quite put out when I told him we would wait a little longer. I sent him off to find some sustenance for the road."

Reed nodded, helping himself to the leftover bread. "Thank you, Aldarin. Though I must claim a few more moments of your time. If you would be so good as to saddle my horse for me? I only need a few minutes."

Aldarin looked at him curiously with his ice-cold eyes and, just as before, Reed felt the knight knew exactly where he was going. "Of course," he said. "There are some things that must be done. We will wait for you by the village gate."

Reed nodded again and left the hall, heading down through the square and out of the palisade into the woods beyond. There weren't many trees, no more than thirty or so grouped around the lake, its mirror-like surface broken only by the occasional gust of wind.

He was alone. It was still early, and most of the villagers slept. Birds fluttered in and out of the branches, twittering amongst themselves. A family of toads called to each other across the water. Reed closed his eyes and let the calm and tranquillity of his surroundings wash over him. For the first time in days, he felt at peace.

After a few quiet moments, he moved further into the woods, heading unerringly towards one of the bigger oak trees, its huge leaves dappling the forest floor with shadows. A crude cross had been cut into the trunk and below it, a small detailed carving of a fish, positioned as if it were swimming up the length of the tree from roots to canopy.

"Hello, Mother," said Reed softly. "It has been a long time, too long, since I came to see you last." He heard a sound behind him and saw a fisherman pulling his hide boat down into the lake. Another reminder of what might have been.

"I feel I need to explain. They say time flows differently up on the wall. The monotony becomes a kind of addiction, a comforting certitude that every day when you wake up, things will be the same. And then those days become weeks, the weeks become months and then ... years. Years and years of menial, repetitive boredom. And I was convinced I was happy. There was no need for me to change, no need for me to return here, to force myself to understand that you are gone, that you are not coming back, and that you and Father have left me all alone."

He felt a wetness on his cheeks and wiped his face with the backs of his hands.

"It has taken the death of many friends, and the help of an honourable — if rather strange — man, to set me back on a path that I think will lead me to better myself. I am sorry, Mother, I must leave you again, but this time I believe it is for the right reasons. I miss you. I miss Father. I hope I will find a way to make you proud. And I will do what I can to come back and see you again one day." He touched two fingers to his lips and placed them lovingly on the carving of the fish, then turned and made his way slowly back to the village.

The square was gradually coming alive as the men and women of Jaelem began their day. Aldarin and Nidore were waiting for him by the gate. Aldarin had locked his helm in place and was mounted on a massive chestnut shire horse with hooves bigger than Reed's fist. Nidore sat upon a pale grey mare. He wore a striking green fitted jacket with gold buttons and tall black riding boots. A wafer-thin rapier hung from a belt at his side, a short bow and quiver of arrows strapped to the saddle behind him. The clothes and weapons were spotless, meaning they had been either thoroughly cleaned or seldom used. Reed suspected it was the latter.

"C'mon, Reed!" huffed Nidore impatiently. "We'll never leave this Pit-forsaken place at this rate!" He gestured to his left with an immaculate gloved hand and Reed saw a sorry-looking piebald horse tied to a post near the palisade with his spear and camping gear on its back.

Sighing, he untied the reins and clambered up into the saddle, steadying himself as best he could against the pommel. He had only been on a horse a handful of times and couldn't remember much more than unpleasant feelings of chafed thighs and aching buttocks.

Turning, he saw Fernshaw had come to see them off, a gaudily-clothed figure waving furiously from the steps leading to the village hall. Reed raised his hand in reply, took a last, long look around the square, then nudged his horse forwards out through the gate and on to Arelium.

≼

The three men set off at a slow trot and soon left Jaelem behind. The horses were sturdy and well-fed, used to travelling along the windswept trails between the villages scattered all over the plains. The road to Arelium was well marked, growing wider and more used as the day drew on.

Nidore was a very different travel companion from Aldarin. The knight spoke little, lost in contemplation, eyes fixed on the road ahead. Nidore talked constantly, mostly about himself, only stopping to drink from his flask or to point out some of the more interesting landmarks as they passed by.

And so, over the next few days, Reed learnt a great deal about Nidore del Conte, first and only child of Lord Loré del Conte, vassal to the Baron of Arelium and one of the richest nobles in the southern valley.

His mother was Fernshaw's sister-in-law, a petite woman with flaming red hair, who worked as a florist for many years before catching the eye of the young Loré who, infatuated, had proposed within months. And so Nidore's mother had left her flowers behind to become lady-in-waiting to the Baroness herself.

The del Conte family owned a sprawling country estate, but Nidore had spent most of his childhood living in the town keep with his mother. These early years were quite solitary ones as most of the other nobles with lands outside Arelium only brought their families to court on rare occasions. In fact, the only other person of comparable age had been the Baron's daughter, Jelaïa, and she had always seemed more interested in her maps and scrolls than in playing hide-and-seek or stealing freshly-baked pancakes from the kitchens.

Once Nidore came of age (at approximately fifteen or sixteen if Reed understood correctly), he received instruction in politics, the arts, and the use of the rapier. The thin, wiry

sword didn't look very dangerous but Nidore assured them
that, if used correctly, it could cause some serious harm.

His father was mostly absent. Things had cooled somewhat between the noble and the red-haired flower girl, and
del Conte came to court only when his function demanded
it. Loré had been designated 'Protector of the Realm', and as
such was responsible for keeping Arelium safe from dangers
both without and within. In practice, the Barony was firmly
allied with its neighbours and had been for many years. The
only real threats to the realm were bandits and wild animals,
little match for a cortege of fully-armoured knights.

Reed had enquired about the 'White Wolf', Listus,
the Baron of Arelium, a man whom he had never met, but
Nidore was quite evasive on the subject of his liege lord.
Loré and Listus, both sons of noble families, had known
each other for years and cultivated a long-standing tradition
of permanent competition dating back to their childhood.

Listus admonished his vassal for his lack of respect,
while Loré reproached the dictatorial nature of the Baron's
rule, arguing that the nobles should be more involved in
running the Barony. This open challenge had sent an undercurrent of unease rippling through the lords and ladies of
Arelium, one that could upset the fragile balancing act the
Baron was trying to preserve.

They had been travelling for three days when they heard
the cries for help. The horses had been following the dirt
road through a patch of woodland, twisting and turning
between the trees. Nidore called the place Kaevel Forest.
Night was fast approaching, the early twilight filtering down
through the leaves, casting strange shadows on the ground
and making it difficult to see more than a few paces ahead.

Aldarin was first to hear the faint sounds of battle and he spurred his horse forwards with a great shout, the others close behind.

Reed crouched low in the saddle, stray branches whipping and snapping close to his head as his horse plunged through the densely-packed undergrowth. He set his spear horizontally against his body, blade aimed low like a makeshift lance. The path opened out into a large clearing, bordered on all sides by a thick screen of trees forming a natural wall. Three wagons formed a rough defensive triangle in the middle of the clearing, beset on all sides by greylings.

The caravan had obviously been ambushed as they were setting up camp for the night. One elderly man lay sprawled on his back a few yards from the wagons, entrails spilling from his open stomach, sticks of kindling scattered around his steaming innards. Others had been attacked while unpacking great metal-banded chests of food and supplies, or while pitching canvas tents in a semi-circle around a fire pit. One of the tents had caught alight, sending plumes of smoke coiling up into the darkening sky, reminding Reed of the signal fires on the wall. He saw dead men, women, and children, bodies clawed and mauled indiscriminately.

Only three were still alive, two men and a woman, hunkered down together inside the paltry shelter offered by the wagons. One man had a crossbow and was firing blindly into the attacking greylings. The other man was in bad shape, one arm hanging uselessly at his side, his leather doublet drenched in blood. He held a longsword in his other hand, swiping desperately with wide, unfocussed strokes. The last of the survivors, a pale-skinned woman with long, curly black hair and a stained sky-blue dress, had a dagger

grasped in two trembling hands, her terror-filled eyes darting anxiously around the clearing as the enemy closed in.

Aldarin thundered deep into the mass of greylings, the
huge iron-shod hooves of his shire horse trampling two of
the creatures underfoot. The Knight of the Twelve slashed
left and right with his battle-axe, hurling the greylings back
in a shower of black ichor. One of the attackers had managed to avoid the blade by ducking instinctively at the last
moment and it scuttled forwards, raking its claws across the
horse's flank. The animal gave a snort of pain, rearing wildly
and shaking Aldarin from its back. He fell heavily, but was
soon upright again, eyes cold and calculating, axe flicking
out like a snake's tongue at any of the enemy that got within
range.

Reed followed close behind. An arrow whistled past his
ear as he galloped forwards and he spared a glance back to
see Nidore at the edge of the clearing, another arrow already
nocked on his bow, the string drawn back taut against his
cheek. With a supple twang, he sent a second shaft following the first, the steel tip striking a greyling through its open
mouth and sending it spiralling to the ground.

Reed aimed well and speared a creature through the
neck, the impact sending the thing flying backwards to col-
lide with one of its kind. A high-pitched scream rang out
over the clearing. Reed saw that several of the greylings had
managed to breach the perimeter of the wagons and had
fallen upon the wounded swordsman in a flurry of teeth and
claws. The crossbowman was hopelessly trying to reload his
weapon, fear and sweat making his hands slip on the coarse
string. The woman cowered behind him, sobbing.

Reed cursed and tried to wheel his horse towards the

wagons but the animal shied and bucked in panic, nearly throwing him off. With an angry cry, he leapt from the saddle and sprinted towards the beleaguered defenders, vaulting up and over the flat back of one of the carts. He arrived in time to see a greyling jump onto the crossbowman, talons opening his throat in a spray of arterial blood.

Two others were still crouched over the unlucky swordsman, oblivious of Reed's presence. He sprang at the first creature, thrusting his spear through its back, then quickly withdrew the blade and sliced diagonally at the face of the second, cleaving it from ear to chin. The creature collapsed with a confused sputter.

The last of the greylings turned at the sound, bulging dirty yellow eyes fixed on Reed. Before it could move to attack, the dark-haired woman stumbled forwards and stabbed it hard between the shoulder blades with her knife. It gave a shriek of surprise and started to swivel back around, but the woman hurled herself at the creature and stabbed it again and again in a frenzy, the knife rising and falling in a torrent of viscous black rain. The greyling thrashed and kicked, then lay still.

The woman stood panting over the grey-skinned body, a feral look in her eyes. She focused with some difficulty on Reed, who was staring at her in astonishment.

"What in the Pit's name are these things?" she said, fear and anger distorting her voice. She raised her knife defensively. "And for that matter, who in the damned Pit are you?" She glanced past the wagons to see that Aldarin and Nidore had killed the remaining greylings and were picking their way carefully among the bodies, silencing the wounded. An eerie quiet descended on the clearing.

Reed wiped the worst of the blood and gore from his spear with the corner of his cloak and laid it against one of the wagon wheels. "That will take a while to explain," he said tiredly. "And time is of the essence. I hope our actions have proved that we are no threat to you. The rest will have to wait."

"Friend Reed!" Aldarin's deep-pitched voice echoed across the clearing as he approached. "We should not tarry, there may be more of the greylings in the trees."

"How did they get here so fast?"

"I fear our detour south to Jaelem may have been more costly than we thought. For while we were forced to turn south for horses and supplies, our enemies have been trav-elling steadily northwards since they breached the wall." Aldarin paused and bowed his head briefly. "Captain Yusifel must not have been able to hold them long, much to my regret." He scanned the glade, counting the number of dead.

"I do not see many of their number here," he continued. "This is an advance group, a scouting party perhaps, sent to reconnoitre the lay of the land and report back. It is but an unfortunate coincidence that they came across this caravan."

The pale woman pushed her way past Reed and stood toe-to-toe with Aldarin, trembling with rage. She was forced to tilt her head back to look him in the eye. "Now listen here, *Sir Knight*," she said, the words laced with sarcasm. "I don't know where you and your kind have been hiding for the last few years, but the rest of us want nothing more than to go about our lives without getting drawn into your petty little skirmishes here. My father and I have been trad-ing silks and fabrics down on the plains since I was a little girl and now that he's gone," — she gestured to the body sprawled among the kindling — "it's up to me to keep the business running, starting with getting all this merchandise to Jaelem."

Aldarin was rather startled by this outburst, but before he could reply Nidore interceded smoothly. "My Lady," he said with a courteous bow. "You are right, of course, my travelling companion spoke a tad rashly. Allow me to introduce myself: Nidore del Conte at your service, son of Lord del Conte and heir to the family name. I fear it would be unwise to travel further south in the next few weeks; there are many more of these creatures roaming the plains. In fact, the people of Jaelem are a few short days behind us, travelling to Arelium to ask for asylum. If it pleases you, I would be honoured to escort you there myself, and petition the Baron to hear your case in open court. He is a most respected and generous man; he will be able to help you."

The woman seemed to calm a little and take stock of her surroundings. The knife slipped from her fingers as she straightened her blood-stained dress. "Thank you, Sir Nidore, I accept your generous offer. If you would just give me a few moments to gather my things?" She drifted over to one of the chests, heaved the lid open and started stuffing various items into a canvas bag. "I'm Veronassandra, by the way, Veronassandra Angelson, but most people just call me Verona."

Once Verona was packed and ready, there was nothing more to do but decide how to dispose of the dead. Nidore suggested burning the bodies, an idea that was quickly discarded as a fire would not only reveal their position to any enemy scouts, but also risk setting the closely-packed trees alight, potentially burning through acres of forest.

In the end, they had no other choice but to leave the bodies in the clearing, laying the corpses together in a long line and covering them with the tarpaulin from the tents. Aldarin disappeared into the underbrush and returned with two sizeable branches, which he fashioned into a makeshift cross.

The moon was shining brightly by the time they were done, and all agreed it would be best to ride hard through the night, stopping to rest during the day once they had cleared the forest. Verona had changed into a simple pale-green blouse and black leggings, and wrapped herself in a dark-blue riding cloak. A heart-shaped silver locket hung on a chain around her neck. She swung herself up easily behind Nidore and the four travellers pushed on towards Arelium, leaving the line of dead to be reclaimed by the forest.

The rest of the journey to Arelium was mostly uneventful. The forest gave way to grasslands, which slowly became fields of cattle and wheat, where farmers toiled away at the hard earth. The road was deserted save for the odd heavily-laden cart travelling between farms or, more rarely, a merchant caravan heading south to trade with the villages on the plains.

Aldarin stopped and warned all those he could, urging them to turn back, or at least find a good spot to hide from the greylings arriving from the south. He was not a charismatic speaker, but his voice exuded calm and confidence, and his message was delivered with such assurance that few doubted the truth of it — however far-fetched it may seem.

Others were swayed by his sheer physical presence. He

continued to sharpen his axe and polish his armour on a daily basis and the gleaming interlocking metal plates sparkled as he gestured with his hands and arms. He rarely took his helmet off, even under the blistering noonday sun, leaving only his intense blue eyes visible in the shadows of his face.

Verona spent the first few days in silence, although at night they could all hear her crying softly in her sleep. Nidore whiled away the hours of the day talking gently to her, seemingly not troubled by the fact that she never spoke back. He told her of his time spent growing up in Arelium, sharing the various funny and embarrassing ways his group of friends played practical jokes on each other to pass the time.

It was during one of these stories, involving a half-open door, a rope, and a bucket of sheep dung, that he heard a muffled chuckle and turned to see Verona smiling back at him, her eyes shining. From that moment on, her heavy veil of sorrow lifted ever so slightly, and she started talking back to Nidore, pressing him for details or pointing out inconsistencies as his stories became more and more ludicrous.

On the afternoon of the sixth day, they got their first look at Arelium. It had been raining since mid-morning. The horses were tired and cold from plodding through the mud and puddles. The path took them up a steep incline and as they crested the hill, the fortified town came into view in the valley below, a distant smudge of grey on the banks of the River Stahl.

"At last, we have arrived," said Aldarin tiredly. "Let this be the end of it." He tapped his mount's flank lightly with his heel and the sodden beast moved slowly down the hill, rivulets of rainwater dripping from its mane and tail.

And so, after a week of anticipation, Reed would finally get to meet the Baron.

CHAPTER 7

ARRIVALS AND DEPARTURES

"I really don't care about long-standing tradition. Tradition is far too often used as an excuse to justify stagnation. Just look at your ledgers. My agricultural holdings bring in more than half the coin of the entire Barony, and yet trade edicts are still signed daily by Listus alone. Oh, and don't think that whole 'Protector of the Realm' thing will buy him any peace. Sending me scurrying left and right, chasing down feral dogs and wild boar. Tell the Baron to tread carefully, for a chained wolf can only suffer so much before biting off the hand of its Master."

LORÉ DEL CONTE, VASSAL TO THE BARON OF ARELIUM, 424 AT

⁓

J ELAÏA WATCHED THE servants scrub at the dry spots of blood staining the floor of the hall. They had been at it all afternoon, unsuccessfully for the most part, the hot water and suds doing little to remove the gory smears.

The day was drawing to a close. More servants moved silently in and out of the hall carrying bundles of wood and flint, lighting the braziers set in the walls.

Her father stood at the head of the table, dressed for war. His gold-plated armour was a magnificent work of art. The gauntlets and vambraces were engraved with curling thorns that spiralled up his arms and legs to frame a delicately bossed wolf's head embedded in the centre of his breastplate. Multiple riveted sheets of metal formed a stiff gorget around his throat and lower face. His bastard sword, shorter in length than a longsword but with a wider fuller, lay sheathed on the table top within easy reach.

Since the attack on the Baron's life, things had changed. Four men had died in the assault; two halberdiers and a couple of minor vassals invited to receive the Kessrin delegation. Now, the few remaining nobles staying at the keep had been sent back to their countryside manors. Five crossbowmen stood to attention on either side of the hall, with two more posted just outside the keep's entrance. All visitors, without exception, were stopped and searched, and the castle grounds were patrolled day and night by a vigilant squad of halberdiers.

The Baron himself had become more introverted and brooding. He blamed himself for the deaths of his two guardsmen, deaths that could have been averted if he had been less complacent.

Praxis had also been hard on himself, working tirelessly to make some sense of the chain of events leading to the assassination attempt. He sent scouts along all the major roads leading to and from Arelium, looking for any trace of the Kessrin's passage into the valley.

In the end they got lucky, a huntsman from the western woods found five fresh corpses buried in a shallow grave just north of the border. The heavy rain of the last few days had turned the loosely-packed earth to mud and exposed enough of the bodies to attract the local wild animals.

The dead men were clearly Kessrin, stripped down to their underclothes. They all bore wounds to their backs; small punctures made by some sort of dart or crossbow bolt. Praxis had the bodies brought back to the keep and examined by the Baron's healer, but nothing could be gleaned from his post-mortem dissection.

From there the trail went cold. With no survivors and nothing of import among the assassins' belongings, there was not much more that could be done. The five dead members of the unfortunate Kessrin delegation were sent back home, accompanied by an armed guard and a letter of warning from the Baron to his counterpart in Kessrin.

For one thing was sure: the attackers must have known when and where the Kessrin delegation would be travelling, their ambush had been well-timed and well-prepared. The integrity of Baron del Kessrin's court was compromised. Either one of his vassals was spying for the enemy directly, or the information had been obtained from one of his subjects by some other nefarious means. In either case, the events merited further investigation.

And now more travellers had arrived from outside the valley, begging for an audience with the Baron, claiming they had urgent matters to discuss. They stood at the end of the hall, three men and a woman, rainwater dripping from their soaked clothes and bodies to pool on the floor.

Two of the men Jelaïa already knew. Nidore, one of the

only court nobles she would call a friend, had changed since she last saw him. His once carefree face was etched with worry lines, partially hidden by a bedraggled mess of blond hair. The fine clothes he wore were ripped and torn from days on the road, spattered with dirt and a darker, sticky substance that could be tar or blood. He stood with his shoulders hunched and his eyes downcast.

The second man, Jelaïa remembered, was called Aldarin, the Knight of the Twelve. She had seen him four or five times in her life. He often appeared in Arelium without warning to converse with the Baron alone, never staying more than a few hours before heading out again on some urgent mission. He was from Kessrin, or somewhere near Kessrin, dwelling in a temple on the coast with other members of his Order. She saw he still carried his double-bladed axe slung over his back. The fact that the Baron had allowed the knight into his hall with a weapon was an enormous sign of trust, more so now than ever, and Jelaïa relaxed slightly.

Behind the knight were two newcomers she had never seen before. A middle-aged man with greying hair and beard stood closest to the door. He was wrapped in a faded red cloak under which he wore a grey leather surcoat embroidered with a setting sun, very similar in style to one of the banners adorning the hall. One of the Old Guard, then, come from the Pit.

Next to him, looking exhausted, was a young woman, perhaps only a few years older than Jelaïa. Her alabaster-white skin was in stark contrast to her lustrous, curly black hair that reached half-way down her back. She was wringing water from the corner of her night-blue riding cloak, adding to the puddles already mottling the floor.

Aldarin went down on one knee with a creaking of metal. "My Lord Baron, Lady del Arelium, Sir Praxis, you have my thanks for receiving my travelling companions and I in your home at this late hour. May I present to you Merad Reed, of the Old Guard, and Veronassandra Angelson, a silk trader whom we met on the road. We have come with all haste from the Pit, and I would speak to you about what we found there." He glanced at Praxis and Jelaïa. "It concerns matters we have not discussed openly until now."

"Things have changed," replied the Baron gruffly, motioning for the knight to stand. "I think the time for keeping secrets and running around in the dark is over. If you have something to say, you can say it in front of my steward and daughter. Praxis saved my life not three days ago, he has proven his loyalty and trust to me many times over."

"Very well," Aldarin acquiesced. "As I told you when we last met, a little over a month ago the priestesses of my temple felt a weakening in the wards surrounding the Southern Pit. It was deemed wise that I should be sent to investigate this occurrence and report back."

Jelaïa saw Reed lean forwards with interest, as if he was hearing this information for the first time.

"When I arrived at the Pit, nothing seemed to be amiss. It was only once I was upon the walls that I could feel it, a pulsing, oppressive energy that seemed to emanate from the Pit itself. And the more I stayed on the wall, the stronger the feeling became, trying to worm its way into my mind and fill it with dark thoughts. I studied the wards themselves and many were faded or destroyed altogether, whether through

erosion or sabotage I do not know. And before I could investigate further, the Pit was attacked by greylings."

The Baron raised his eyebrows in surprise. "Greylings?
There haven't been any greylings around here for hundreds
of years. My grandfather told me that *his* father had routed
a small band of them out in the forests near our southern
borders, but even then, I'm not sure that story wasn't just to
scare me out of going hunting there. Are you sure about this?"

"Are we sure?" came an irate voice and Jelaïa saw that
Reed had come to stand beside the Knight of the Twelve,
simmering with suppressed rage. "I got a fairly good look
at one of them, my Lord, just after it slit my friend's throat.
Got to see plenty more, too, as they ripped my fellow watchmen to pieces and fought over the limbs torn from their
bodies. They wanted to keep them, as trophies, you see?
Maybe if you had deigned to come down to the Pit yourself,
you would have known my comrades' names!"

"Enough!" roared the Baron, his steely eyes flashing
dangerously. "You address the Lord of Arelium, not some
half-brained peasant. Do not take that condescending tone
with me again or I will have you removed from my hall."

Reed clamped his jaw shut, but continued to stare daggers at the Baron as he fought to control himself. Jelaïa
thought that if looks could kill the Baron would be a human-
shaped mess on the floor.

"My apologies, my Lord," said Aldarin formally. "My
companion is still quite shaken from what occurred. He lost
both his friends and his home in one night. For while we
did manage to beat back the initial assault, the forces we left
behind were in no fit shape to repulse a second wave. The
wall has fallen."

The Baron scowled and looked down at the hand-drawn map of Arelium spread out on the table. In the bottom-left corner, an ominous pitch-black blot of ink represented the Pit. "Very well. Go on."

"After seeking aid in the village of Jaelem, we pushed north and met the creatures a second time in Kaevel Forest."

"Kaevel Forest, but that's only four days away," said someone in a strained voice and Jelaïa realised it was her own.

"That is correct, my Lady. We killed what we believe to have been an advance party to a much larger force making its way up from the plains. I would think they are only a few days from the entrance to the valley."

"Thank you for this," said the Baron, all anger having left his voice. "I must admit when you first told me of your mission, I dismissed it as another fool's errand but I was wrong. I have been wrong about a number of things recently; it is time for that to change."

He turned to Reed. "And do not think I do not know who you are, or the sacrifices you have made Merad Reed. I receive regular reports from the wall, always have, and they are always taken seriously. Not one month ago, Praxis and I ordered stone to be brought from the Morlak quarries to reinforce some of the dilapidated towers. And I have met with Captain Yusifel many times. He is" — he caught himself — "he *was* a fine man, always putting the Old Guard first before anything else, including his own well-being. I would like to have more soldiers like him. You can be proud of who you are and what you have done. Thanks to your efforts, we can stop this before it has even begun. Come, stand with me."

He turned back to the detailed map of Arelium. The others gathered around the table. "We will not be taking any chances. We must act swiftly and with a great show of strength. A mounted response would give us the best chance of crushing them before they arrive in the valley." He tapped an area on the map with a gauntleted finger. "Praxis! Send word to the nobles. Tell them the security of the Barony is compromised. I want them and any cavalry they have available armed and ready within the hour. We leave tonight."

"I do not think that would be wise, my Lord," said Praxis calmly.

"What do you mean, man?" replied the Baron, glowering at his steward.

"You have already survived one attempt on your life, my Lord, I see no need for you to go rushing off headlong into another battle."

"I disagree. The people need to see me. I have always led from the front, Praxis, I won't have anyone tell me I am a coward."

"I am quite sure no one would say any such thing of you my Lord," said Praxis with a thin smile. "In fact, from what I understand, recent events have only consolidated your good standing with the people of Arelium. The town theatre staged a wonderful re-enactment of the attack, and people cheered when you broke Diacrosa's nose."

The Baron mellowed somewhat at this, but would not be dissuaded. "Maybe so, Praxis, but someone needs to keep those nobles in line. They are fine knights individually, less so when they are asked to fight and coordinate with others."

"I'm sure Lord del Conte can deal with the nobles," replied Praxis smoothly. "He has been doing a first-rate job as Protector of the Realm. And I seem to remember that when he took charge of the militia in your absence several years ago, he routed those bandits quite effectively."

"Yes, he would like to take charge, I'm sure," said the Baron testily. "He'd like to do more than just take charge of my knights, too, if he could. I've seen him skulking around the corridors of the keep, trying to worm his way into my good graces. And leaving his son here to go after my daughter."

"If I may, my Lord," said Nidore tentatively, his face reddening, "I don't think that's—"

"Oh quiet, Nidore!" snapped the Baron. "Anyone with two eyes and a brain can see what's going on. At least your father has some military experience, which is more than you have to offer."

"Thank you for enlightening me, my Lord," said Nidore tersely through clenched teeth. "If you would excuse me, I am greatly fatigued by the journey from Jaelem. I will return to my father's manor to rest." He turned without waiting for the Baron's reply, and stalked from the hall. Verona opened her mouth to say something, caught a warning glance from Aldarin, and shut it again.

"That was badly done, Father," admonished Jelaïa. "Whatever your problem is with Lord del Conte, his son has nothing to do with it."

The Baron removed his gauntlets, throwing them onto the table with a clink of metal, and pinched the bridge of his nose. "You are right, Daughter, as you so often are. I have had difficulty mastering my emotions of late. I'll apologise to him when we return."

"Thank you, Father."

"You have to admit though, he is a rather annoying young man, prancing around here in his fine clothes and his blond ponytail."

"Father!"

"Right, right, sorry. I still think I should lead my own men into battle. Praxis?"

The steward was shaking his head. "I really didn't want it to come to this, my Lord, but you are being awfully stubborn. Would you remove your gorget, please?"

The Baron gave Praxis a sour look, but did as he was asked, undoing the hinged clasps that secured the gold-plated slats to his breastplate. The gorget came free, revealing a blood-stained bandage wrapped around his upper neck.

"Your cut's still bleeding?" said Jelaïa.

"I didn't want to bother you with it, Daughter," replied the Baron guiltily. "It is healing, slowly, but I break the surface of the skin each time I turn my neck, making the Pit-spawned thing bleed again." He deflated slightly, suddenly looking more his age. "Very well, Praxis, you win. I will stay here. Del Conte will lead the assault on the grey-lings. I suppose if I'm lucky, he'll fall to a stray claw and I won't have to see his infuriating smirk anymore. Aldarin, is there anything else?"

"My fellow initiates and I are few, but well-trained in the art of war," said Aldarin carefully. "If you call upon my temple for aid, we will stand by you and the people of Arelium."

"No need for that," scoffed the Baron, dismissing the idea with a wave of his hand. "My own knights will be sufficient. And besides, we do not have time to wait."

"Very well." Aldarin bowed his head respectfully. "In

that case, would it be possible for myself and my fellow companions to take advantage of your hospitality for a while longer? Reed cannot travel south while the way is blocked and Verona will need to spend some time here consolidating her business. As for me, I would rest for a few days before returning to my temple."

"Of course, Aldarin," the Baron replied. "It's the least we can do to thank you for your service. I will have guest chambers prepared for you all here in the keep, new clothes brought for you, and fresh horses ready for when you leave." He summoned one of the servants positioned discreetly around the hall. "This man will see you lodged and fed. We will have ample time to discuss your journey in greater detail tomorrow."

The meeting was over. The three travellers thanked the Baron and followed the servant from the room.

～⑥

The mustering field in front of the barbican was a swirling storm of people and horses. Squires ran after their masters, bent double with swords, lances, and shields. Stablehands were giving the animals a last grooming or cleaning leather tack. Nobles shouted noisily for servants to strap on breastplates, helms, cuissarts, and barding.

The grass of the field was getting churned into muck from the hundreds of shod hooves and armoured feet. Four great bonfires had been lit, one at each corner of the area. The whole place stank of sweat, straw, and smoke.

The rain had dwindled to a drizzle and the first of the evening stars could be seen through the thinning clouds. A

cool breeze blew down from the river, tugging at the fluttering standards and pennants. Each of the noble houses had
its own colours and coat of arms: prancing lions, winged
birds of prey, horned stags; a veritable menagerie of creatures
dancing in the wind.

Jelaïa watched the muster with her father. She sat side-
saddle on a snowy-white mare, her fur-lined hooded cloak
keeping out most of the cold. The Baron, still in his resplendent gold armour, looked agitated; pacing his horse back
and forth, bellowing words of greeting or advice, and fiddling with the gorget around his neck.

Jelaïa could tell he was itching to join them, but she was
glad he had decided to stay. Whenever he left for battle, his
wife, the Baroness, worried herself sick, spending long hours
in her chambers and eating little. Lord del Conte would be
up to the task, she was sure of it.

The man himself suddenly appeared at the edge of the
field, almost as if she had willed him into existence. Nidore's
father was tall and handsome, much like his son, with short,
blond, expertly-styled hair. He was as charismatic as he was
arrogant: Jelaïa had heard many tales of the mistresses dotted
around his estate and everyone knew he rarely slept in his
own bed. Despite this poorly-kept secret, he was well-liked,
particularly among the nobles. She watched him move slowly
through the throng of knights, clasping hands and chatting
amiably. He stopped in front of her, flashed a perfect smile,
then turned to her father.

"Listus, how nice of you to come and see us off!"

Jelaïa winced inwardly. Loré del Conte was one of the
only people to call the Baron by his first name and she knew

it irritated him immensely. She saw her father grit his teeth before replying.

"It is my prerogative as Baron to inspect my troops before they engage the enemy, Loré, as you well know. And please address me by my title. We are not boyhood friends chasing chickens around my father's yard anymore."

"Of course, of course," said del Conte with an easy grin. "In any case, I came to tell you we are ready to march, we await but your command."

Jelaïa saw he was right, the Baron's vassals and their men had finished their final preparations and formed into ranks on the field, ten abreast. She had to admit it was an impressive sight. Each knight carried a highly-embellished shield and lance displaying his personal heraldry. Multi-coloured plumes and crests decorated polished helms of all shapes and sizes. Most of the horses wore padded coats, but some had full barded armour with ornate chanfron headpieces, the hostile horns and spikes transforming the animals into something more primal and dangerous.

Del Conte hauled himself into the saddle of his own barded warhorse and locked his helm in place. His horse pawed at the ground nervously.

"Loyal vassals!" came the Baron's booming voice. "Let me tell you why you are here! Arelium is under attack! As we speak, dark creatures are spreading like a plague through our lands, killing our merchants, murdering our women and children, burning our crops that we have worked so hard to grow! This cannot stand! Our ancestors stood shoulder to shoulder with the Twelve and sent these snivelling cowards back into the holes from whence they crawled forth! Will you help me do it again? Will you help me protect my subjects and avenge the fallen? Will you do your duty?"

A deafening cry answered the Baron's words, echoing off the curtain wall, cutting through the silence of the night. Horses shied and reared. Knights banged rhythmically on painted shields and steel breastplates, adding to the din.

"ARELIUM!" yelled the Baron, his words somehow rising above the tide of sound.

"ARELIUM! ARELIUM! ARELIUM!" came the reply uttered by a hundred mouths. And Jelaïa found herself chanting it too, swept up in a moment of passion and loyalty.

The knights kicked their horses into a gallop and charged off the field into the night, the ground beneath them rumbling and trembling from the mass of steel and flesh.

Jelaïa and her father watched them go, then wheeled their horses back towards the keep.

All that was left to do now was wait.

CHAPTER 8

THE STORY OF THE TWELVE

"We are not your rulers. We are not your enforcers. My brothers and sisters have always been teachers first, warriors second. We will abide by any decision you choose to make. But look at what your stubbornness is costing you. While you argue amongst yourselves, your people are dying of hunger and disease. Every second you remain divided is another step down the path to your own damnation. So ask yourselves, is it really worth doing nothing at the risk of losing everything?"

MAKARA, TENTH OF THE TWELVE, 2 AT

✧

REED'S GUEST CHAMBERS were bigger than the entire barracks of the Old Guard. He struggled out of his travel-worn clothes and hobbled across the room on aching feet to the ornate four-poster bed. Sinking down gratefully into the soft feather mattress, he was asleep within minutes.

A stooped, balding servant dressed in the red and white livery of Arelium was waiting patiently by the door when he awoke, blurry-eyed, the next morning.

"Good morning, Lord Reed," said the man, his face expressionless. "The Baron apologises but he will not be able to meet with you today, being detained by matters of State. I'm sure you understand."

Reed grunted and searched around for the clothes he had left in a tangled heap on the floor the night before.

"I took the liberty of dispatching your attire to the laundry," said the servant, somehow making the word *attire* sound like an infectious disease. "I have laid out a selection of vestments for his lordship, to your left near the window. To your right is a range of breakfast foodstuffs with fresh apple juice and white wine. I am afraid you will have to eat in your room, the kitchens are closed this late in the morning."

"This late? How long have I been asleep?"

"It is shortly before noon, my Lord," answered the man, a tad reproachfully. "Of your fellow travellers, only Sir Aldarin is still here, in the garden I believe. Lady Veronassandra has departed to her townhouse on business and Lord Nidore has not yet returned from his family estate."

"Thank you," Reed replied. "There is no need to address me as 'my Lord', I am lord of nothing and no one. My name will suffice."

"Of course, Lord Reed," said the servant with a taut smile. "I will do my best."

Reed got the impression he would do nothing of the sort.

"If there is nothing else, I will leave you to get dressed and eat ... unless you need some further assistance with one of these tasks?" The man waited, one eyebrow cocked inquisitively.

"No, no, of course not," said Reed, a bit more hurriedly than he had meant to.

"Very well." The servant bowed low and retreated gracefully, shutting the door quietly behind him.

Reed's stomach gave a warning growl and he wandered over to the breakfast table. It was overflowing with food and drink: bread rolls with cream and butter, fresh strawberries, hard-boiled eggs, milk and cheese, yoghurt mixed with honey, sugary pastries, piping-hot porridge, and much more. Reed attacked with gusto, trying everything he could get his hands on, and washing it all down with a generous helping of apple juice.

Once satiated, he turned his attention to his new wardrobe. True to his word, the servant had chosen a wide selection of doublets, blouses, and hose including some bright pink and purple pieces that would make Fernshaw proud. Reed settled on a simple leather doublet with steel buttons, an ivory-white undershirt, and cinnamon-brown trousers. It felt strange not to be carrying a spear or sword, but the Baron's orders were strictly enforced, and his weapons were still in the hands of the keep's guard. Pocketing a couple of blueberry pastries, he set off to explore.

Reed happily spent the next few hours discovering the layout of the keep. The six-storey-high building was home to over a hundred people, all serving the Baron and his family, who occupied the entire top floor. The fourth and fifth floors were reserved for the Baron's guests and high-ranking servants. Lower floors housed a small private library brimming with scrolls and books, two guardrooms, garderobes, an indoor training room complete with wooden figures and hand-drawn targets, storerooms, and kitchens. The great rectangular meeting hall was situated on the first floor, just above the cellars, ice houses, and more servant quarters.

The keep was separated from the rest of the town by a crenellated wall surrounding the inner courtyard. It was here that Reed found the stables, smithy, tannery, and round-topped bakery. A gaggle of geese and hens squawked and clucked in a wireframe coop next to two cows and a starved-looking goat. A dirt path led around the side of the keep to an enclosed hedged garden about eighty yards long.

The hedges were high and thick, and when Reed entered the garden through the wrought-iron gates, the hustle-and-bustle of the castle servants faded to a distant murmur.

The garden itself was exquisitely designed and maintained. Gravel paths wove in and out of orange marigolds, hanging purple passionflowers, white meadowsweet, lavender, and bergamot. The centrepiece was an ornate, round fountain topped with a marble statue of a woman. She had been carved standing on the tips of her toes, hair flowing down her back, bare arms stretched out in supplication as if she were receiving a gift from the sun. Water bubbled up from her cupped palms and splashed down into the pool below.

Decorative stone benches were placed around the fountain. It was on one of these that Reed spied the massive shape of Aldarin. The knight was dressed in a simple sky-blue tunic, scarred face turned towards the smooth curves of the statue. He carried, as always, his double-bladed axe. The weapon had been wrapped carefully in strips of cowhide tied together with leather thongs.

Reed sat down next to him and for a while neither man spoke, enjoying the tranquillity of the garden and the soft gurgling of the water.

"I believe she is one of the Twelve," said Aldarin finally. "Though I cannot be sure. So much has been lost." He sighed a melancholy sigh.

"What happened?" asked Reed. "Where did the Twelve disappear to? Where are the Knights of the Twelve? And what in the name of the Pit are those foul creatures you keep calling greylings?"

"That is a long story," said Aldarin ruefully.

"Lucky we have plenty of time, then," retorted Reed.

Aldarin gave a short chuckle. "I do enjoy your company, friend Reed. It is very refreshing for me to have a companion who speaks plainly and does not hide behind rank or protocol. Very well. If you wish to know more, I will go back to the very beginning."

"Roughly four hundred years ago, the men of this world were split into hundreds of separate warring tribes. They squabbled over territory and raw materials, grinding each other down in pointless skirmishes. The tribes grew weak, their numbers dwindling as they lost more and more of their own to battles, disease, and the hostile landscape. It was then, during these grim times, that calamity struck.

"A series of massive tremors wracked the lands, opening great chasms and funnels in the earth. Villages were swallowed whole, livestock crushed by falling rock. Mountains collapsed in on themselves, creating rubble-filled craters. Cracks formed along riverbeds, draining lakes of water, their fish suffocating on dry land. The seas churned with white foam, ten-foot-high tidal waves obliterating those foolish enough to have settled too close to the coastline. I do not know what caused this wanton destruction: there is little written testimony that has survived intact. Most of what the scholars in my temple have taught me is based on oral histories handed down from generation to generation, so there is much we still do not comprehend.

"What we *do* know is that these violent earthquakes opened up passages deep in the earth and gave the greylings and their kin a means to re-join the surface. Thousands of them swarmed out of the pits and hollows that now scarred the land, a throbbing, swirling, disorganised mass. At first, they didn't travel far: as I told you back at the Pit, the sun is anathema to creatures that have spent their whole existence in the dark. Their first forages into human territory were swiftly repulsed by the hardy men and women of the fractured tribes, but these early victories were short-lived.

"You have only met the greylings, friend Reed, but there are other things that lurk far beneath the earth. I have seen drawings of larger creatures, taller and broader than myself, sturdy and muscular. They are darker-skinned than the greylings, more resistant to sunlight also. Accounts in the temple archives speak of skin as hard as bark, stronger and tougher than leather. Instead of claws they have short, stubby fingers much like our own, and are able to wield primitive weapons with great efficiency.

"But even more troubling is that they all carry barbed whips; whips they use liberally on their greyling cousins. A few dozen of these creatures can turn a disorganised rabble into a respectable fighting force, such is the fear they inspire.

They fight from the rear, flogging the greylings forwards, mercilessly beating those who refuse to obey. It is for this reason we have named them threshers, and they are infinitely more dangerous than what you have faced up until now."

Aldarin stopped and rolled his shoulders, working the kinks out of his back. "Let us pause awhile, friend Reed, my throat is parched and my stomach empty. We shall eat and continue our history lesson this afternoon."

Reed nodded and followed the big knight to the kitchens, trying and failing to match Aldarin's long strides. The Baron and his court were still detained so they ate among themselves, savouring two large servings of roasted pheasant and baked potatoes in a rich plum sauce. Reed tapped a barrel of mead. The foamy amber froth stuck to his beard and moustache as he drank, much to Aldarin's amusement. After dining, they returned unhurriedly to the garden, which was still empty save for a lone gardener trimming an unruly lavender bush.

"Now, where was I?" asked Aldarin.

"The threshers," prompted Reed impatiently.

"Ah, indeed. Despicable creatures. I have yet to see one in the flesh. Maybe one day I will get to test my own skills against one of the beasts. Wouldn't that be a sight!"

"I'm not sure it would," said Reed. "Would you please continue?"

"Of course. There have been scattered reports of other types of creatures, some small and spindly, others large and ferocious, but again, much of what was known has been lost. Suffice to say that over time, the attacks on the human tribes became more disciplined and inventive. Ambushes were planned, traps were laid. The threshers took prisoners who they then used as bait. They would employ diversions and illusions to split the human forces, ensnaring them in pincer movements or attacking from the rear. The greylings were, of course, expert diggers, and they used their knowledge of the underground paths and tunnels to catch the enemy unawares, bursting out of the ground in the middle of villages, slaughtering the unsuspecting inhabitants.

"Now, our ancestors were a brave and resilient people, born into a lifetime of hardship. Only those who could adapt to the harsh living conditions and frequent attacks survived past early childhood. They fought back stubbornly with everything they had: slings, swords, axes, and spears. But it was not enough, and slowly the human tribes were pushed back.

"It was then, in the darkest time the human race has known, that the Twelve appeared. We still have no idea where they came from or who brought them into existence, but they pulled the scattered tribes back from the brink of extinction. First and foremost, they gathered the various tribal chiefs together and convinced them that if they did not lay aside their petty internal squabbles they would be annihilated. The next time the greylings attacked, they would face a unified line of defence.

"Secondly, they lent their considerable skills and knowledge to the race of men. I have told you of my patron, Brachyura, who taught us how to build great walls and towers — and how to defend them effectively. Others imparted their expertise with the bow, the sword, the lance, or the shield. They taught us how to ride in formation, how to shoot from the saddle, how to splint and bind broken bones. We learnt the importance of terrain in battle, when to attack and when to retreat. A wealth of information, shared willingly and unconditionally.

"A decisive battle was fought many miles north of here, on a wide stretch of grassland not unlike the plains surrounding the Southern Pit. A substantial host of greylings and threshers had been spied moving towards one of the villages and the Twelve decided it was time to halt the advance."

Aldarin paused and cleared his throat.

"We are lucky, friend Reed, that Brachyura was present on that fateful day and recorded much of what he saw. I will try to relate it to you as best I can.

"The united human tribes attacked at dawn, the rising sun at their backs in the hopes of blinding the enemy. They were outnumbered over ten to one, but filled with courage and a thirst for revenge after years of humiliating defeats. And with them stood the Twelve.

"The two armies crashed together in a discordant explosion of sound. In the centre, a sizeable contingent of men had been armed with great rectangular shields, designed to overlap with others to form an impenetrable wall of metal, five feet high. The fronts of the shields were smooth and slippery, leaving no purchase for the claws of the greylings that found themselves boxed in, trapped by the shieldwall in front of them and pushed forwards by the whips of the threshers from behind. The defenders, armed with short, sharp-edged glaives, stabbed through strategic openings in the wall into the press of bodies, wreaking havoc amongst the attackers.

"Behind the shieldmen, a spread of archers aimed high over the front line, peppering the greylings with arrows and setting alight deep ditches filled with pitch or tar that had been prepared the night before. Light mounted cavalry harassed the enemy flanks, fighting to get through to the threshers and trample them under hoof.

"Greylings died in their thousands and yet still they came on, bounding over the bodies of the dead, hammering their claws at the shieldwall, slashing, biting, and scratching at every exposed piece of human flesh. Each time a human warrior fell, the creatures flowed into the gap like grains of sand, leading to desperate and bloody melees as the defenders fought to reform the line.

"The threshers turned their whips on our horses, the barbed tips ripping easily through muscle and bone. Riders were thrown from their saddles as the horses went wild with panic, others running amok or fleeing back towards relative safety.

"At that moment, dark clouds covered the sun. The greylings, taking the fading light as a sign, uttered a triumphant shriek and surged forwards with renewed vigour. The shieldwall buckled, the front row of men was pushed back into their comrades. Resistance was crumbling.

"And then the Twelve entered the fray.

"You must understand, Reed, that the Twelve were more than just men and women, something greater. Of course, I have never seen Brachyura in the flesh, but there is a life-size statue of him before the gates of my temple. The statue is ten feet high, Reed! Imagine twelve such demi-giants fighting together in unison. Twelve of the greatest minds the world has ever seen, each one playing to the others' strengths and weaknesses, parsing and analysing hundreds of possible outcomes to each and every action."

Aldarin's eyes glittered with an almost religious fervour.

"The men who fought that day told their sons and daughters they had witnessed a miracle. The Twelve formed a circle, then walked slowly and calmly from behind the shieldwall through the enemy lines, slaughtering the greylings. They were untouchable, invincible. If one of the Twelve missed a strike, he or she was redeemed by a watchful brother or sister.

"Once through the greylings, they separated into groups and took apart the entire rearguard of threshers, cutting them down to the last beast. It was a massacre. Hundreds slain by twelve.

"And the most amazing thing? None of them was wounded, not even a scratch. Some say they were barely even winded.

"As far as we know, it was the first and last time the Twelve took to the field together. Once the battle was won, they separated, travelling throughout the surviving tribes and helping them take back what had been lost.

"And so, over the course of several years, the greyling threat was ended. The enemy was forced back underground. The smaller holes and chasms were filled with dirt and rubble, or flooded with water. Six pits, too large to be filled, were enclosed in thick stone walls designed by Brachyura himself. One of these six you know too well, Reed; you have been guarding it for most of your adult life.

"The Twelve established what you now know as the Council of Baronies, men and women drawn from the tribal chiefs to oversee the territories and maintain the alliance between factions. When the Council was deemed autonomous, the Twelve withdrew from their roles as warriors and politicians, retreating into seclusion to found the Knightly Orders and build a place for them to stay.

"As for how and when they disappeared, I will have to disappoint you, for we simply do not know. There are no records pertaining to anything useful, and believe me when I tell you that my Order has been searching for answers to this mystery for a very long time."

Reed was overwhelmed by everything he had just learnt. Six pits! Threshers! It was as if a whole new world had opened in front of his eyes, one ripe with secrets. He spent the rest of the afternoon and early evening picking apart the knight's tale, questioning him relentlessly on the battle of the Twelve, the forming of the Council, the guarding of the pits.

Aldarin answered what he could with patience and good humour, breaking off only when the setting sun no longer warmed the stone seats, the chilly twilight air forcing them back inside for a late supper of cold meats, cheese, and strong red wine.

It was late when Reed returned to his chambers, his face flushed from a few too many cups of drink. He was slowly drifting off to sleep when a loud metallic chiming startled him awake. Someone was ringing the bronze bell fixed to the roof of the keep. He stumbled out of bed, pulled on his trousers and threw open the door, nearly running into the servant who had brought him breakfast that very morning. The clanging sound was even louder here, reverberating around the spiral staircase.

"What's going on?" he yelled, raising his voice above the din.

The man just shook his head and pushed past him down the stairs. Reed followed, running through the Great Hall and out into the courtyard. There he found the Baron, buck-ling his sword to his side as one of the stablehands saddled his horse.

"My Lord, what has happened?" repeated Reed.

The Baron looked up. "Del Conte has returned," he said, grimly. "But something is wrong. Something is very wrong."

Without another word, he leapt into the saddle of his horse and galloped out into the night, leaving Reed alone in the courtyard, the frenzied chimes of the alarm bell ringing in his ears.

CHAPTER 9
THE FALLACY OF PRIDE

"Out of Kaevel Forest at last. What a depressing, muddy, rat-hole of a place. Good riddance! We are in the home stretch now, let me tell you. And I for one am looking forward to a warm fire and a nice, soft, feather mattress. And maybe a glass of wine or two."

AUGUSTE FERNSHAW, MAYOR OF JAELEM, 426 AT

❧

J ELAÏA'S EYES FLASHED open as the alarm bell rang. Before she could do anything more than clamp her hands down over her ears, the doors burst open and Mava bustled in carrying her Lady's fur-lined riding cloak.

"Hello, M'lady," she said, her bubbly voice wavering between excitement and trepidation. "Looks like the cavalry has returned! I'm sure you'll want to go down and meet them? Your father is already on his way!"

"What? Yes, right, of course," said Jelaïa groggily, fiddling with her hair. "Help me do something with this stupid brown mop on my head. And bring me a basin of cold water, would you please?"

Less than ten minutes later, she was running swiftly down the stairs to the stables where her horse was already groomed and saddled. A group of halberdiers stood smartly to attention nearby, ready to escort her down to the barbican. Jelaïa waved them away irritably. "I think I can make it a few hundred yards without being set upon by assassins," she said, shouting over the noise. "And could someone tell whoever is ringing that Pit-spawned bell to stop? He must have woken half of Arelium by now!"

She caught up with her father just outside the main gate, surrounded by soldiers. The old Baron was staring at the horizon, searching for some sign of movement. His breath misted in the night air.

"Father!" called Jelaïa. "What news?"

"I'm not sure. The night watch saw some activity at the edge of the valley, maybe horses, maybe not. It can't be del Conte, it's too soon!"

A pinprick of light flickered in the far-off darkness, somewhere high in the hills beyond the valley. They waited in silence as the light grew closer, revealing the shadowy forms of two horsemen, riding hard. The lead rider held a flaming torch in one hand, its dim glow illuminating the road ahead. The second cavalier was slumped in the saddle, both hands gripping the reins tightly. As they approached the last hundred-yard stretch, he slipped from his stirrups, tumbling to the ground with a cry.

"By the Twelve!" cursed the Baron, urging his horse

forwards. The fallen man's helm had rolled free when he fell and Jelaïa could see it was Loré del Conte, his face a mask of blood.

Her father reined in his steed and hurried over to where del Conte lay on his back in the road. The other rider was del Conte's squire, a young foppish noble barely old enough to hold a sword. Tears streamed down the squire's cheeks. His clothes were torn, his face and hands scraped by stray branches. The horses had been ridden hard, their swollen tongues lolling from open muzzles, their flanks lathered with sweat.

"Fetch the healer!" yelled the Baron. Del Conte shifted at the sound of his lord's voice.

"Listus?" he rasped. He turned his head painfully towards the Baron and Listus del Arelium saw the damage the enemy had wrought on his old rival. Claw marks ran down the left side of del Conte's face, cutting deep into his cheek. His left eye was gone completely, nothing left but a bloody socket. A second set of lacerations ran horizontally across his forehead. Fresh blood trickled from three thin incisions down into his remaining eye and along his nose. His half-open mouth was missing several teeth, forever ruining his perfect smile.

The rest of his body bore more red scratches and one leg was twisted sideways at an impossible angle, surely broken or fractured.

"By the Pit, man, what have they done to you?" said the Baron, thickly. The town healer appeared, his bulging bags of herbs and medicines bouncing up and down as he jogged towards them. Jelaïa hurried after him, holding rolls of bandages and a canteen of water.

The Baron found Loré's armoured hand and grasped it firmly. "Stay still, try not to talk," he whispered.

The healer was a kind-faced, rotund little man, still wheezing from the effort of his run down from the keep. He blanched when he saw the noble's mutilated face, but recovered quickly. Setting his bags down on the ground with a clink of glass vials, he produced a pestle and mortar, and started grinding some herbs into a thick paste.

"The wounds suffered seem to be quite extensive, my Lord," he said, adjusting his half-rim spectacles that were slipping down his nose. "I will give him something to make him sleep, then we can bandage the worst of it here. I would suggest a litter of some sorts to get him back to the, um, keep, where I can start with the stitches."

"Of course, of course, whatever you think best," replied the Baron distantly, his eyes never leaving the injured man.

"Wait!" murmured del Conte. "Not yet. I must make my report."

"Bah! Make it tomorrow, man! When you are feeling better!"

Del Conte grasped the Baron's arm and their gazes locked. "Tomorrow will be too late," he said quietly. "Please, Listus."

The Baron paled visibly at hearing this, but after a brief hesitation he nodded once.

"Healer, make him comfortable and give him something for the pain. Then you can set about binding his legs and forehead while he talks. Jelaïa, get the man some water. You there!" he motioned to the squire. "Give your torch to my daughter and go find something we can use to carry him up to the keep. Right, del Conte, you've got ten minutes, then you are going to get some rest, even if I have to knock you out myself."

Jelaïa brought the canteen to the injured man's lips and he took a long drink. The healer offered him a vial of dark brown viscous liquid which he swallowed, grimacing.

"Trying to poison me, healer? What in the Pit's name was that foul muck?"

"Just something of my own concoction to help you focus, my Lord," said the healer humbly.

"Disgusting," said del Conte. He shuddered and hacked a sliver of blood onto the dirt road. "My Lord Baron, if I may proceed? Very well. After we parted ways, our party left the valley in good spirits and rode hard through the night, stopping only to rest the horses. We proceeded past the outer farmsteads with little resistance. The men were joking that you had sent us off on some wild goose chase to get a little peace and quiet."

His lips twitched into a gruesome half-smile revealing broken teeth. "It was near midday yesterday when we spotted the smoke. At first, we thought it was some sort of bonfire, but I'm afraid it was something else entirely. A refugee train had been attacked by the enemy, twenty or thirty caravans set on fire. Judging by the damage done, it appeared we had only missed the attackers by a couple of hours. The wind carried the smell of burning wood and the metallic stench of spilt blood. We soon saw the refugees, or what was left of them at least.

"The greylings had dismembered the men, women, and children, piling their corpses in a gory pyramid-shaped heap twenty yards away from the caravans. I would guess there must have been about a hundred bodies. In front of that grisly mound of dead flesh, a stake had been hammered into the soft earth. We were still far away, but could see a man was tied to it, his arms bound together high above his head. He was naked, and covered in welts and bruises. His face was a bloody ruin, but he was alive, his head cocked as if listening for something.

"I recognised the man despite his bruised and battered body. I recognised him because I knew him well, I was there at his wedding. It was my brother-in-law, Fernshaw, Mayor of Jaelem."

Del Conte coughed, a rough, grating sound coming from somewhere deep inside his chest. The healer, who had finished bandaging the lacerations covering the arms and legs, looked at him anxiously. "My Lord Baron, his body won't take much more of this, he needs to rest."

"You hear that, del Conte?" said the Baron gruffly, "Let's hear the end of it."

"Yes, yes, Listus," replied the noble, beckoning Jelaïa forwards for more water. "I should have realised then that something was wrong. Where were the enemy bodies? Why had they kept Fernshaw alive? There would be no logic in leaving a man bound to a stake in the middle of nowhere unless they thought he would be found. Alas, at the time my mind was flooded with a seething red haze devoid of all logical thought, and I am sure my men were similarly affected by the gruesome tableau that stretched before us. I didn't even stop to send out scouts or discuss options with my captains. All I did was draw my sword, and urge my steed forwards into a canter, bellowing some angry war cry. I could see my brother-in-law agonising less than a hundred yards away and my only focus was to reach him as fast as possible. My fellow knights raced after me with their lances held high.

"I got closer and closer, so close I could see the blood running down Fernshaw's face. I could see they had blinded him and had sealed his mouth shut so he could not see or speak. And a great fear hit me in the stomach like a ball of lead. But it was too late. The ground opened up before me and my horse plunged straight into a concealed trench, packed with greylings.

"The riders behind me did all they could to halt their reckless advance, pulling hard on their reins and gouging their mount's sides with their spurs. But even as they slowed, the second rank crashed into the back of the first and the whole chaotic jumble of horses and men tumbled into the ditch where they were set upon with animalistic fury."

He winced as the healer laid a padded dressing over his empty eye socket. "Give me some more of that vile elixir, would you?"

Listus leaned over him and tipped more of the vial's contents directly into del Conte's mouth.

"Thank you. So, in just a few minutes, my stupidity had lost us the only advantage we had over the foe: the speed and power of a heavy cavalry charge. Even worse, down in the filth of the trench the enemy had the upper hand. Some of the knights had fallen badly, breaking bones or twisting limbs. Others had been crushed by their own horses, more still pinned down by the press of bodies and animals, drowning in the thin layer of murky water that filled the bottom of the trench.

"The survivors were weighed down by their armour, those with metal greaves or sabatons getting stuck in the mud. There was not much room to swing a weapon in such an enclosed space so axes and spears were rendered useless. Only those armed with swords or daggers stood a chance of defending themselves.

"I myself had the good fortune of being thrown free of my falling horse. I slammed into the opposite wall of the trench, my helm protecting me from the full force of the blow, but dazing me nonetheless. Before I could get my bearings, two of the wretched creatures jumped me. The first aimed a slicing cut at my legs, the second grasped my helm in both hands and tried to yank it off.

"Luck smiled on me yet again as I realised I had kept hold of my sword during my tumble. I quickly decapitated my first opponent and stabbed the second as he ripped at my helm. This brief respite gave me time to take in the massacre happening all around me.

"The nobles of Arelium are brave, hardy men, my Lord, but there was nothing they could do. They were outnumbered four or five to one, and the greylings exploited this advantage, needlessly sacrificing some of their number in a frontal assault so others could dart in from behind. I saw greylings climb up the slick walls of the trench then turn and leap back down below onto the unsuspecting soldiers.

"I decided then that there was not much I could do in the trench. A dead horse crushed against the wall opposite me gave me enough extra height to pull myself out.

"As I crawled out of the trench on my hands and knees, I saw that the second half of my forces was faring little better. Greylings were pouring out of even more concealed pits and trenches. They were attacking the horses as much as the riders, and the sound of the beasts braying in pain was terrible to hear."

He coughed again, louder this time, and the healer shot him a warning glance.

"Yes, I have nearly finished, the last part needs to be told. Because I saw something then that I had never seen before. The greylings were not alone. Three massive, hulking creatures stood close by. One of them wore some sort of metal breastplate and carried a barbed whip. The others both held black stone axes."

"Threshers," said the Baron in disbelief.

"I have not heard that name," admitted del Conte, "but it certainly fits them well. I knew the battle was lost but I thought that if I could somehow take down these three creatures, some of us might at least escape with our lives.

"I hit the first of them with a heavy two-handed swing. I put all my fading strength behind the blow, crying out in anger as I did so. We have fought together many times before, Listus. You have seen what I can do. A blow like that should rip a man in half. But it barely broke the thing's skin. I had done nothing more than make it aware of my presence. It glanced at me contemptuously and growled a string of syllables to its fellows in a mocking tone. They laughed, a deep barking sound intermingling with the dying cries of my men."

Bright red blood leaked from the corner of his mouth. The Baron frowned and gave him the last drops of liquid from the vial. Del Conte swallowed with difficulty.

"I realised then I was going to die. A kind of quiet peace came over me. I slipped into my duellist stance, body turned, my right leg behind me, sword raised above my head. The thresher lunged forwards. I pivoted and let its charge carry it past me, hitting it twice in its exposed neck. My cuts were weak, but I must have hit an artery as a geyser of black blood fountained from the wound and it crashed to the ground.

"My cry of victory was cut off by the second beast, its stone axe whistling towards my face. I caught the axe with the flat of my blade, the power of the blow pushing me to my knees. A kick from the third thresher sent me reeling backwards into the trench. Greylings swarmed over me, raking my arms and legs. The last thing I remember is the greyling that took my eye, sitting on my chest cackling at me as I passed out from the pain.

"My squire was the one who found me, half-buried in the muddy sludge at the bottom of the trench. He was one of the only survivors. We had left him with the pack horses a few hundred yards up the road. He pulled me out and got me onto one of the spare mounts. We've been riding hard ever since."

He gripped the Baron's arm feverishly. "Don't you see, Listus? This couldn't wait until tomorrow. They'll be here by then. Thousands of greylings. And thanks to my foolishness, we have lost the only means to stop them."

Loré del Conte's remaining eye closed with an exhausted shudder, and he lost consciousness.

CHAPTER 10

A COUNCIL OF WAR

"The shantytown? I hate that place. I've lost more men patrolling that ramshackle hive of pestilence than I have anywhere else. I don't know why the Baron allows it. Burn down half the shacks, clear the path to the docks and get some proper housing down there. Then maybe my watchmen will stop looking for excuses to avoid doing the rounds."

ORKAM, CAPTAIN OF THE ARELIUM TOWN GUARD, 424 AT

❧

ALDARIN HAD JOINED them in time to catch the end of del Conte's alarming news, and he quickly stepped in to gather the injured noble in his arms, picking him up as if he weighed nothing more than a small child.

"Let us not wait for the stretcher, I will carry him. I would suggest we convene in the Great Hall as soon as possible," he said sombrely. He moved away, his great strides carrying him quickly back to Arelium and the healer's dispensary.

The Baron was still crouched on the dirt road, staring at the warm blood staining his right hand. Loré's blood. Jelaïa came up behind him, pulled off her glove, and laid her hand on his shoulder. They remained motionless for a few moments, father and daughter, the Lord of Arelium and his heir.

"He was a fool," said the Baron softly. "An arrogant, pompous, stuck-up fool. And he was also brave, daring, altruistic, and caring." He gave his daughter's hand a squeeze and heaved himself wearily to his feet. "His life is in the hands of the Twelve, now. Let us use what information he has given us to prepare the best we can. Someone find Praxis. And bring me that Reed fellow; he has fought the greylings twice now, his insight may be of some use to us."

They led the horses back through the dark streets to the keep. The alarm bell had woken many of the keep's occupants and they arrived at the Great Hall to find it alive with servants, nobles, and soldiers. Fires burned brightly in their iron braziers, illuminating a cluster of men who stood heads bowed over the map of Arelium, Praxis and Reed among them.

"We must prioritise the supply trains," Praxis was saying as the Baron approached. "If we can bring enough food inside the town walls to hold out until winter, the cold and the snow will do our work for us."

"Foolishness!" said a bull-necked, stocky man with a pug nose. He wore the livery of the Baron's town guard, a captain's golden emblem pinned to one shoulder. His thick, sloping eyebrows gave him a permanent scowl.

"Please elaborate, Orkam," said Praxis dryly.

Orkam ran his hand over his shaved scalp with a dry scratching sound. "Time spent gathering supplies is time lost preparing the defences. We need pitch and spikes for trenches, tar for the walls, steel and leather, wood and fletching. Three months of stores will not do us much good if the greylings can simply walk up to our front door and take it all."

"Reed," said the Baron sharply.

Reed looked up, startled. "My Lord?"

"You are here because, apart from Aldarin, you are the only person in Arelium to have faced these things twice and lived. The knight will join us once he has seen to Loré. In the meantime, I would have you tell us what you can. How can we defend against such creatures?"

Reed coloured as the half-dozen men gave him their undivided attention.

"I ... I ... am most honoured, Lord Baron," he stammered. "From what I have seen, they are small but agile, driven by a fierce, almost sadistic anger. Individually, they are weak and disorganised: I managed to kill several of them in single combat myself. As a group, however, they are much more dangerous. At the Pit, a small force of guardsmen held them at bay with a simple spearwall, until they were overwhelmed from behind and slaughtered." He paused, remembering the sacrifice of Yusifel and his men. "I believe we can use our knowledge of such defensive tactics to our advantage."

"Maybe," said the Baron, stroking his beard in thought. "However, both times you faced the greylings they were acting without the support of threshers. That will not be the case here as—"

"What?" interrupted Reed, forgetting himself. "There are threshers coming too?"

"Yes. And that reminds me. I am afraid I have bad news. You must have heard by now that del Conte's pre-emptive attack has failed. But there is more. The refugee caravan from Jaelem was ambushed. No survivors."

Several of the nobles gasped, and even Praxis looked pale, the half-smile he always wore falling from his lips. Reed could only stare in shock. "No survivors? Fernshaw?"

The Baron shook his head. Reed slammed his fist down on the table in frustration, making the miniature figures tremble.

"But, that's impossible," he said. "They set off only a few days after us! The wagons would make for slow going, of course, but they must have been over halfway here!"

"They were. The convoy was attacked north of Kaevel Forest. We have but a day or two at most before Arelium is under siege."

The news hit the war council like a hammer to the chest, and they looked at each other in stunned incomprehension.

"But ... I mean, there is no time," began one of the nobles in a faltering voice. "What can we—"

The double doors banged open with a resonant clang and Aldarin marched into the room, his face grave. "Apologies," he said, inclining his head to the group of men. "I thought it right to make Lord del Conte comfortable before joining you. As of yet, he has not regained consciousness. The healer tells me the Twelve will decide tonight if he lives or dies. I have sent word to Nidore, he will want to spend as much time with his father as he can."

"Thank you, Sir Knight," said the Baron. "I would welcome your advice as to what to do next."

Aldarin glanced down at the map. "Our position here is both a blessing and a curse," he said, pointing at the tiny carved icon representing the fortified town. "The river valley is flat and wide. With no elevated ground, we will not have a height advantage over the enemy, and they will not have to struggle uphill to reach us. What's more, the large open space before the walls will give them ample room to muster and manoeuvre."

"None of that sounds good," growled Orkam, the guard captain.

"Indeed. But the flat land also means we will have an excellent view of the enemy. There is minimal forestation, nowhere the enemy can hide or conceal troops, save for the estates and farmsteads. Even better, the town is right up against the river and the greylings detest running water. They cannot swim through it and they cannot dig under it. The only way to encircle us would be to cut through the hills or mountains and try to find a crossing point, which would lose them weeks of time. It will push them to try for a frontal assault. I believe this is where we must concentrate our defensive efforts."

"You talk of the valley as if it were empty, Sir Knight," said Praxis. "But it is not. What would you have us do with the farmers and their families that work the land out beyond the gates? The nobles? The traders? We cannot abandon them."

"The boats!" said Jelaïa suddenly. She pointed to the small ship icons positioned on the paper river. "We can load the barges and canal boats with people and send them down the river towards Kessrin. A day should be enough to get the outlying villages on board."

"That's actually … not a bad idea," said Praxis, his half-smile returning. "And we can requisition any cargo of interest to help with the siege."

The Baron was shaking his head. "The women and children can leave but the able-bodied men must stay and help defend the town. We have lost our cavalry; the walls are all we have left. If they are poorly defended, the farmers will have nothing to return home to."

"They are not soldiers, my Lord," said Orkam. "Most of them have spent more time holding a hoe than a sword."

"A hoe can be a dangerous weapon in the right hands," interjected Aldarin seriously. "I was always taught that a weapon can be used as a tool, and a tool used as a weapon. If these men are brave and willing, they will be of much use to us. Any man can be trained in the art of war, but some things like courage and steadfastness are not so easily found."

"Hah! There is plenty of both among the men of Arelium," said the Baron proudly. "And what of the wall itself, Aldarin?"

"It appears to be of sufficient height," the knight replied. "The curtain wall was poorly designed though. It should be one long, concave curve that allows a man standing at one end to see its entire length. The wall here twists and turns like the body of a snake, full of blind spots. If you will allow it, I will attempt to place your soldiers as judiciously as possible."

The Baron nodded.

"As for the shantytown," Aldarin continued, "I would advise we dismantle it and use the wood for other things. We must deny the enemy any sort of cover between the valley and the wall."

"Very well," said the Baron. "This is what we will do. All able-bodied men in the valley are to be conscripted into the town's defence, apart from the boat captains and their crews. The militia will be split into three groups: those who have some skill with a bow will be armed accordingly. The others that show some combat proficiency will be issued with spears and halberds. Reed, I would like you to train these men—"

"I'm not sure I'm the right person for that," said Reed.

"Nonsense, man. I told you — Yusifel sent me regular reports. You trained a bunch of the new recruits when they joined the Old Guard, this will be no different. Oh, and Reed? Come over here."

Reed moved nervously to stand before the Baron.

"On your knees." The Baron drew his bastard sword. Now Reed was closer, he could see the ivory-white pommel was styled as a wolf's claw embedded with rubies. He dropped to one knee and bowed his head.

"Merad Reed. As is my right as Lord of Arelium, and as witnessed by the men of this court, I hereby raise you to the rank of Captain of the Old Guard, Commander of the Southern Pit, with all the titles and honours that such a rank entails." He tapped each of Reed's shoulders lightly as he spoke. "May the Twelve guide you, Sir Merad Reed." The Baron sheathed his sword and pulled the startled guardsman to his feet with a grin.

"Right, now as captain you only answer to Praxis, Orkam, and me, understand? Don't let anyone else boss you around."

"Yes, my Lord," said Reed. He was trying to process

what was happening, but things were changing so fast. *Mother*, he thought. *It is happening. I have been given the chance to prove myself.* Glancing across at Aldarin, he saw the tall knight studying him seriously. He caught Reed's gaze and gave him a broad wink.

"The third group," the Baron was saying, "will be given picks, axes, and shovels. I want the land before the wall as clear as possible, bring down everything you can. The wood recovered from the houses can be turned into stakes, spears, and arrows. The stakes can be hammered straight into the ground around the wall, and we'll spread half the pitch we have out there too. The rest can be used by the archers on the ramparts. Orkam, make sure we have a good supply of arrows. The greylings are unarmoured. Between the stakes, the pitch, and the arrows, we should be able to bring a good number of them down before they reach the walls. Praxis? How many men can we conscript from the valley?"

"A thousand, two thousand maybe."

"And the town guard, Orkam?"

"A couple of hundred, my Lord."

"Very well. It will have to do. Cavalry?"

"We have plenty of horses, but no riders," replied Orkam glumly. "We could maybe muster a dozen or so from your personal guard, no more."

"We'll use them. Put together a group of mounted scouts and send them out into the hills and mountains near our borders. I agree with Aldarin's assessment of the terrain, but it pays to be prudent. Send a rider to Kessrin and another to Morlak. They must be informed. Anything else?"

"Father?" said Jelaïa timidly.

"Yes, Daughter?"

"What about the wounded? Food? Water? We will need to discuss rationing and distribution."

"Agreed. We'll turn the Great Hall into an infirmary. Jelaïa, I'll need you to take some men and bring the healer here. And find some volunteers to help treat the wounded. Praxis, I want you to liaise with my wife, work out the best way to store what we have and how to feed everyone. I suggest you start by turning the guest rooms and other unnecessary facilities into larders."

Praxis nodded.

"Well, if that is all—"

"My Lord?" interrupted a deep voice.

"Yes, Aldarin?"

"I … I have a confession to make." The habitually confident knight was avoiding the Baron's gaze. He looked almost sheepish. "I feel I must beg my Lord's pardon; I have disobeyed you."

"I see," said Listus, his steel-cold eyes narrowing dangerously. "It is maybe not the best of times to be telling me this, Aldarin."

"No, my Lord, I agree. However, it is of some import to our plans, if you would allow me to continue."

"Yes, yes. Spit it out, man!"

"I know you told me not to send word to my temple but I could not, in good faith, let my fellow initiates stay uninformed and shuttered away. We have all sworn oaths to help and protect the people of this land."

"What did you tell them?"

"I told them …" Aldarin swallowed. "I told them they were needed here, that they must put aside their books and scrolls and take up their axes and armour. I told them to mount their war steeds and sound their horns. And I told them to ride here with all haste. They are but a few, no more than a hundred or so if they all heed the call. But they are valiant and strong."

The Baron marched up to Aldarin, who towered above him, and looked up into the knight's scarred, honest face. Then, much to everyone's surprise, he grasped the man's arms in his own and pulled him close in a bearlike embrace.

"You are one amazing fellow, Aldarin," he said, releasing the surprised knight and grinning his wolfish grin. "And I for one am most pleased you did not listen to the rantings of a stubborn old man. You may have just given us a bit more of a chance! Right, you all have your orders. I propose we reconvene here tomorrow at dusk." He turned to leave.

"My Lord Baron?" asked Praxis, stopping the Baron in his tracks. "What shall we do with what we can't harvest? What we can't bring into the town?"

The Baron's grin faded and his face became as hard as granite.

"Burn it," he said. "Burn it all." And without another word, he strode from the hall.

CHAPTER 11

FRIENDSHIPS GAINED AND LOST

"Yes, Son, I know I told you we would spend the afternoon together, but I just don't have the time. In fact, I'm going to be very busy over the coming months. Very busy indeed. I suggest you go and see your mother instead. Now leave me alone, Nidore. I have a lot of work to do."

LORÉ DEL CONTE, VASSAL TO THE BARON OF ARELIUM, 417 AT

❧

J ELAÏA POUNDED ON the door of the healer's house for the third time. The dispensary was situated on the main street, just outside the inner wall protecting the keep. Its glazed windows were filled with vials, pots, labelled jars, dried flowers, and herbs, piled haphazardly one on top of the other. Jelaïa thought that if she hit the window hard enough, she could probably send them all crashing to the ground. She readjusted the hem of her fur-lined cloak.

"Healer!"

Her voice was swallowed up by the commotion behind her. It was just past midnight, but the town guard had lost no time in following the Baron's orders, rousing the towns-folk and sending riders to the outlying hamlets. Men were being herded towards the keep where they would be sorted, armed, and armoured. Women and children hurried down the slope in the opposite direction towards the barges. In the midst of it all, a group of halberdiers in the bright red colours of Arelium directed the flow of traffic as best they could, shouting and waving their arms.

The two men hand-picked by Praxis to serve as Jelaïa's bodyguard exchanged a smirk when they thought she wasn't looking. She bit her lower lip in frustration and was just about to attack the display window when the door creaked open and the small round face of the healer appeared in the crack, glasses askew.

"Oh, it's you. What do you want?" he asked. "I need to stay with del Conte. His breathing is much too shallow. It's not good, not good at all!"

"I am sorry to hear that," Jelaïa replied. "But I have orders from the Baron. You are to pack your bags and move up to the keep. We are turning the Great Hall into an infir-mary. Please do so as soon as you can."

"Um. I can't just leave del Conte!"

"No, of course not. The men accompanying me will help you transport him to one of the cots in the keep."

"My Lady," said the nearest guard. "Lord Praxis was quite specific—"

"I know what Lord Praxis said, I was there!" snapped Jelaïa. "I will not wait around doing nothing. You will go with the healer and find me again later. And if Lord Praxis is not happy about it, he can come and tell me himself!"

"Yes, my Lady," said the guard in a suitably subdued voice. He inclined his head sharply to his fellow soldier and they moved past her into the shop. The door slammed shut with a thud.

"Right," murmured Jelaïa, pushing a stray lock of chestnut hair from her eyes. The infirmary needed nurses. Mava and some of the chambermaids had volunteered almost immediately, but it wouldn't be sufficient. Where to look for more? Her eyes roamed the packed street in front of her. On the far side, a swinging sign caught her eye: a coloured roll of silk overlaid with a stylised needle and thread. It made her think of the silk merchant's daughter, Verona-something. It was as good a place to start as any.

She steeled herself then launched into the press of bodies filling the road, pushing horizontally against the rolling tide of people entering and leaving Arelium. She made it to the other side with some difficulty, and was breathing hard as she rapped on the door of the silk merchant's shopfront. The door wasn't locked and swung open on creaking hinges.

The interior was a disorganised mess. Rolls of silk spilled untidily from bags and chests, carpeting the floor with a jumbled mismatch of garish colours. More fabric was draped over the chairs and tables. Behind the counter at the back of the shop, a shimmering light filtered down from a set of wooden steps leading to the second floor. A small candle or lantern, perhaps.

"Hello?" called Jelaïa. She advanced through the room

cautiously, picking her way around fallen stacks of merchandise. Dust drifted down from the ceiling and she could hear the muffled bumping of someone moving around.

Jelaïa was starting to regret leaving her escort with the healer. She moved slowly up the stairs, arriving on the first floor above the shop. It was here that the silk merchant and his daughter lived. The floorboards were covered by an expensive-looking silk rug that spanned the length of the room. A set of beds was pushed against one wall, with two wardrobes and a tiny desk next to them. On the opposite wall, a washbasin and mirror stood next to a narrow opening that must lead to some sort of privy; while at the far end of the room, a wide bay window illuminated a hooded figure hunched over a travelling chest.

"Excuse me?" said Jelaïa tentatively.

The figure gave a startled jump and its arm whipped round, lightning fast. Jelaïa saw a flash of steel and something sharp whistled inches past her cheek and thudded into a timber cross-beam.

"Hold! Hold!" she shouted in panic. The figure rose, pushing back its hood, revealing the pale features and long black hair of Veronassandra, the silk merchant's daughter. She looked visibly shaken.

"Oh, by the Twelve! I am so, so sorry, Jelaïa. Are you all right?" she stammered.

"I think so," Jelaïa replied, staring at the throwing knife embedded in the wood not far from her face.

"I've been jumping at shadows ever since we were attacked in Kaevel Forest and I lost my father. Luckily I'm not as good at throwing knives as he is!"

"Err, yes, quite! I suppose I should have called out a bit

more assertively too. I'm not what you might call an expert on social interaction."

"That makes two of us," said Verona, coming to sit on the end of one of the beds. "We were always travelling, or planning to travel. I don't think I've ever stayed more than a couple of nights in the same place. And even when there was time to go out and mingle, my father was never far behind. Though I suppose that's no excuse for me throwing a knife at you." She smiled ruefully and offered Jelaïa her hand. "Friends?"

"Friends." Jelaïa smiled back, giving the hand a quick shake. It was cool and smooth, like a piece of carved marble. "Let's forget about it. Just remember to check who it is next time; your aim may be a bit off but your speed and technique are spot on!"

"Agreed! So what's going on?" asked Verona. "I nearly fell out of bed after getting woken up by the clang of that alarm bell! Sorry for my appearance, by the way, my hair must look awful!"

Jelaïa looked enviously at the other woman's perfect hair, full lips and suggestive curves; and decided it would be best to say nothing.

"Anyway," Verona continued, playing with the silver locket she always wore. "The town crier has been shouting himself hoarse for the last hour, saying we are under attack, that all women and children must evacuate the city. Is that true? It's the greylings, isn't it? They've reached the valley." She shuddered involuntarily.

"I'm afraid so," Jelaïa replied. "My father sent some men out to stop them, but they failed. He thinks they will arrive by nightfall tomorrow. We are doing what we can to prepare."

"I thought as much. I was just getting ready to leave. You know what's ironic? Yesterday, I was thinking that I'd finally managed to make friends with someone, and for once I wouldn't have to leave again and lose it all. And now that's just what I'm doing. Will you tell Nidore I will always remember his entertaining stories, and that I hope to see him again one day?"

"Nidore? Nidore del Conte?"

"Yes. The man who helped me fight off the greylings and brought me to Arelium. He said you two knew each other?"

"We do, a little. I'm afraid his father was part of the advance force the Baron sent beyond the valley. He returned alive, but terribly wounded."

Verona's face fell. "Oh no. I'm sorry, I'm so sorry. I can only imagine what he is going through. I don't know how I would have managed without his comfort. Does he have someone to grieve with?"

"I … don't know," Jelaïa replied honestly. "I haven't seen him since we were all together in the Great Hall and he left for the del Conte estate out in the valley. Praxis sent word of his father's condition, but I'm not sure he's arrived yet. I didn't see him with the healer."

"I see." Verona sat in silence and Jelaïa could see some sort of internal conflict playing out behind her eyes. Finally, she nodded once and stood, her gaze purposeful and unwavering.

"He did so much for me, I cannot leave him like this. He may need my help. I will stay."

Jelaïa felt a flicker of guilt somewhere deep in her breast.

She had known Nidore for years and, although they had never been close, she did like and care for him. And yet she hadn't even thought to find him, to comfort him in the hours since his father's return. *What a great leader you'll turn out to be*, she thought. *You can't even make time for one of your subjects. What will you do when you have to attend to the needs of thousands?*

She waited outside for Verona to gather a few personal things. The silk trader's daughter was sent up to the keep with instructions to find the healer and make herself useful. Nidore would come looking for his father sooner or later.

Jelaïa spent the next few hours roaming the streets and alleys, searching for other potential volunteers. Much to her dismay, nearly all the houses and shops were already empty or barred shut, their doors and windows covered with planks. The night drew on, and the flow of people down to the barbican slowed to a trickle. Her eyes started to itch from lack of sleep. After another fruitless hour of searching, she gave up and returned to the Great Hall.

The map and table were gone, replaced by rows and rows of military-style cots and bedrolls. Women hurried to and fro, stacking cupboards with bandages and utensils. A pan of boiling water bubbled over the fireplace, ready to be used to sterilise the healer's tools and, in some more serious cases, the wounds themselves.

Lord Loré del Conte lay asleep on one of the cots near the fire, his mutilated face made even worse by the strange shadows cast by the dancing flames. Nidore and Verona sat by his side. The merchant's daughter had her arm around Nidore's shoulders and was speaking to him in a low, mellow voice, her other hand on his knee. The young noble was weeping openly, tears rolling unchecked down his cheeks.

Jelaïa hovered by the doorway. The scene was so intimate she wasn't sure she wanted to interrupt. But then her decision was made for her as Nidore raised his head and saw her standing there. He wiped his eyes with a silk handkerchief and waved her over. His blond hair was still a mess, hanging wild and unkempt around his tear-stained face. As he looked at her, she could see no trace of the charming, laughing little boy who had chased her around the courtyard when they were young. Nidore had aged ten years over the last few hours. Grief had cut deep lines across his forehead and around his eyes. His once smiling lips were pressed tightly shut, thin and bloodless. He fixed her with eyes devoid of all emotion.

"My Lady, I am surprised to see you here," he said coldly. "I would have thought you had better things to do."

"Nidore, I am so sorry about your father," she said, and moved to take his hand in hers, but he quickly drew it away.

"Are you, Jelaïa? Is that why you rode to my estate as soon as you knew?"

"I didn't—"

"You did not, no. Neither did the Baron. In fact, he sent one of the town watchmen to tell my mother and me that my uncle had been tortured, humiliated, and killed, and that my father was dying. My mother went completely mad, you know, screaming at the top of her voice and tearing at her hair. We had to lock her in her own room to stop her from running out of the house in her nightgown. I have left orders with my servants to escort her to the barges tomorrow at first light. They will carry her bound and gagged if they must."

Verona squeezed his knee and he looked across at her, his face softening.

"When I arrived at the keep, I thought I would find my father alone. But that was not the case. Verona was sitting here, holding his hand and telling him of our battle with the greylings in Kaevel Forest, telling him how she was proud of what I had done. She has done more for me and my family this night than the lords of Arelium have done in twenty years."

"It's not what you think," said Jelaïa, exasperated. "I saw my father speak to Loré, there was compassion in his eyes, compassion and respect. Your father showed unbelievable bravery and resilience. But do not forget the greylings are coming, Nidore! We will have time to grieve once all this is over. For now, my father needs to organise our defences and the evacuation of the town as swiftly as he can; a few hours could make all the difference."

"Why did the Baron choose my father to lead the expedition?" asked Nidore suddenly.

"I ... I don't know. He wanted to go himself, but Praxis dissuaded him. I think the decision weighs heavily on him even now."

"Do you know what I think?" said Nidore, his voice wavering dangerously. "I think your father knew what a threat the del Conte family posed to his iron grip on the Barony. Listus is an old, feeble wreck of a man whereas my father was — *is* — in the prime of his life. He is well-liked by his fellow nobles and the lower classes. His aggressive trading deals have brought great riches to the valley. His military prowess has kept our borders safe and unmolested. Your father must have been afraid of him, and rightly so."

"Nidore, I don't think—"

"DON'T INTERRUPT ME!" Nidore shouted, and the hall fell silent; nurses and servants rooted to the spot. A bedpan fell to the ground with a clang.

"Your father *did* perceive him as a threat, and was looking for a way to rid himself of our family, plotting with that snake Praxis to do just that. I see now that it was all a ploy. The Baron mocking me in the Great Hall when I returned so I wouldn't interfere with his plans. The steward innocently advising him to stay in the keep. The Baron ordering my father to ride to the slaughter in his stead. It was so easy."

He chuckled sadly. "And for all those years he belittled me, ridiculed me, scorned me even. It was simply petty jealousy and fear of what I might become. The fool that I was, continuing to praise his merits to all I met while he trampled me into the dirt. My only regret is that it has taken the death of my father to make me realise what I had become."

He was on his feet now, quivering with anger. Jelaïa saw the thunderclouds gathering in his eyes and knew there would be no reasoning with him now, not tonight. She brushed past him and with a heavy heart slowly climbed the spiral stairs to her chambers on the top floor.

As she pushed the door open into the room, she was assailed by a soft, orange glow emanating from the windows overlooking the valley. At first, she thought it was the early rays of dawn chasing away the night. But then she smelt the smoke and knew it was something else.

Jelaïa del Arelium stood by the window and watched as the fields and farmsteads of her inheritance were consumed in a raging storm of fire.

CHAPTER 12

THE GIRL AT THE COUNTRY FAIR

"I cannot overstate the importance of leadership. A proficient leader must learn to apply a philosophy of balance to all aspects of his command. For every disciplinary action, there must be an act of mercy. For every word spoken in anger, another spoken in praise. And if he is the last to arrive on the field of battle, it is paramount that he be the last to leave."

ZYGOS, SEVENTH OF THE TWELVE, 19 AT

❧

"NO, NO, YOU idiots! By the Pit, have you been listening to anything I've been saying?" shouted Reed as the makeshift spearwall collapsed in a heap of wooden sticks and bruised conscripts. The sun was peeking shyly over the wall of the keep, bathing the inner courtyard with dawn's first light.

Workers had spent the night dismantling the animal pens and outbuildings, relocating the smithy and tannery to abandoned buildings outside the inner wall. The empty space before the keep was now large enough to fit about a hundred men from Reed's command. Over four times that number waited on the mustering field before the barbican.

"All right, all right, let's take five minutes. Go get some water or something to eat." He pulled the morion steel helmet from his head and threw it to the ground. His greying hair was wet and sticky with sweat. He knew the Pit-spawned thing offered good protection against blows to the head and neck, but the weight of it constantly pressed down into his scalp and restricted his movements. *I'm an officer now, I can wear what I want*, he thought petulantly, silently vowing never to put the headgear on again.

He scratched at his beard idly. The dour servant who had fed and clothed him on his arrival in Arelium had since become some sort of personal assistant, carrying missives to and from the other captains, organising the billeting of the men and the troop rotations. Reed had found out his name was Jeffson. The man continued to treat Reed with the same respectful indifference as when they had first met, seemingly unfazed by Reed's change in rank and status.

The only time Reed had seen a crack in the man's calm facade was shortly after his oath of fealty to the Baron. Jeffson had pressed a wrapped package into Reed's hands and backed away hurriedly, muttering something about looking the part.

The crinkly paper bundle was hiding Reed's Old Guard uniform, washed and repaired. The vermilion cloak had been scrubbed clean of blood and dirt; the holes in the leather surcoat sewn up by a precise, dexterous hand. The sun emblazoned on the surcoat's torso shone like the beacon of hope it had always meant to be. A golden pair of crossed swords had been added to the right sleeve just below the shoulder: the sigil associated with the rank of captain. And best of all, the leather clasp of his cloak had been replaced by the embossed silver wolf's head of Arelium.

Jeffson had been invaluable, working tirelessly through the night. They had agreed it would be nigh on impossible to train each and every spearman before the greylings arrived; they had neither the time nor the space. Instead, they would pick and instruct the most promising recruits, men who would be raised to the rank of sergeant. They would then pass on what they had learnt to the rank-and-file.

At least, that was the plan. Reed soon discovered that even the better of the conscripts were cruelly lacking in discipline and coordination. They tripped over each other's practice spears or hit their neighbours in the face when changing formation. Reed shouted and mocked, threatened and cajoled; nothing he did could make the men move as a cohesive whole.

Jeffson appeared as the bruised and dirty recruits returned to the courtyard. He wore a bulky leather satchel overflowing with scrolls. He looked disapprovingly at the spattered uniforms and raised an inquisitive eyebrow at Reed. "I see you are pushing the men hard, my Lord. I would perhaps suggest not exhausting them completely or all the enemy will need to do is step lightly over their slumbering bodies."

"Thank you, Jeffson, you are very perceptive, as always," replied Reed, his tone laced with sarcasm. "Perhaps you have an idea about how to remedy the situation?"

"Oh, my Lord, I am but a servant of the Baron, I would not presume to meddle in the affairs of the *noblesse*, as it were." He pulled out a wad of papers and dropped them on the bench next to Reed. "Letters from the Baron, his wife the Baroness, Praxis, Orkam, and the barbican captain, my Lord." He somehow managed to sound smug despite the droning monotone of his voice. He turned towards the keep, whistling under his breath.

Reed had only known Jeffson a short time, but he had an inkling the man was trying to tell him something. "What are you humming?" he asked.

"A little ditty called '*The Girl at the Country Fair*'," Jeffson replied without looking round, his back to Reed. "It is danced throughout the valley on the first day of spring. Hundreds of villagers and farmers moving rhythmically in perfect harmony. It truly is a sight to behold!"

Reed felt himself smile. "Thank you, Jeffson."

"For what, my Lord?" the balding servant replied blithely, and he left Merad Reed, Captain of the Old Guard, to try the spearwall one more time.

❧

"Right, gather round, men," said Reed, beckoning them closer. "You." He pointed to a broad-chested giant of a man, his face red and peeling from long days spent in the sun. "What's your name?"

"Ferris, Lord Captain, Sir!"

"Just 'Sir' will be fine, Sergeant Ferris. Tell me, do you know the words to the '*Girl at the Country Fair*'?"

"Err, yes my Lord, I mean Sir."

"Well out with it then, loud as you can. The rest of you, form ten ranks of ten and show me the steps."

Ferris cleared his throat noisily and began to sing in a strong, jovial voice:

"I saw a girl at the country fair, prettiest I could see,

Saw a girl at the country fair, her name was Marjorie,

Saw a girl at the country fair, but she didn't want to dance with me,

But she whisked me off for a tumble in the loft and next year we were three."

The song continued for several more verses, the hero of the song gaining more and more children with each couplet. Reed was barely listening, his eyes fixed on the men before him, twisting, whirling, and stamping their feet in rhythm to the song. In perfect rhythm.

"By the Twelve, Jeffson, I owe you for this," he murmured as Ferris bawled out the last chorus to a smattering of applause.

"Thank you, Sergeant," said Reed. "You have, without a doubt, woken up the few people in Arelium still asleep." There was some laughter among the recruits.

"Now grab your weapons and give yourselves some room, we're going to form a spearwall three ranks deep." The men groaned.

"Positions!" continued Reed unfazed. They formed into three concave lines.

"Not you, Ferris, you stay here with me. Now this is what we are going to do. Apologies to everyone within earshot, but Ferris is going to sing again." More groans. "When you hear the first '*see*', I want the first rank to drop to one knee and brace spears. At '*Marjorie*', the second rank will place their spears on the right shoulder of the man in front of them. And finally, at '*dance with me*', the third rank will slot their spears through the spaces left open by the second rank. Begin!"

When the first slightly off-key '*see*' echoed around the yard and forty men dropped onto one knee in near-perfect unison, Reed knew he had cracked it.

They spent the next few hours using the rhythm of the song to work through different formations: splitting the wall into smaller independent groups, creating openings to lure in opponents or let through friendly troops, moving forwards or backwards while maintaining a coherent block, and quickly changing the orientation to face attacks from the flank or rear. Once Reed was satisfied, they swapped their practice batons for real weapons and did it all again.

Ferris had practically lost his voice by the time they had finished, but by then the song was no longer needed to be sung; each man could now hear the beat in his head as he went through the motions.

Reed was pleased, and sent the men down to the mustering field where the rest of his spearmen were attacking crude targets painted on bales of hay. To Ferris, he gave a handful of copper coins, telling him to find a flagon of ale or two to wet his parched throat.

Alone at last, he leafed through the missives Jeffson had left him. The Baron's note was the most interesting, detailing how his men were to be divided into three groups. The first would line the curtain wall, supporting the archers. The second was to be placed just behind the barbican, the section that would in all likelihood bear the brunt of the enemy assault.

The third and final group would be placed near the keep, to be deployed as reserves or to hold off any greylings that made it over the outer defences. He skimmed through the notes left by Praxis and the Baroness pertaining to food rationing and set off for the barbican, stopping on the way down to grab a couple of freshly-baked loaves and a leg of ham.

He passed under the two imposing portcullises and stepped out into what had once been the shantytown. The rickety wooden huts and shacks had been completely dismantled and their remains carved into sharp stakes.

Workers were pounding the stakes deep into the ground, covering a swathe of grassland with the evil-looking spikes. To the distant north-west, he could see the last of the cargo barges moving ponderously along the river. The women and children would be safe, for a while at least.

Beyond the spike traps, the lush green fields and farm-steads had been reduced to a scorched and barren wasteland. The fires set by the Baron's men had burned themselves out, prevented from spreading closer to the town by deep earthen ditches. They left behind charred husks of timber-framed buildings and blackened earth. Flakes of grey ash spiralled through the air like snow.

Only some of the more opulent manor houses with stone walls had resisted the ravenous flames and even these were being raided for food and supplies. Reed knew the enemy must be denied sustenance and shelter, no matter the cost, but it was a terrible sight nevertheless. How long would it take to restore Arelium to its former glory if the greylings were pushed back? Some of those farmers had been working the land for generations, their livelihood passed down from father to son. Years of labour and hardship lost in one night.

"Make way!" came the sudden cry and Reed threw himself to the side, narrowly avoiding a trio of mounted scouts as they hurtled through the gatehouse and down the paved highway towards the hills on the far side of the burnt-out valley.

He picked himself up and saw Aldarin close by, directing a group of men with long poles. Reed was not surprised to see the knight once again fully armoured, his plate and pincer helmet adding more height to his already formidable size. He towered over the workers, relaying orders in his deep, calm voice. Reed ambled over, chewing contentedly on a mouthful of ham.

"Sir Knight!"

"Friend Reed!" replied Aldarin, grinning. "The mantle of captain suits you well, methinks. It will not be long before it is me calling you 'Sir'."

Reed grimaced. "I sincerely hope not, I can barely keep it together as it is. Any more responsibility and I will start tearing out what little hair I have left!"

Aldarin laughed: a rich, melodious sound that did much to raise Reed's spirits. He grinned back and offered up a loaf of bread, which Aldarin accepted gratefully.

"How fare the defences, Aldarin?" Reed asked.

"The first hours were slow-going," his friend replied through a mouthful of crust. "The cold sapped our strength and working at night made it difficult to see. Once the Baron set the fields alight that was no longer a problem, of course. We now have stakes twenty yards deep and lines of pitch beyond. I don't think we'll have enough wood for many more."

"And the walls?"

"The walls are a problem. Too many places to hide. Take the protruding tower behind me, for example. It provides its occupants with an excellent view of the wall on either side, but blocks the exact same view for the soldiers on the ramparts. And if the tower is taken, the enemy will have the perfect defensive foothold. And there is another thing to consider." Aldarin gestured to the men with their poles. "You saw what happened at the Pit. The greylings scaled the walls there in minutes. It will be more difficult for them to do so here, the mortar is stronger and much better maintained. I have sent a detail of men to requisition pots and cauldrons that we will fill with boiling water and any other foul liquids we can find. Lastly, we are coating the exterior stonework with animal fat and vegetable oil."

"That will make it very slippery indeed."

"Precisely. A rather unconventional method I must confess, but if it slows them down just a little, they'll be easy prey for our archers."

"Not bad, Aldarin, not bad at all. I don't know how—" Reed stopped mid-sentence. Jeffson was scurrying across the mustering field towards him.

"How does that man always seem to know where I am?" he grumbled. "I fear I will have to leave you, Sir Aldarin. I will see you this evening for supper."

The men grasped wrists just as Jeffson arrived, and Reed let himself be pulled back into a maelstrom of war council meetings and paperwork.

It was late afternoon when the scouts returned, pushing their horses as hard as they dared.

The Baron was waiting for them before the keep. The lead scout dismounted fluidly and fell to one knee.

"They have reached the hills, my Lord."

"How many are they?"

"I ... I don't know, my Lord."

"What do you mean, you don't know! Hundreds? Thousands?"

"More, many more. I could not count them all, my Lord ... I ... I could not count them all."

"Very well. Praxis, get this man something strong to drink. And sound the bell."

Soon the rhythmic clanging echoed once more through the streets of Arelium.

The enemy had arrived.

CHAPTER 13

THE CLIFFS OF KESSRIN

"Have you ever seen such savage beauty? Such resilience? They were here long before I walked this earth and they will persist long after I am gone. When I look upon these towering cliffs of jagged rock, I see everything my Order must represent. Steadfastness. Resistance. Strength. Protection. These will be the tenets of my knights. And it is here that I will build them their temple."

BRACHYURA, FOURTH OF THE TWELVE, 41 AT

෨

ALDARIN AND REED stood shoulder to shoulder, looking down into the valley below. A rolling tide of darkness blanketed the land, thousands upon thousands of screeching, howling greylings. They scampered back and forth just out of arrow range, scratching at the ground and hurling excrement at the distant walls. Threshers paced among them, lashing out with their whips at any of their kin that broke the line.

The infernal cacophony of sound smothered the defenders, so loud and high-pitched they had to raise their voices to be heard. The sun was fleeing the sky, the last rays of daylight ebbing away as if chased by the advancing horde.

The curtain wall was alive with a flurry of final preparations. Young boys ran along the ramparts with lighted torches, igniting the cast-iron braziers. Fletchers and their apprentices filled wicker baskets with arrows. Reed's spearmen were being herded into place and given some last-minute instructions by the squad sergeants. One man in a coarse black robe and sandals was reading aloud from the Book of the Twelve, ignored by all but the most fervent soldiers, who bowed their heads or grasped various amulets and trinkets.

"Why are they waiting?" asked Reed, fiddling with the metal clasp of his cloak.

Aldarin turned his head, features fading into the shadow of his helmet. "They will attack shortly after nightfall, I think. Remember their aversion to strong sunlight. It won't be long now."

Reed grunted. He watched one of the distant threshers catch a stray greyling and break its neck before throwing its broken body into a crowd of its fellows.

"May I stand beside you?" Nidore looked like a man in need of a good night's sleep. His pale skin accentuated the dark circles under his bloodshot eyes. His hair was bound in a loose ponytail, but it had been poorly done and several stray wisps hung across his face.

The young del Conte was dressed for battle. A steel

breastplate shielded his upper body while leather trousers and boots offered some protection to his legs and feet. His longbow and a quiver of arrows were slung across his back. The arrows looked exquisite, far more expertly crafted than the goose or chicken fletching mass-produced for the Baron's archers. The feathers were long, dense, and black. A hawk, maybe, or some other bird of prey.

"Of course, friend Nidore," said Aldarin politely, making room. "How fares your father?"

"Loré has still not woken. The healer tells me he has done all he can. Do you know his leg was broken in two places? That he has three cracked ribs? The endurance and willpower to ride for hours in that condition are beyond my understanding."

Nidore gave a grief-stricken sigh. "I was never close to my father. He spent more time away from his home than in it. He hated coming to court. Once my mother and I became permanent residents there, I saw him even less. I resented him for that. I thought he didn't want to see me, was ashamed of me for some reason. I see now that nothing could be further from the truth. All that time away from us was to protect our house's interests, and the interests of Arelium. It was not his family he was avoiding by not coming to court, but the Baron himself."

"I do not know your father well, friend Nidore," said Aldarin, "but I have heard he is a brave and kind man. And last night I witnessed first-hand his devotion, not to the Baron, but to Arelium itself. If there is a man who can survive such terrible injuries, it is he."

Nidore smiled sadly. "I wanted to stay with him, but Verona persuaded me to come to the wall. She promised me she would not leave his side and I trust her. We have a connection, whether it is through loss or loneliness I am not sure, but it is something I have never felt before. She has brought me great comfort. I… I think that when this is over, I may ask her to stay with me a while longer."

He pulled a silk handkerchief out of his sleeve and looked at it thoughtfully before stuffing it away. "She told me the noble house of del Conte needs to be represented on the wall and she is right, so here I am."

He squinted at the distant mass of figures. "What would you say, Aldarin, a couple of hundred yards?"

"More like two hundred and fifty," the knight replied. "Well out of accurate range. Some of our stronger bowmen may be able to make a shot that far, but at great cost to precision and penetration. Best save the arrows for when they get closer."

"Hmm," said Nidore and drew the longbow from his back. "The Baron's guard are armed with yew bows, strung with hemp. Each bow is the same: same height, same curvature. The archer must adapt his stance and his posture. He is forced to bend his body to use his bow. It should, of course, be the other way around. The weapon should be made to fit the man, not the man the weapon."

He pulled one of the black-feathered arrows from the quiver and nocked it with a practised gesture. "My father had a new bow made for me every year. Some of my best memories are hunting with him. I never wanted to disappoint him so I trained for hours a day in the weeks leading up to the hunt."

He drew back the bow fluidly, closed one eye and

sighted along the length of the arrow, the bowstring taut against his cheek.

"My optimal accurate range was about three hundred yards."

He breathed in, held his breath, and loosed.

Two hundred and fifty yards away, a thresher howled in pain as Nidore's arrow took it in the eye. It clawed at the shaft, ripping it out in a spurt of black blood.

"An eye for an eye," said Nidore calmly. "I will avenge my father. And for every wound inflicted upon him, I will return it to the enemy ten-fold."

Reed could only nod.

The sky was turning a darker shade of blue save for a slash of red, the colour of raw flesh, on the western horizon. It reminded Reed of the burning fields of corn. A babble of voices from the barbican drew his gaze. The Baron had arrived, appearing on the flat roof of the gatehouse like an avenging god.

He was clad, as always, in his extravagant golden armour, shining like a beacon in the setting sun. His squires must have spent hours polishing and buffing every inch of metal. The embossed wolf's head looked alive in the flickering firelight. The wolf's ruby eyes glimmered. To the Baron's left stood Praxis, sleek and dangerous in a tight-fitting black leather cuirass and shoulder guards. He wore two stiletto-like daggers strapped to either thigh. On the Baron's right, a member of his personal guard held aloft the battle standard of Arelium, the leaping white wolf snarling in defiance at the enemy.

The Baron had chosen his position well: the barbican was the highest point of the wall, visible to all the men

manning its southern portion. They fell silent as their Lord
started to speak. The Baron was a veteran of a hundred battles and knew how to pitch his voice perfectly, carrying easily
over the shrieks and screams of the distant greylings.

"Men of Arelium! I am glad! At first I thought you
would not all get to kill your first greyling, but it appears
there are enough for all of us!" Nervous laughter rippled
along the wall and even though he was too far away to see,
Reed knew the Baron was grinning his feral grin.

"For it would be a shame indeed if, when you return to
your wives and children and they ask you what you did here,
you have nothing to tell them! I look upon these foul creatures, desecrating the land we have spent so long nurturing,
polluting our air with their stinking bodies. I look, and I do
not feel fear, I do not feel sadness, I feel anger. Anger at what
they have already taken from us, at what they would take
from us still. Anger for the lives they have already claimed,
for the widows and orphans they have made. Enough!"

All along the wall, men stood straighter, raising their
weapons in salute. All except Nidore. The noble stared
straight ahead, purposefully ignoring the Baron. He was visibly shaking, his face unreadable.

"I gaze down upon them," the Baron continued, "and
I think of the ocean. A roaring, crushing mass of waves and
water. The ocean is wild, unpredictable, and dangerous. A
man who ventures deep into the sea at night is risking his
life, no matter how strong or how fearless he is. But then I
think of the tall cliffs of Kessrin. Every day and every night,
those cliffs are pounded relentlessly by the cold waves; beaten,
pummelled, and battered with no respite, all the way back to
when the Twelve walked the land. And they are still standing!"

The Baron leapt up onto one of the crenels, moving with an agility that belied his age. He looked around and spread his arms wide. His voice rose to a shout.

"My countrymen, my subjects, look around you! It is here that we will stop the incoming tide! We are the cliffs of Kessrin! And just like those cliffs, we will be battered and beaten, but we will not give in! For it is not in our nature! We will resist! And we will prevail! For we are the men of Arelium and we will defend what is ours!"

The Baron drew his bastard sword with one swift flourish and held it aloft, returning the salute.

"The enemy taunts us, screams at us, but they do not know us! Let us tell them who we are! We are Arelium! ARELIUM! ARELIUM! ARELIUM!" The Baron yelled, punching his sword into the air.

"ARELIUM!" came the echoing shout from a thousand lips. The sound gained momentum as more and more soldiers took up the chant, from the walls, to the gatehouse, to the town below, up as far as the keep. Soon the enemy could be heard no more, the battle cry swelling to a crescendo, resonating across the valley.

"ARELIUM! ARELIUM! ARELIUM!"

And as the last crimson light faded from the western skies, the greylings began to move.

꙳

There was no coordination in the first assault, no semblance of order, nothing more than a writhing crowd of churning bodies pushing towards the wall. The enemy moved quickly, hunched over on all fours, scampering along the ground like beasts.

Initially, Captain Orkam had been given command of the archers, but he quickly deferred to the Baron when it became apparent the old man wanted to take charge himself. He called the signal horn blowers to his improvised command post on the gatehouse roof and told them to await his orders.

The front line of greylings hit the spike traps at speed, with gruesome results. Pushed forwards by their own momentum, hundreds were impaled on the pointed shafts of wood. More crashed into them from behind, forcing them deeper and deeper into the deadly field of stakes. The greylings in the second and third rows suffered the same fate, propelled onto the spikes by those behind or unable to slow down in time.

It was eerily similar to the disastrous cavalry charge Loré del Conte had made only days before, except this time it was the greylings suffering the consequences of their own foolhardiness.

The threshers laid about with their barbed whips and the assault slowed to a crawl. Greylings milled about uncertainly, awaiting further instructions.

"Now!" ordered the Baron, seeing his chance. The signal horns blew two short, sharp notes, and the sky was filled with the buzz of a thousand arrows.

The encroaching darkness made it difficult to pick targets, but it mattered little, as the enemy had nowhere to run. In front of them stretched the field of stakes, choked with the dead and dying. Behind them, packed rows of greylings. The hail of arrows descended upon them like a swarm of locusts, puncturing flesh and bone like paper. Hundreds and hundreds of the creatures fell shrieking to the ground, killed or wounded. The greylings panicked, turning their backs on the defenders and pushing against their kin in outright hysteria. Fights broke out as the trapped front lines tried to escape.

"Again," said the Baron grimly, and another deadly sheet of metal rain sluiced across the battlefield. The threshers grunted and roared in frustration; and finally, the enemy was routed, running back beyond arrow range. There was no thought for the injured. Reed could see bodies squirming among the trench of stakes and shafts, left to bleed out and die.

A resounding cheer rang along the length of the wall. Men laughed and clapped each other on the back, adrenaline pumping through their veins.

"First blood to us, eh, Aldarin?" said Reed with a grin.

The Knight of the Twelve didn't return the smile. "'Twas but a test. Those losses mean nothing to them, they still outnumber us fifty to one. They will be back, and we must be ready."

Reed sighed as his short-lived elation trickled away.

"It's going to be a long night."

CHAPTER 14

THE DOLEFUL HORN

"Ignorance will be the cause of many lost battles. How can you formulate an effective plan of attack if you are incapable of predicting how the enemy will react to it? I know you do not think my skills important, that my role in the coming conflict is insignificant compared to that of Brachyura or Dhanusa. But I can offer you something they cannot. I can tell you how they think."

MITHUNA, THIRD OF THE TWELVE, 3 AT

I T WAS THREE hours before the greylings attacked again. Great cauldrons of stew had been brought down from the keep and ladled into wooden bowls. Reed poked around his portion with a questing finger and was pleased to see it contained real carrot, not a rodent in sight.

The Baron moved among his men, smiling. He would

grasp wrists firmly with the men of one group, tell a bad joke to another, share a war story with a third, draw his sword to show a fourth. He didn't stay long, but Reed could see the effect he had. The soldiers laughed louder, smiled more openly. Most of them had only seen the Baron from afar, an untouchable figure of authority who, as their liege lord, had the power to grant them life or death. Stepping down from his ivory tower to mingle with his subjects was an obvious move, but it worked well nonetheless.

"Reed! How goes things?" asked the Baron, grinning broadly, Praxis hovering behind him like some guardian angel. "Heard you had a nice little sing-a-long this afternoon instead of doing some actual training, eh?"

"Yes, my Lord. I mean, no, my Lord. Well, I suppose a bit of both, my Lord."

"Excellent. Excellent. If we can't spear them to death, maybe singing will work! I heard that big chap, Ferris. By the Twelve, he's so out of tune I thought someone was butchering a family of pigs! Good job in any case. Heard the men were calling you old Sunny. Must be nice to have a nickname. Suits you."

"I get the old part, my Lord, but why Sunny?"

The Baron pointed to the crimson sun emblazoned on Reed's surcoat. "You're still the only member of the Old Guard here, and that makes you special."

"I suppose I am. The last and only."

"In Arelium, yes. We'll have you link up with one of the other chapters when this is all over; get you sorted out."

Reed's eyebrows shot up in surprise. "Other chapters, my Lord?"

"Of course. Don't be a fool, Reed. I know the good

Knight of Brachyura has been telling you of our past. Who do you think guards the other pits? There are six pits and six chapters. Closest one must be up in the Redenfell Mountains over in Morlak. We'll send you there with a full escort once the enemy has been routed here."

"Thank … thank you, my Lord."

"Unless you'd rather stay here. That was a fine idea, using the song to get them all in step. I could do with a few more drillmasters."

"I am honoured, my Lord. You have given me much to think about."

"Right, yes! Make a note of that, Praxis!"

"Yes of course, my Lord," said Praxis, rolling his eyes. "Let me just get out my paper and ink that I always carry with me when I go into battle."

"You are quite an insufferable fellow, Praxis," said the Baron amiably. "Maybe that is why you are still unmarried, eh? We will have to do something about that too!"

The Baron meandered away, his armoured sabatons clinking on the stone paving.

Reed found himself weighing up the two options in his head. He still felt a sense of duty towards the Old Guard, towards Yusifel and the promise he had made. But those memories were fading fast, replaced by the fine meals and lodgings at the keep and the afternoons spent in conversation with Aldarin, surrounded by the marble statues and blooming flowers. He pushed the decision to the back of his mind; something to come back to another day.

He finished his soup, wiped his mouth with the edge of his cloak and stared out into the night. The sky was cloudless and the stars twinkled like distant jewels. The gibbous moon shed enough light for him to make out the chittering army of greylings positioned just out of arrow range. They were much quieter now, their far-off screeching lost in the nocturnal wind.

There was something else; a faint rumbling he could barely hear, but getting steadily louder.

"Aldarin!" he cried, scanning the horizon.

"I fear they are mustering," said the tall knight. "We would do well to prepare." His blue eyes pierced the darkness. "Look, there! In the ruins of that old manor house!"

Reed looked where the knight was pointing, but could see only shadows within shadows. Dark shapes darted between broken stone columns. Then, as he watched, the enemy revealed themselves. Fifty, sixty, then a hundred threshers emerged from the remains of the manor, each of them taller and broader than Aldarin.

There was something different about them and it took a moment for Reed to realise they were armoured. Crude sheets of rusting iron were strapped to their chests, arms, and legs. Bowl-shaped helms covered their heads. They bore no weapons, but each thresher held a massive metal shield, a rough, rectangular plate of iron, seven feet high.

"Sound the horn!" Aldarin yelled and soon after, the baleful wail resounded along the wall. Men threw down their half-finished meals and grabbed their weapons. The threshers advanced, twenty abreast. One of their number barked a guttural grunt and the metal shields were brought forwards, held high to protect their faces. With a clank, the shields locked together.

"By the Twelve! They are ... forming a shieldwall," said

Aldarin in a disbelieving voice. "That is not possible, they have never acted in this way before."

"Maybe not. But *we* have. Maybe they learnt from us," Reed replied sourly. "You told me that four hundred years ago, the Twelve trained our ancestors in the art of the shieldwall. I fear we may have underestimated the enemy. Del Conte said they built trenches to ambush his cavalry, and now this."

The shieldwall advanced, slowly at first then picking up speed. Greylings scattered as it approached the wall. Those not fast enough were trampled underfoot.

"Bowmen!" came the Baron's cry from the barbican and a thousand archers nocked arrows. The first rank of threshers came into range and the bows thrummed, sending their deadly shafts whistling towards the enemy. With a harsh cry, the second and third ranks of threshers raised their shields flat above their heads. There was a deafening sound akin to hailstones hitting a tin roof as the arrowheads hit the metal shields. Two or three threshers stumbled and fell, pierced by a lucky shot. The shieldwall barely slowed.

The signal horns sounded four short blasts. "Fire arrows!" cried Aldarin. The archers around him covered their arrow tips in oil-soaked rags and plunged them into nearby braziers. Pinpricks of light flared up along the battlements. The archers let fly again, adjusting their aim. The arrows soared from the walls, trailing tails of fire. They landed among the hidden lines of pitch laid by Aldarin's workers earlier that day. The sticky black resin caught fire immediately with a whoomph, and a wall of flame burst into life between the threshers and the defenders, belching grey smoke into the night sky.

A ragged cheer came from the wall, but it was short-lived.

The threshers did not falter, only increased their speed. They were practically running now, thick, muscular legs pumping up and down in unison. The first rank hit the wall of fire without slowing. The thirsting flames lapped around the shields, but did little damage. The second and third ranks followed.

"Fire at will!" the Baron called as the threshers ploughed into the line of stakes, scattering them like a bunch of twigs. They were less than a hundred yards from the barbican now, the spikes not slowing their progress. Arrows ricocheted off metal as archers looked for chinks in the shieldwall.

Reed saw Nidore draw, inhale softly, and send one of his black-fletched arrows into an exposed foot, causing the thresher and the three behind it to trip and crash in an undignified heap. They were quickly peppered with arrows. As the group drew closer, more and more archers found their mark. Less than fifty threshers reached the barbican.

The Baron looked down on them with contempt. "Oil!" he ordered and great, steaming leaden pots were dragged to the machicolations overlooking the gatehouse. It took two men to overturn each pot into the murder hole, sending a cascade of boiling hot oil down onto the attackers. Inhuman choking screams fountained up from below.

Reed could see the shields melting from the heat, fusing to the hands and heads of the threshers. Molten drops of metal and oil trickled down through the gaps. Dark grey skin puckered, smouldered, and burned. He looked away in disgust.

"Arrows," said Aldarin softly and the men around him responded, firing on the dying wretches below, ending their suffering.

The signal horns blew again and fletchers appeared on the ramparts, running to fill the wicker baskets with more shafts.

"They would not have done that for us," said Nidore hotly.

"Exactly," Aldarin replied. "And it is one of the many things that makes us better than them. As long as we remember that, friend Nidore, we will be fine."

"Maybe *we* will, but my father will not."

"I—" Aldarin paused and stared. "What are they doing now?"

A group of greylings were digging out of arrow range, sending great clods of burnt earth into the air. Threshers stood behind them, egging them on with cracks of their whips. Dirt piled up on either side as the holes became deeper. More threshers with battered metal shields arrived.

Placing the shields on the ground, they started loading them with soil. Once the shields were overflowing with dirt, they pulled them forwards like sleds, sheltered from missile fire by their fellows. They spread out before the impassable wall of fire and started shovelling the earth onto the burning pitch, smothering the flames. Parts of the conflagration sputtered and grew dim. Great plumes of smoke billowed over the battlefield as patches of fire went out, obscuring the enemy from view.

"We cannot fire through that," muttered Aldarin despondently. The defenders could only stare at the vaporous smog and wait to see what came through it. Veiled shifting forms rippled in the fog. Suddenly, with a deafening roar, a great host of greylings poured out of the mist.

"Arrows, at will!" shouted Aldarin, not waiting for the

signal. A whistling drone filled the air once more, reaping a savage toll on the attackers. Hundreds fell, and hundreds more came in their place. The Baron was right; the enemy was like a tidal wave, rolling forwards to crash into the wall with unstoppable force.

The first greylings reached the wall and leapt upwards, looking to sink their claws deep into the ancient stone. Aldarin had done well, however, and the coating of fat made the face of the wall soft and slippery. The archers were firing point-blank, releasing shafts straight down from their positions without bothering to aim. The soldiers stationed around murder holes upended boiling oil or pitch with horrific results.

And still the enemy came.

Slower-moving threshers had reached the base of the wall now, using their shields to provide some shelter to the greylings. Bodies started to pile up and the greylings used them to climb higher.

"Spears!" came the cry and the archers, their reserves nearly exhausted, stepped back from the ramparts to give the spearmen room. Reed moved closer to the battlements. A hundred or so yards down the line, he could see Ferris yelling orders to his squad. Their eyes met and Reed gave him a brief nod.

The first greyling to reach the top of the wall took a spear through the mouth and fell soundlessly back into the press of bodies below. It was quickly replaced by two more. Reed leant over the parapet and saw one of the creatures three feet below him. It had a thick rope tied around its waist, trailing behind it down to the ground. He thrust his spear into its right arm, causing it to lose its grip and tumble down out of sight.

Another creature gained a footing not far from Aldarin, and he hit it hard in the jaw with a gauntleted fist. An archer to his right screamed as a greyling leapt over the battlements and landed on his chest. Nidore ran to the man's aid, putting his rapier through its neck.

Reed pushed an enemy off the top of the wall with the butt of his spear and took a minute to survey his surroundings. His section was clear, but the gatehouse was under heavy assault. Greylings had gained a foothold on the barbican roof and managed to secure four or five ropes. Threshers were slowly pulling themselves up. Reed saw a flash of gold as the Baron fought to repulse the attack.

Just as Reed was about to help, he heard his name called from further down the line. It was Ferris, surrounded by greylings.

"Dammit!" spat Reed and ran towards him. The first greyling, intent on Ferris, had its back to him. He skewered the thing through the chest and threw himself at a second attacker, ducking a swing to the face and bringing his spear up hard into its groin. Ferris came to his aid, slicing the tip of his own spear across a greyling's throat.

"Sunny!" He grinned. "It's good to see you!"

"By the Pit, Ferris, you could at least say 'Sir'—" Reed started to say, then he saw the monstrous form of a dark-skinned thresher pull itself up behind Ferris.

"MOVE!" Reed shouted, and Ferris whisked round, but not fast enough. He caught the thresher's fist on his shoulder, and Reed heard a crack of bone as the man dropped to the ground.

The thresher's eyes swivelled from Ferris to Reed. It snarled, needle-sharp teeth flashing in the firelight. It was unarmed, but its spade-like hands were the size of Reed's head. It would not need weapons to kill him.

Suddenly, it barrelled forwards, faster than Reed thought possible. A huge fist hurtled towards his chest. He blocked hastily with his spear, deflecting the blow. A second punch took him in the stomach. It felt like he had been kicked by a bucking horse. Air exploded from his lips and he collapsed, moaning.

The thresher stood over him and said something in its guttural tongue. It raised its foot to crush his skull. Reed couldn't move, only scream his rage and defiance as the foot came down.

Then Aldarin's axe hammered into the thresher's chest.

The Knight of the Twelve withdrew his weapon with a sick, squelching sound, spattering Reed with black blood and shards of bone. The thresher toppled from the wall and crashed onto one of the roofs below.

"Friend Reed," said Aldarin, pulling the winded captain to his feet. "You should not wander off like that."

Reed, clutching his aching stomach, opened his mouth to reply when five long blasts of the signal horns sounded mournfully.

"Five? What does five mean?" he asked, grimacing with pain.

Aldarin looked at him in alarm. "It means the Baron has fallen," he said. "The Lord of Arelium is dead."

CHAPTER 15
SCALPELS AND LIPSTICK

"You see this pale, yellow, bell-shaped flower with a purple centre? We call it henbane, very useful in the right hands and quite deadly in the wrong ones. Ah, this little white plant with purple spots? Hemlock, excellent for the pain. And last but not least, Echinacea, with its beautiful pink petals. For infections and disease. Maybe the most important of them all. It would be a shame to win the war against the greylings just to die from sepsis, eh?"

KUMBHA, ELEVENTH OF THE TWELVE, 17 AT

⊷

J ELAÏA WIPED THE sweat from her brow and loaded more logs onto the crackling fire. The Great Hall was already stiflingly hot, but the healer had assured her that constant heat was necessary to help protect against infection. She grabbed a tray of surgical instruments and started pushing the blades into the hottest parts of the flames to sterilise them. The makeshift infirmary was still practically empty, less than a dozen beds filled with injured men. One of the wounded had told her that the greylings had tried to attack the wall with metal shields, but had been soundly pushed back by the defenders. She had seen the Baron's cooks heaving great cauldrons of soup out into the courtyard, so presumably the fighting had stopped for the time being.

Her mind wandered to those she knew and cared for stationed up on the ramparts. Her father of course, Aldarin, Reed, Orkam, Nidore … and Praxis. She had found herself thinking more and more about Praxis, with his jet-black hair, twinkling eyes, and all-knowing half-smile.

He had been her father's advisor for a good ten years now, replacing the previous steward: an old, wrinkled grouch of a man who had died peacefully in his sleep. In those early days, she had followed him around like a puppy, hanging on his every word, infatuated with him like so many other teenage girls.

Then she grew older, and maybe a little wiser. She had stopped fawning over him and had started challenging him, using her own growing knowledge to poke holes in the policies he presented to her father. And he went from ignoring her to actively seeking her out when he needed a second opinion or a sympathetic ear.

She could now tell the difference between the polite laugh he used publicly to avoid offence, and the deeper, more authentic laugh that rippled from his lips when they were together.

What was he to her now? Her father's steward? A

colleague? A friend? Or something else? She sighed and picked at the knot of the nurse's apron that the healer had told her to wear. The more she thought about it, the more she realised that there *was* something else, perhaps something worth exploring, once all this was over.

"More scalpels for you!" came a voice from behind her. Verona sauntered into view carrying a tray laden with surgical equipment and two steaming bowls of stew.

"Is there room for one more on that bench?" she asked, then sat down without waiting for a reply. She wore the same white gown as Jelaïa, her long dark hair drawn back into a crude ponytail that only further emphasised her striking pale face and prominent cheekbones. She was barely sweating as if unbothered by the heat.

She really is quite beautiful, Jelaïa thought, suddenly conscious of her own unruly hair and plain features. She picked up one of the bowls from the tray and let the mouth-watering odours of cooked meat and carrot wash over her. Her stomach growled, reminding her she had missed supper that evening to help set up the infirmary beds. She brought the bowl to her lips and took a deep sip, relishing the taste of the viscid broth as it slid down her throat.

The heiress and the silk trader's daughter sat in companionable silence.

"I'm sorry for Nidore," said Verona abruptly. "Grief and pain make us say things we do not really mean."

"Of course," Jelaïa replied. She had not seen Nidore since their previous altercation.

"He is … at a crossroads, I think. He has been holding back a lot of anger towards your father, towards his own father … and to you. Sometimes, he tells me he wishes Loré would wake up so he can apologise for not being the son he needed to be. Other times, he wishes his father would stop fighting to survive and die so he can take his place as head of the family estate, and finally regain some of the power and recognition he believes he deserves. I have done my best to help and console him, but it will take time, a long time, for things to get better."

Jelaïa nodded. "I am partially to blame. He was right about that. He was always so nice to me ... I think maybe he had a bit of a crush on me, to be honest. And I definitely knew I had him wrapped around my finger. Poor Nidore. He deserves better."

She put down her bowl and straightened her nurse's gown. "But what he said about my father was wrong. I've been involved in the running of the Barony since I turned eighteen and, while Loré and the Baron are certainly not friends, there is a lot of mutual respect there. You can see it in the way they grasp wrists and look each other in the eye. My father sent Loré out against the greylings because he trusts him, and trusts his loyalty. Nidore is incorrect to presume otherwise."

"I'm not sure—" Verona started to reply, but was cut off by the alarm bell ringing insistently from the roof of the keep. "Another attack," she said.

The healer swept into the Great Hall like a cantankerous mole, the lenses of his glasses fogging up in the heat. "Verona, Jelaïa, let's get ready," he squeaked, handing out face masks and hairnets. The door opened once more, this time revealing the fraught silhouette of Baroness del Arelium. She hurried in, tying a nurse's apron tightly around her considerable waist.

"Mother!" said Jelaïa reproachfully.

"Yes, yes. I know, I know, your father told me to stay in my quarters, but I'll be damned to the Pit if I just sit around doing nothing!" She grabbed a jug of fresh water and a stack of mugs.

"Ladies!" said the healer timidly, "If I may have a moment of your time? Thank you. Just a quick reminder of how things work here. I will be posted by the door with this, um, tube of lipstick kindly provided by her Lady."

The little man blushed and Jelaïa covered her mouth with her hand to hide her smile.

"I will mark each and every patient as they arrive. One cross for the lightly wounded: scrapes, abrasions, superficial cuts, and the like. We don't have enough beds to hold everyone so they'll just need a quick bandage and a pat on the back, then we'll send them on their way. Two crosses for the more seriously wounded: broken bones or deep wounds. Breaks will need to be set and splintered, wounds washed out, cleaned, and stitched up. Serious, but not life-threatening. We'll set them up in the cots along the eastern wall. And lastly, three crosses for the most urgent cases: bleeding arteries, crushed lungs, fractured skulls, that sort of thing. I'll deal with them first. Cots by the fire would be best if there are enough left. Questions?"

The Baroness raised her hand.

"Yes, um, my Lady?"

"Healer, how do you expect to sort patients and operate at the same time? It all sounds a bit counterproductive to me, no?"

"Well, I mean, in my experience—"

"I have myself read a great deal on the subject and

received some training as a nurse when I was younger. I consider myself quite capable. I will sort the arriving patients, leaving you time to care for them."

"Um. Very well, my Lady."

The muted sound of the signal horn bled through the walls.

"Arrows!" whispered the Baroness, wringing her hands.

"They can't be far from the walls, then," said Verona grimly.

The nurses waited in the silence of the Great Hall. They didn't have to wait long. Minutes later, the doors slammed open and a lanky young man in the livery of the Baron's guard stumbled into the room, his face caked with grime and soot.

"They've made it past the pitch and stakes!" he shouted wildly. "They'll soon be at the wall!"

Jelaïa could see out through the open double doors, down as far as the distant town walls. Fire and smoke blackened the night sky.

Men started to trickle into the infirmary, some carried on stretchers, others helped along by fellow soldiers.

All bore claw marks, bites, and scratches. The worst had suffered cuts across the neck or upper thighs and were bleeding profusely. The Baroness calmly examined each soldier as they arrived, marking them with one, two, or three crosses with a methodical swipe of lipstick.

The nurses led the injured to the cots, cleaning the wounds with hot water and lemon, comforting the men as best they could. Jelaïa carefully removed the leather cuirass of a soldier who had taken a blow to the chest. Two deep, diagonal cuts had sliced through the protective leather and pierced the skin below. Luckily the gashes were shallow enough to avoid stitches, but the man grimaced in pain as Jelaïa staunched the bleeding with a cloth soaked in lemon juice.

"How goes the defence?" she asked him tentatively, trying to keep her voice calm and neutral.

"We are holding, M'lady," the man replied. "They've reached the wall, but we are pushing them back."

"And did you, by chance, see Praxis, the Lord's steward?"

"Aye, the steward and the Baron were at the gatehouse, right in the thick of it. They both seemed fine when I left."

"Thank you, Sir. You bring me good news!" said Jelaïa with a smile, and she felt as if a weight had been lifted from her shoulders. Picking up the soiled towel and bowl, she headed to the end of the Great Hall where wicker baskets had been left by the keep's servants for dirty laundry.

As she passed the cots, someone whispered her name. Turning, she searched the rows of wounded men.

"Jelaïa," came the whisper again, much closer this time.

She looked down and saw with astonishment that Loré del Conte, first and most powerful of the Baron's vassals, was awake, fixing her with his one remaining eye.

"Loré!" cried Jelaïa, rushing to his side. "We were so worried! You have returned to us! How are you?"

"I feel like I've been trampled underfoot by a raging bull," said del Conte slowly in a rasping, halting voice; his disfigured lips and broken teeth slurring his words. "What did I miss?"

"The greylings are here, Loré, but we are beating them back. Your strength and courage gave us time to prepare."

"And where's Listus, then?" he coughed.

"Out on the ramparts, leading the defence."

Del Conte nodded and looked around with some difficulty. "And of course my son's not here to greet me as I wake.
I did not expect otherwise."

"Your son?" came the strong voice of Verona as she
moved to join them. "Your son sat by your side day and
night from the moment you were brought in here, holding
your hand and changing your urine-soaked clothes when
you were too weak to reach the chamber pot. He talked to
you for hours on end, pleaded with you, prayed for you,
helped you."

"Well, I—"

"And he is not here now because he is out on the wall
with the other defenders of Arelium, representing the house
of del Conte."

Loré snapped his lips shut. Something resembling pride
glimmered deep in his single eye. "I'm sorry, I spoke hastily,
you are right." He tried to raise himself onto his elbows and
fell back onto the cot with a wince.

"It seems I am to remain ... indisposed for a short
length of time. Perhaps Jelaïa, you or Lady ..." he squinted
at Verona. "I'm sorry, I do not know you, my Lady."

"I am no Lady. Veronassandra, silk trader's daughter.
Verona."

"Very well, Verona. Maybe one of you would oblige me
by telling me what in the Pit has been happening while I've
been having my little nap?"

Jelaïa glanced towards the door to the Great Hall where
the trickle of men had become a flood.

"Gladly, Lord del Conte, as soon as I am no longer

needed elsewhere." She dumped her dirty towels into the basket.

Five short horn blasts blew into the hall.

Loré del Conte let out a terrible moan. He flailed around with his hand and caught a handful of Jelaïa's apron, pulling her close with a strength that belied his weakened condition.

"The Baron!" he croaked. "The Baron is in trouble!" This final effort was too much for the noble; his eyes rolled back in his head and he lost consciousness.

CHAPTER 16

THE TRAMPLED BANNER

"My Lord. It has been an honour."

PRAXIS, STEWARD TO BARON DEL ARELIUM, 426 AT

"WHAT?" EXCLAIMED REED. "No, that's not possible, not the Baron, we must have misheard."

"That is what the signal means, friend Reed."

"No, no, there must be some mistake." Their part of the wall was free of greylings for the moment; the defenders slicing and stabbing at any enemy shapes that made it as far as the battlements. The gatehouse, however, was not faring well.

"Aldarin, with me!" said Reed decisively, and set off at a jog for the barbican, shouting at the men in front of him to let him pass. He heard the distinctive jangle of metal and knew that Aldarin was following him.

They quickly reached the end of the ramparts where three wide steps gave access to the gatehouse roof. The roof itself was a chaotic whirlwind of men and greylings, with two or three threshers commanding their lesser kin, spurring them forwards towards the soldiers of Arelium. More and more greylings were scrambling over the battlements, many of them trailing coarse ropes to make the climb easier for others. There was no sign of Praxis or the Baron.

Reed saw with no small amount of pride that a squad of spearmen had formed a crude spearwall at the top of the steps, preventing the enemy from moving off the roof. Several of them saluted when they saw him approach.

"Report!" he said, raising his voice above the clash of steel and the cries of battle.

One of the men pushed his way to the front and Reed saw it was Orkam, his shaved scalp stained with blood.

"We are holding them here! But we can't move forwards, we're the only thing stopping them from taking the ramparts!"

Aldarin had remained silent, studying the ebb and flow of the skirmish with his azure eyes. "There is no need for you to accompany us," he said in his deep voice. "If you would simply let me through, I believe I can reach the Baron unaided."

He moved back a few paces and unslung his double-bladed axe. Murmuring something softly to himself, he kissed the silver 'Brachyura' engraved into the haft.

Orkam nodded. "Ready."

Aldarin jogged forwards, slowly picking up speed. As he

reached the spearwall, Orkam barked a command and two files turned ninety degrees to the left, creating a slim corridor just wide enough for the knight to pass through. He crashed into the greylings on the other side, scattering them like a bowling ball hitting a row of pins. Two unlucky survivors lying in the knight's path were brained by the butt of his axe as he continued towards the far end of the barbican roof.

Reed sprinted after him, hearing the clack of the spearwall locking back into place once he was through. He could now see what Aldarin was aiming for, a furtive splash of black and gold less than fifty yards away.

The Knight of the Twelve attacked relentlessly and Reed marvelled at the man's skill. Aldarin's eyes were always moving, his mind analysing and planning, his upper body constantly repositioning to counter enemy attacks.

He was barely swinging his axe, only orientating the sharp edge to block the greylings as they jumped towards him, cutting through flesh and bone like a butcher's cleaver. Much like when they had fought at the Pit, the greylings were packed tightly against one another, hoping to use their superior numbers to overwhelm the defenders. But it left them little space to manoeuvre, and no latitude to escape Aldarin's axe.

Suddenly, the press of bodies vanished and Aldarin arrived on the edge of a small semicircle. In its centre, Listus del Arelium lay sprawled face down, bleeding from a series of cuts across his forehead. Reed saw with horror that his left arm was missing. All that remained was a raw, oozing stump protruding from the damaged remnants of the Baron's golden armour. The standard of Arelium lay in the dirt next to him. The proud white wolf had been trampled by a multitude of clawed feet and was encrusted with grit and blood.

Over the unconscious form of the Baron stood Praxis, breathing hard, a dagger in each hand. The steward's black leather armour was battered and torn in several places but, apart from that, he seemed to bear no other injury. He was holding his own against the greylings; Reed counted nine dark-grey corpses on the ground before him.

As Reed watched, two more of the creatures tried to rush the steward. Praxis parried a claw strike from the first attacker and put his dagger through the eye of the second, popping the orb with a spatter of gelatinous matter. Quickly withdrawing his weapon, Praxis spun around and drew it sharply across the stomach of the remaining greyling. Reed was hit by the stench of half-digested meat as the greyling's innards splashed onto the paving slabs. The other greylings backed further away, snarling.

Praxis saw them now and favoured Reed with one of his half-smiles. "Reed! Or should we be calling you Sunny?"

"You should most definitely not," said Reed flatly. "What is the Baron's condition?"

Praxis' smile vanished. "Not good, I'm afraid. I've managed to staunch a lot of the blood but he's not a young man anymore. We need to get him to the healer as soon as we can." More greylings attacked, quickly dispatched by Aldarin.

"Very well, Sir Praxis," the knight said. "May I suggest you carry the Baron off the wall and escort him to the infirmary? There are stretchers and horses waiting down below."

"Agreed," said Praxis, holstering his daggers. He managed to get one arm around the Baron and hauled him to his feet. Listus groaned. His eyelids fluttered, but he didn't regain consciousness.

"Sorry about this, my Lord," muttered the steward and began half dragging, half carrying the Baron towards the stairs.

"Wait a minute!" said Reed and, discarding his spear, he knelt down to pull the standard of Arelium out of the muck. "We need to take back the gatehouse or the wall is lost. And for that we need a bit of hope. The men must see the Baron is still alive. Aldarin, will you help me?"

"Of course, friend Reed." Aldarin's baritone boomed across the battlefield and out along the wall.

"Men of Arelium. Do not despair! Your Baron is wounded but not dead! And with your help, he will live to fight another day! But he needs you now! See how your colours have been tarnished" — Reed held the standard aloft — "see how they defile your town. We cannot accept this, we will not accept this! Let us push forwards! Let us throw them from our towers! Cast them from our walls! Send them back to the Pit from whence they came! Who is with me? Arelium! Arelium!"

"ARELIUM!" came the answering cry and Reed turned to see Orkam dissolve the spearwall and lead his men forwards in a desperate charge.

"ARELIUM!" echoed down the wall. Arrows appeared overhead, hitting the enemy furthest from where they stood and knocking them off the roof. Nidore had gained the barbican, the thin point of his duellist rapier stabbing left and right; a complement of men from Ferris's squad protecting his flanks.

A deafening growl came from straight ahead and a

couple of threshers loped towards them, batting away any greylings that got in their way. They were taller even than Aldarin, their massive, thick-skinned bodies towering over the two men.

"Stay back, Reed," warned the knight as he turned to meet them.

The threshers attacked simultaneously. Aldarin blocked a vicious sword cut to the face and took an axe to the shoulder, denting his hard metal plate. He switched stance, holding his axe like a spear and jabbing forwards in a flurry of short thrusts. The thresher stumbled back clumsily, clutching its chest and Aldarin followed through with a powerful over-head swing, splintering the thing's ribs and burying the axe deep into its torso, releasing a cascade of black ichor. The thresher shrieked in agony just as its companion hit Aldarin hard from behind, forcing him down on one knee.

Reed sprang to his friend's aid and caught an elbow to the head. He fell heavily, stunned. The thresher ripped Aldarin's axe from his grasp and threw it well out of reach. Flexing veiny muscles, it locked both hands behind the knight's back and pulled him close in a vice-like hold.

Aldarin had lost his helmet and, for the first time, some-thing akin to doubt flickered across his features. The thresher squeezed tighter, laughing into its opponent's face, blood and spittle dribbling from its putrid mouth. Aldarin strug-gled as the breath was pushed from his lungs, the bones of his ribcage straining against the pressure. A dark veil began to obscure his vision.

Then Aldarin drew back his head and head-butted the thresher in the face. The thresher let out a surprised cry. Aldarin's forehead hit it again and again. With a nasty crunch, the thresher's nose shattered. It released its grip and recoiled from the knight in amazement. Aldarin, his face battered and bruised, chased after it and hammered his fist into the thing's face four more times. Finally, with a roar of effort, he grabbed the thresher's head in both hands and gave a short, sharp jerk to the left, breaking its neck with a resonant crack.

The surrounding greylings scattered, howling and chittering in panic. A great cheer went up from nearby defenders as the massive thresher toppled lifelessly to the ground. They assailed the disorganised enemy with renewed vigour, slowly forcing them back towards the battlements. Only one thresher remained, cornered by Orkam and a handful of veterans.

They used the superior range of their spears to great efficiency, darting forwards in groups of two or three to hit the thresher in its blind spots before retreating. Finally, inevitably, the thresher fell, bleeding from a dozen wounds. With the last of their leaders gone, the remaining greylings fled, scampering on all fours over the wall and back to their brethren below.

"Arelium!" came the cry from a hundred mouths, then five hundred, then a thousand as news of the rout spread up and down the wall. Men sang and cheered, grinning and laughing. Others sank to the ground in silence.

Reed saw one man sitting with his back against the ramparts, tears streaming down his cheeks, the decapitated head of one of his friends sitting in his lap. Another was on his knees, rocking back and forth muttering '*No no no*' under his breath, his eyes focussed on the dead and the dying strewn over the roof of the gatehouse.

Orkam quickly formed a group of volunteers to go among the wounded, carrying those who could still be saved off the wall and offering a quick, merciful death to the less fortunate. The frenetic sounds of battle were no more, replaced by the celebrations of the victorious and the moans of the injured.

Nidore and Reed met in the middle of the roof. The young lord was sporting a new cut on his cheek and looked exhausted. His rapier hung slackly in one hand, covered in black ichor.

"Nidore, thank you," said Reed, smiling and grasping the man's wrist. Nidore did not return the smile, his eyes still hard and bitter behind his mane of golden hair.

"I did not do this for you. Or for him," he said.

Reed looked him squarely in the eye. "Good," he said. "I am glad. A man should not fight because his Lord tells him to, or because his friend tells him to. He should fight because he believes it is the right thing to do. And it *is* the right thing to do, Nidore, whatever grudge you hold against your liege lord or your father. If we had not held the gatehouse this night, the greylings would have reached the keep by now, slaughtering the wounded and the nurses. They would have butchered Verona without a second thought. You helped prevent this Nidore, and you should be proud."

Nidore opened his mouth to reply, then shut it tight. With a curt nod, he turned and was lost in the crowd of cheering soldiers.

Reed shook his head. There was so much hate in the young man now, an ever-present bubbling rage that would be hard to quell. He could only hope that given enough time those feelings would fade and the happy, boisterous young man Reed first saw in Jaelem would return.

He joined Aldarin and Orkam at the wall. The gruff guard captain was recounting the assault on the gatehouse, his hands gesticulating wildly as he described each attack and counter-attack. Aldarin listened without moving, his battered face unreadable.

"Reed!" the knight cried, visibly relieved. "That was closer than I would have liked." He winced and probed his bruised face with one enormous hand. "I may have lost my calm a little at the end there; my teachers back at the temple will not be pleased."

Orkam gave a deep-throated chuckle. "We are certainly glad to have you with us, Sir Aldarin. If you had not dealt with those two threshers, things might have turned out quite differently. And the shieldwall! By the Twelve, Reed! I admit I thought the Baron was going senile when he chose you to train our conscripts, but only a fool would say that now. You'll have to let me buy you an ale or two when this is all over."

"With pleasure, Orkam. I haven't had time to try any of the local stuff yet, but I'm sure anything you have here will be better than the awful swill the Old Guard brewed at the Pit. We used to use the leftover dregs to clean the moss and lichen from the walls!"

Orkam laughed again. His mirth was infectious and Reed soon found himself smiling too.

"So what next, Aldarin?" he asked.

The Knight of the Twelve was observing the greyling horde that covered the valley floor. The enemy had lost thousands since the siege began and yet their numbers barely seemed diminished. More and more threshers were arriving to bolster their ranks, grouping together in bands of ten. The new arrivals were much better equipped: at least half wore primitive metal helms and breastplates, or carried the same rectangular shields that had been used to counter the fire trenches.

"Looks like you won't be able to head-butt all of them, eh, Aldarin?" said Orkam, pointing out some of the more heavily armoured threshers. "Lucky you've still got your axe or you'd be in trouble."

"Indeed," said Aldarin pensively, rubbing his jaw. "I'm not sure what they will do now. There are only a few hours of night left. If they want to attack again before the sun comes up, they will have to do so immediately."

"What would you do, Aldarin?" asked Reed curiously.

"I would order another assault, without hesitation. We are still reeling from the last one. Our supplies are low." He indicated the empty wicker baskets and iron pots. "We have no arrows and no oil; they could approach the wall with little resistance. No time to clear the ramparts either; we would be hindered by the bodies of the fallen. And last but not least, we do not know the fate of the Baron. That man was essential for morale, his opening speech alone did more to strengthen our defences than any stock of arrows or field of tar ever could." He tapped his forehead with a gauntleted index finger. "Most people don't understand that most wars are fought and won in the minds of men."

"What do you mean?" prompted Orkam. He was listening intently.

"Have you heard of the ambush of Hellin Pass? No, I suppose you wouldn't have. Towards the end of Brachyura's life, he rarely ventured forth from his temple, dedicating all his time to teaching and writing. Word came about a village less than a day's ride away that had been attacked by greylings, the men slaughtered and the women and children abducted. Brachyura took a group of thirty knights and went to find them. It was a trap. They were lured into a narrow defile, a dead end with no way out. Thousands of greylings, threshers, and other species long since forgotten attacked them relentlessly for a week. A *week*. Guess how many of them perished?"

"All of them?"

"No. None of them. When the relief force arrived, it found all of them mauled and battered, but alive. One of my old temple masters said his great-grandfather was there that day. I asked him how they survived. The answer was simple: Brachyura told them none of them would die. He told them every morning when they woke, before every enemy assault, before every sunset. And such was his strength of character that they believed him. Convince a man he is invincible and he will be unstoppable. The Baron is essentially trying to do just that."

"Right," said Orkam. "But we are talking about thirty Knights of the Twelve and one of the Twelve themselves. If they are all anything like you, I don't think they'd need much convincing."

"You have missed the point, friend Orkam, but I thank you for the compliment."

Fresh reserves were lining the wall, their clean-shaven faces and spotless red and white uniforms in stark contrast to the dirty, tattered tunics of those who had been fighting the greylings since sunset. Weary groups of spearmen and archers made their way to the stairs and ladders leading off the battlements, leaving a few encouraging words of advice behind them. The new arrivals, in no immediate danger, began heaving the bodies of the enemy over the wall, clearing the ramparts.

"Orkam, it looks like now is the time for that beer," said Reed tiredly. "Will you be joining us, Aldarin?"

"Thank you, but no. I do not need to rest. I will stay for a while." He retrieved his helm and locked it into place, his scarred, olive-skinned face once more hidden from sight.

Reed stopped at the top of the stairs. Something made him glance back. The knight was standing immobile, arms crossed, staring out into the night; the bright steel plates of his armour reflecting the pale moonlight. Reed remembered the shock and awe he had felt when first meeting him, a legend made real.

Reed did not have many friends, but he was glad Aldarin was one of them.

"May the Twelve keep you safe," he murmured. "I will see you again soon."

He could not have been more wrong.

CHAPTER 17

A MEETING OF
BROKEN LORDS

"Why are all men so incredibly stubborn? One of the soldiers came to see me today; his training baton had broken while sparring in the yard. A two-inch piece of wood stuck in his thigh! I offered to remove it, but he refused. Didn't want to get laughed at for getting injured during practice. A week later, it was much worse. I pleaded with him to leave the front line, to come here for treatment. Again, he refused. He didn't want to look weak in front of his squadmates. Another week, and he was brought in on a stretcher. Stupid man! I had no other choice but to amputate."

KUMBHA, ELEVENTH OF THE TWELVE, 31 AT

᪥

THE INFIRMARY STANK of blood, sweat, urine, and death.

The cots had been filled within the first hour, and

injured men now covered every inch of available floor space, packed together like sardines. All but the most serious cases were diverted to the courtyard where servants had laid out mattresses and pillows from the guest quarters, and lit great bonfires in an attempt to keep the soldiers warm.

Nurses bustled around the wounded; changing sheets, emptying bedpans, bringing food and water, and offering what little comfort they could.

The Baroness had not moved from her spot by the door, interrogating each new group of men for news of her husband. Since the doleful lament of the signal horns, they had heard nothing more. None of the soldiers arriving at the infirmary knew whether the Baron was still alive, only that the gatehouse was still under heavy assault.

Jelaïa was assisting the healer in his third amputation of the evening, cleaning his instruments and doing her best to soothe the pain of the poor young archer whose foot had been ripped to shreds by a greyling's claws. The creatures deliberately covered their nails with dirt and excrement, spreading infection among the wounded as a result.

The healer was using a metal bone saw, his round face red with effort as he drew the blade back and forth just above the patient's ankle. The archer, barely eighteen, had mercifully passed out from the pain. With a final crack, the saw broke through the tibia and the mutilated foot came free.

Jelaïa swallowed hard, then bound the stump as tightly as she dared with a linen cloth soaked in lemon juice. All that remained was to find the man a spot on the ground near the fire and hope to the Twelve he would survive the night.

"I'm not sure how much longer I can do this," said the healer tiredly, washing his bloodstained hands in a bowl of fresh warm water. He had lost his glasses some time ago and heavy bags were forming under his bloodshot eyes. A thin shadow of stubble dotted his chin and neck. Jelaïa was fairly sure the man had not slept since Loré del Conte had returned to the valley.

"Do you not have anyone else to help you, healer? An apprentice, maybe?" she asked.

"Two apprentices, aye, but they're not much use for anything other than mixing concoctions and gathering herbs. One of them did help a midwife deliver a child once. Wouldn't eat red meat for a week after." He gave a wry smile. "Serves me right for not taking on a partner when I had the chance. I'll carry on for tonight at least; we'll see what tomorrow brings."

Jelaïa spied Verona through a crowd of nurses and patients. She was feeding a bowl of stew to Loré. The noble was still pale-faced and weak, but had managed to move himself into a sitting position despite the discomfort it obviously caused him. Verona saw her watching and gave a short nod and a resigned smile.

There had been a constant flow of wounded since the second assault began. Most of the early arrivals bore claw marks, but once the threshers had gained the walls, the injuries were much more serious: fractured skulls, crushed limbs, and broken bones. The leather and steel armour worn by the Baron's conscripts did little to soften the blows. Armour offered no protection against fists harder than solid rock and, for each man injured, she knew another would be found dead on the ramparts.

Luckily, she did hear of some extraordinary escapes too. Ferris, the ruddy-faced bear of a man under Reed's command, had been thrown off the wall by one of the threshers only to land on a thatched roof below. The tightly-packed straw had cushioned his fall and, apart from a few bruises, he was miraculously unharmed. Between that and his vocal performance in the training yard, he had become a sort of mascot for the conscripted spearmen, a position he was already exploiting by making his unit buy him drinks.

A sharp shriek from the Baroness heralded the arrival of Praxis and Listus del Arelium. Praxis was covered in blood, his black uniform hanging off him in tatters. Behind him came two red-clothed guards carrying a stretcher upon which lay the Baron in his golden armour. Silence engulfed the hall as its occupants stopped and stared.

"Over here, quickly now!" cried the healer, pulling on a pair of thin leather gloves and striding over to the makeshift operating theatre set up by the fire. The guards, straining with effort, lifted the Baron onto an oak table covered in dirty sheets. Listus was conscious but dazed, his eyes moving in and out of focus, his mouth opening and closing as if trying to speak. The Baroness pushed past the soldiers to grasp his remaining hand in her own, sobbing.

Jelaïa moved to join them, but was stopped by the restraining hand of Praxis on her arm. "You need to give them some room," he said quietly. "Let the healer do his job." Jelaïa tried to shake him off, but the world was spinning around her, and she stumbled forwards, half-tripping over her nurse's apron.

Praxis caught her before she could fall and she spent a few moments pressed against his chest, his arms around her. He smelt of oil and leather mixed with blood. Embarrassed, she pushed herself away, trying to hide the sudden flush spreading from her neck to her cheeks.

"P ... Praxis, thank the Twelve, you are all right!" she stammered. "Are you injured?"

"What?" Praxis looked down and seemed to notice his stained tunic and trousers for the first time. "Ah no, my Lady. I'm afraid it is not my blood but that of your father. I managed to get a makeshift tourniquet around his arm once we were off the wall, but he had already lost a fair amount of blood."

"What happened?"

"Greylings ... threshers ... we were overrun. The greylings came up the wall so fast! We couldn't shake their foothold before they managed to get some threshers up and those massive brutes laid into us like a farmer scything wheat. Nothing we did seemed to hurt them. Swords and spears bounced off their thick hides without even leaving a scratch.

"Each time they swung their weapons, men died. Your father tried to rally us, we were starting to form a spearwall, but then three of them hit us simultaneously and the men's resolve shattered. The Baron held them back for a minute or two ... but he doesn't have the strength he had twenty years ago. I saw them wear him down, pummelling at his guard until he was forced to lower his sword. That was all it took for one of them to take his sword-arm off above the elbow." He rubbed his eyes tiredly.

"Oh, Praxis, I'm so sorry."

"I would have died out there too, you know. If Aldarin had arrived but a few minutes later, he would have found my body lying beside the Baron's." He removed his battered leather breastplate and tossed it to the floor.

Jelaïa said nothing. There was nothing to say.

"Praxis!" came a hoarse grumble. The healer had administered some foul-smelling liquid to the Baron and his steel-grey eyes had regained a small amount of lucidity. He was staring intently at them while two nurses worked diligently to remove his pauldrons. A fresh bandage encompassed his upper forehead, obscuring the nasty gash made by a greyling's claws.

"Well, man, what are you waiting for? Attend to me!" he said, then grimaced as one of the nurses brushed against his ruined arm.

"Yes, my Lord, my apologies."

"I suppose you think you deserve a rest after carrying me down from the wall, eh?"

"That would be nice, my Lord."

"Well, that's not going to happen. Too much work to do. Although I suppose you might manage to beat me in the practice yard now. You'll have to spar with me left-handed, of course, it would only be fair."

Praxis looked worried. Maybe the Baron wasn't so lucid after all. "We will have to see, my Lord, won't we? What are your orders?"

"Well, once this bloodsucker" — he scowled at the healer — "gets me back into some sort of fighting shape, I'll need my second set of plate. Then we'll head back down to the wall again, show the men I'm ready to hold the line."

"No, my Lord."

"I'm not going to do this again, Praxis. Last time was enough. And it cost me Loré. I won't give in to you this time."

"I said no, my Lord."

"Now listen, *steward*," said the Baron, his voice growing low and dangerous. "Do not overstep yourself. It is not for you to decide what I can and cannot do. I am your liege lord. I am the lord of all men and women here! And I'll be damned to the Pit if I can't do what I want. I imagine the attack on the wall failed or we wouldn't be talking right now. But they'll be back. We need to look to the men's morale now, Praxis. They need their Baron."

"Oh do be quiet!" came a sharp, high-pitched voice. The Baroness stared down at him, her features a mask of fury. "You are a stubborn, stupid little man and you forget I know everything about you."

"Now see here—"

"Be *quiet*, I said!" The Baroness repeated, raising her voice even higher. "I can see how you grit your teeth and clench your hand, how your body tremors when you move but a fraction. You are trying to hide your pain from us and it's ridiculous. You do not need to be on the wall, Listus. You don't have to control everything. There are experienced people down there, people like Aldarin, who have been trained for this type of situation. Reed has spent most of his life on a wall. Orkam too. Trust them. You need to stay here. Monitor things from your chambers if you wish, the southern window has an excellent view of the barbican."

"You must be joking!" spluttered the Baron. "I'm not going to sit around here while you—" he stopped abruptly and let out a wild scream of agony, startling the wounded soldiers in the nearby cots. Looking down, he saw the Baroness had closed her hand around the remains of his missing arm and was squeezing very softly.

"Wh ... wh ... what are you doing, woman?" he said haltingly, drawing in great heaving breaths to calm the red-hot lines of fire running from elbow to shoulder.

"Proving a point, my husband. Imagine the wall is attacked again. Do you feel that pain? I am barely touching you. What will happen when a greyling hits you with its claws? When a thresher cuts you with its axe? You are defenceless, my dear, and you will die. And the soldiers' 'morale' that you are so intent on preserving will crash and burn."

"She's right, Father," murmured Jelaïa. "As is Praxis. They are both right."

The Baron lay silently on his back, staring up into the rafters of the Great Hall. After a long moment, he spoke.

"Very well, I will heed your counsel this one time. Orkam and Aldarin have command of the wall."

"My Lord—" began Praxis.

"No, Praxis, you will stay here with me. We will set ourselves up in one of the guest bedrooms; one that has a good view of the southern curtain wall, as the Baroness suggested. I'll let you organise a team of messengers to carry my orders to the front lines. Healer! Work your magic on what's left of my arm and give me some more of that disgusting stuff you dare to call medicine."

"It's wormwood, my Lord, effective for the pain but only in small doses. I really don't think it would be a good idea to, um, indulge in much more. I've given you as much as I can without risking some rather nasty side-effects."

"Nonsense, man. I feel better than ever. Now leave me in peace, the rest of you. I'm sure the healer can bandage my arm perfectly well without you all gaping at me." The operating area had been fitted with drapes pillaged from the Baron's bedroom and the healer pulled them closed, transforming the doctor and his patient into two blurred shadows.

"Stupid idiot." Loré was awake, sitting up in his bed and supported by a mountain of cushions. He looked better. A wad of padding covered the wound in his cheek. His ruined eye socket was now mostly hidden by a black eyepatch, with only a hint of puckered scar tissue peaking around the edges. His blond hair had been shorn to stubble.

Despite his injuries, he bore himself well. He had been dressed in a white shirt, crimson-red doublet, and matching britches. His broken leg had been splintered and fixed to a metal articulated brace, hinged at the knee to allow move-ment. It must have cost a fortune.

"Loré!" exclaimed Praxis. "It is good to see you awake!"

Jelaïa could tell the steward was being sincere. Not for the first time, she wondered how much of the enmity between Loré and the Baron was real and how much was political fabrication. Loré had been around her father for a long time, much longer than Praxis, and although she had often seen him contest the Baron's word in public, he was loyal to a fault. *Better the enemy you know than the enemy you don't*, she thought to herself.

"What did I miss? Where's my son?" Del Conte was saying. "Still on the wall?" Verona took it upon herself to recount the night's events and the attack on the gatehouse.

The Baron had been the last of the grievously injured to arrive, and now the frenetic activity of the last few hours slowed to a more manageable pace. The drapes parted with a swish and the healer emerged, exhausted.

"Lord del Arelium is doing well. He passed out a few minutes ago. I suggest we all try to get some rest before the next attack." He tore off his apron and gloves and half-collapsed into a cushioned chair by the fire, snoring as soon as his head hit the fabric.

Jelaïa felt a tug on her sleeve. Verona had removed her apron and hairnet, revealing a low-cut purple dress and the heart-shaped silver necklace she always wore. She looked radiant.

"Loré has asked me to look for Nidore and tell him his father is awake."

"Oh, it's 'Loré' now is it? Not Lord del Conte?"

"Oh, do be quiet. Would you like to come with me down to the wall?"

"Well, I'm not sure that would be a good idea. I still have lots to do here—"

"Don't be silly, you need a bit of fresh air." Verona linked her arm with Jelaïa's and pulled her towards the door. "It'll be fun! Who knows what mischief we will find? And if there is none to be found, maybe we can make some of our own!"

And the two women left the stench of the infirmary for the cool night air of Arelium.

CHAPTER 18
A MOMENT'S RESPITE

"Now listen up. You'll be wanting to put your mug at an angle under that there barrel. Now grab the tap and yank it open, right? Don't half-open it, that'd be stupid. Now let that honeydew beer flow down the side of your cup, and give it a little upwards twist at the end to get that frothy head. There you go! Nothing to it! A perfect brew. Now how about you pour another one for me?"

FERRIS, SERGEANT OF THE ARELIUM 'IRREGULARS', 426 AT

⁓

V ERONA AND JELAÏA found Nidore and the others just as the last of the night stars were fading from a slowly brightening sky.

The greylings had not attacked again and more reserve troops had been sent to the wall. The worn-out spearmen and archers had dispersed, some returning to their homes, others finding quiet spots away from the front lines to rest and recuperate.

Reed, Orkam, Nidore, Ferris, and a small group of conscripted spearmen were sitting on a pile of overturned barrels stacked in the corner of a secluded cobbled square bordered by oak trees. A stone fountain bubbled in the square's centre and another corner was taken up by a two-storeyed alehouse, its wooden struts carved with bunches of barley and twisting hop vines. The alehouse's windows were boarded up with riveted planks, its front door chained shut.

This didn't seem to bother the men much. An enterprising spearman had tapped one of the barrels and was handing out big, foaming mugs of warm ale, much to the excitement of all involved.

Orkam was standing on one of the kegs, his chest puffed out, his hands firmly planted on his hips. "Prithee, return to whence you came!" he bawled in a passable imitation of Aldarin's deep voice. The others chuckled good-naturedly and toasted his performance by raising their mugs into the air. Orkam gave a cheeky bow and jumped down to accept a congratulatory drink.

"Good morning!" said Verona, waving excitedly at the little group.

Nidore had been slouching in a corner, but his head shot up at the sound of her voice. A wide, affectionate grin split his face and Jelaïa saw at long last a hint of the carefree young noble of her childhood.

Throwing away his ale, Nidore bounded forwards and swept Verona up into his arms, twirling her around. Pulling her close, he bent his head and kissed her full on the lips. Verona's eyes widened in surprise, but she did not pull away.

Ferris gave a long, whistling cat-call amid cheering from Reed and the spearmen. Verona blushed faintly, but Nidore did not seem to care, his face radiating joy.

"Verona, I have missed you," he said huskily. "You do not know what you mean to me. If something had happened to you, I ... I don't know what I would have done."

Verona smiled broadly at him. "Nidore, your father is awake and asking for you."

"What?"

"He's awake, Nidore. He's doing all right."

"What?"

"You heard me."

"But ... but he was dying, I saw his face, those wounds ... how could anyone survive that?"

"I don't think your father is just anyone, Nidore."

"No, I suppose not." He sat down heavily on one of the barrels with a sigh.

"Nidore? I thought you would be pleased?"

"I am, I mean, of course I am. It's just ... I had started to grieve, you know? I ... may have said some things in anger that I did not mean." He glanced over at Jelaïa. "If you would forgive me, my Lady?"

"Think nothing of it!" said Jelaïa warmly. "Now away you go. Verona will take you to him. I'll stay here a while longer." She smoothed the folds of her pea-green dress and lowered herself daintily to the ground, leaning back against a cask of ale.

Nidore held out his hand to Verona, who took it gladly and the young couple disappeared out of the square, back towards the keep.

Jelaïa watched them go and found herself thinking of Praxis.

"A drink, my Lady?" asked Reed. He looked tired, but happy. His unkempt beard and tangle of salt-and-pepper hair made him seem even more dishevelled, and he had fresh wrinkles pulling at the corners of his brown eyes. Something else had changed about him too. He exuded a new-found confidence and inner fire that had been sorely missing when she had first met him in the Great Hall. Jelaïa had been surprised when Praxis had told her that it was Reed and Aldarin who had saved the Baron, but looking at him now it didn't seem unlikely at all.

"A bit early for a drink, isn't it, Captain?" she said in a teasing tone.

"It's never too early. And don't call me Captain, it's Reed."

"Or Sunny!" Ferris yelled, wavering on his feet.

"No, no, definitely not. Reed will do fine. So, a drink or not?"

"Yes, please." Jelaïa had never been fond of ale, but the hours spent in the infirmary had made her terribly thirsty and, apart from sticking her head in the square's small fountain, there didn't seem to be any alternatives.

Reed filled a mug to the brim and handed it over before laying his cloak down on the cobbles next to her. Jelaïa took a tentative sip and felt the warm liquid slide down her throat. Not bad at all. She licked the froth from her lips and took another sip.

"Have you seen your father?" asked Reed.

"Oh, yes, I suppose you couldn't know, but he is alive and well ... and very, very grumpy."

Reed laughed. "No change there, then! I am glad. He was inspirational on the wall. You should have seen how they were hanging on his every word. A good man."

"Yes, I suppose he is. I will be taking his place one day. I only hope I will be half as competent as he is."

"Something I have learnt from my meagre few hours in command is to surround yourself with people you trust. I'm pretty much useless by myself, but give me Orkam, Ferris, and Aldarin, and I can get things done."

"Thank you, Reed. That is indeed comforting. And that reminds me. Father is alive but by no means able to fight. He'll be staying in the relative safety of the keep until the fighting is over. Aldarin and Orkam have the wall."

"You hear that?" said Reed jovially to Orkam. "You're in command!"

Orkam turned visibly pale. "By the Twelve, I hope not. I can yell orders at a bunch of men but my tactical expertise pretty much stops there. Aldarin is the strategist, let him coordinate our defences for the time being." He looked at his empty beer mug forlornly. "I suppose I should go and tell him."

"I will go," said Jelaïa, laughing. "You stay here a while longer. If I remember correctly, the greylings don't usually attack during the day and the sun is beginning to come up. I'll be safe."

"Why thank you, M'lady. That is most kind. You'll find him on the gatehouse roof. Don't think he's moved from there at all in the last couple of hours."

"Very well, thank you." Jelaïa drained the last drops of ale and rose to her feet. As she was leaving the square, she could faintly hear Reed asking the others.

"So how does that awful song go again? Something … something … country fair?"

And Ferris, never one to disappoint, began belting out what had become the unofficial marching song of the Arelium conscripts, his raucous voice loud enough to wake the dead.

❦

Jelaïa found Aldarin standing alone on the gatehouse roof, massive hands resting on the head of his double-bladed butterfly axe. He was lost in thought, staring out over the valley as the first rays of light hit the burnt-out farmsteads and ravaged southern fields.

"Sir Knight," she said respectfully.

"My Lady," he replied, inclining his head. "Have you come to appraise the enemy?"

Thousands of greylings still carpeted the land almost as far as the eye could see. Jelaïa was reminded of when she had kicked open an anthill as a child and observed the swarm of little insects scurrying without purpose in every direction.

Some greylings were pulling the bodies of their fallen comrades into great piles already buzzing with flies. Another group was digging crude ditches and trenches, uprooting the few remaining trees and bushes. Surprisingly, a large number were doing nothing at all, staring blankly, their bulbous eyes half-closed.

"It's the sunlight," said Aldarin, following her gaze. "They seem to become more lethargic during the day. Reed and I experienced the same thing when they attacked the Pit."

"And what about the piles of corpses?"

"That is a bit more macabre. Greylings and threshers are omnivorous, but can be driven to cannibalism if there is no other option. I hate to say it but I think they are making sure they have enough food to carry on the siege."

Jelaïa turned away, disgusted. "What is morale like here?" she asked, changing the subject.

"Good. It will be better when the Baron returns."

"Ah. He will not be returning. You have command of the wall now."

Aldarin looked at her in astonishment. "Me? But I am not even a subject of Arelium! The men will never accept my guidance. What was he thinking? No, I cannot accept, he will have to choose someone else."

"Hah! If that's what you really want, you'll have to tell him yourself. He's already in a foul temper, I'm not going to make it any worse."

Aldarin removed his pincer-like helm and ran a hand over his cropped hair. Jelaïa could see an ugly purple welt on his forehead and another colouring his cheek.

"I didn't ask for this. My mission was to investigate the Pit then report back to the temple. They must still be waiting for me." He shook his head.

"Maybe," Jelaïa said. "However, positions of responsibility should not be given to those who *ask* for it, but to those who *deserve* it ... and have the necessary skills to qualify for it. You told me yourself you have been trained in the teachings of Brachyura, one of the greatest strategists who ever lived. I think that qualifies you for the job."

Aldarin's blue eyes bored into hers. A frown came and

went. Then he shrugged and inclined his head to her once more.

"You are right, my Lady. And you would do well to heed your own words, methinks. For you will make a fine Baroness."

"I suppose so, but Baroness of what? Look at my domain!"

Jelaïa indicated the scorched land with a wide sweep of her arm, then steadied herself as her vision trembled for an instant.

Too much ale, she thought. But then she saw the look on Aldarin's face and knew he had felt it too.

"What is it?" she asked. A second slight tremor followed the first, stronger this time. She could see small pebbles vibrating on the ramparts. A metallic clang rang out nearby as one of the iron braziers tipped over, spilling embers and ash onto the paving.

"Aldarin?"

A third tremor cracked a stone slab a few feet from where they were standing. People were shouting now, fear and panic spreading along the wall like wildfire. An overhanging bretèche split apart and crashed down to the valley floor below in a shower of mortar and rubble.

More tremors followed, and men started to scream.

"Aldarin, what's going on?" she repeated in a tremulous voice, steadying herself against the parapet as she felt the ground move under her.

The big knight had sheathed his axe and locked his helm back in place. He strode over to her and lifted her bodily off her feet. She cried out as a nearby section of wall collapsed in on itself, dragging a howling guardsman down to his death.

"We must get off the wall!" Aldarin yelled at her over the cries of terror and the ear-splitting rumble.

He paused, taking in their surroundings, and then exploded into action, running for the stairs behind them as the southern corner of the gatehouse began to collapse with a roar of shattering stone.

"Aldarin!" Jelaïa shrieked. She felt as if her heart was going to burst from her chest.

A two-foot-wide fissure zigzagged out from the crumbling wall, sending paving slabs spiralling down into oblivion. Aldarin dodged sideways as another crack shattered the stone in front of them. They were showered with dust and shards of fallen mortar.

Jelaïa could see the stairs, but they were too far, much too far.

"We're not going to make it!" she screamed at Aldarin. The knight suddenly veered away from the stairs and aimed for the edge of the roof.

"What … what are you doing? Aldarin? Aldarin?"

The knight accelerated, his legs pumping as the world exploded around them.

"Aldarin, stop! No! STOP!"

Aldarin pulled her close and jumped.

CHAPTER 19

WHAT CAME
FROM BENEATH

"When choosing where to engage the opposing force, a smart commander must not be limited by what he can see clearly in front of him. Thought must be given to every permutation, every possible path the enemy might take to reach him. What terrain flanks the battlefield? What lies to the rear? And what lies below?"

BRACHYURA, FOURTH OF THE TWELVE, 43 AT

❧

REED FELT THE tremor only seconds before the gatehouse fell apart. They were a couple of hundred yards away, but the booming crack of split masonry was loud enough to shatter the windows of the houses surrounding the square. Dust and debris were hurtled into the enclosed space by the following shockwave, ripping the tavern sign from its hinges and battering the planks nailed to the front door. One of the barrels burst, filling the fountain with warm ale.

Reed jumped to his feet and grabbed his spear. He could taste the grit and sour beer in his mouth.

"Orkam!" he yelled over the distant rumble. "That came from the wall. Form up the men, we have to stop them getting through."

The bald guard captain hadn't heard him. He was staring mouth agape at the great cloud of dirt hanging in the air over all that remained of the distant barbican.

"Orkam!"

"But it's daylight, Reed, why are they attacking during the day? We were told they wouldn't attack during the day ..."

"Orkam, come on, man. I need you. Gather the men!"

Orkam turned to him in a daze, then his eyes cleared and he nodded. "Sorry, Reed. You're right. There is a time for everything, I suppose." He looked down at his half-full mug of ale still grasped in one hand and tossed it aside with a sigh.

"Ferris!" shouted Reed. "There was a bunch of men down by the bakery; go get them and meet me at the gatehouse." The big man pounded his fist to his chest in an unofficial salute and left the courtyard at a run.

"The rest of you, on me. I want a square, six men wide, two ranks deep. Check your helmets and plate buckles. Remember what you have been taught. We are not going to run. We are not going to break ranks. You will follow my lead." Reed dusted down his vermilion cloak and attached it firmly round his shoulders with the wolf head metal clasp gifted to him by the Baron.

"Spears up!"

They moved slowly out of the square and onto the main road. The dust and smoke were thinning and the remains of the gatehouse were just about visible. The destruction wrought by the enemy was staggering. Nothing remained of the barbican itself; the walls had collapsed in on themselves, smashing the portcullis and metal-plated oak doors that had protected Arelium so well against earlier assaults. Small fires had broken out among the rubble; overturned braziers and barrels of pitch eating away at the wood. Reed wasn't sure how anyone could have survived such desolation.

The surrounding houses had not fared much better. Huge holes gaped in thatched roofs. Glass from shattered windows littered the streets. Falling stones and paving slabs had punched holes in wattle walls and timber struts. Several houses had collapsed entirely under the relentless battering, leaving a smoking mess of cracked tiles and broken furniture.

With the town evacuated, there would be few civilian casualties. For the town guard, however, there was no such luck. Reed could make out crumpled forms in red livery: men crushed by the gatehouse or nearby fallen buildings.

The curtain wall on either side of the barbican was damaged, but miraculously still standing. Teams of archers were firing down into the rubble below at something Reed could not see. Soldiers from the reserve squads were scattered along the main street in small groups, some groggy and out of uniform as if they had just risen from their beds, others still clutching plates of food and drink. One man was sitting alone at an inn table, face hidden in his hands. Another was openly weeping at the sight, comforted by two of his fellow guardsmen.

Reed knew his qualities and his faults. He knew he was

an impatient man, a man easily goaded. He searched for that
hidden rage now and found it simmering deep inside. He let
it loose, using the fires of wrath to burn away his feelings of
fear and doubt.

"Men of Arelium!" he bellowed. "Form up! On me!"
His square of spearmen marched in step down the street, its
ranks swelling as they went. The men's faces were grim and
hard, streaked with grime and sweat. Reed could see anger
in those faces, anger and pain at what the enemy had done
to the place they called home.

More and more spearmen joined the throng, some hastily buckling on breastplates and helmets. The gatehouse
inched closer: a hundred yards, eighty, seventy. Small shapes
were moving among the ruins.

A group of thirty or so men boiled out of a side street,
led by Ferris. The beefy farmer was yelling at the top of his
voice, his face even redder than usual. He took up his place
on Reed's right, wheezing and clutching his right hand.

"Sorry, Sunny. Seems like some of the lads were thinking of staying put, nice an' cosy down by the bakery. Had to
remind them what the penalty for desertion was."

Reed raised an eyebrow as he took in Ferris' bruised
knuckles but remained silent.

They were close enough now to see how the greylings
had brought down the gatehouse. A huge gaping maw,
twenty yards across, marked the entrance to an enormous
tunnel that stretched from one corner of the barbican all the
way back to enemy lines. The opening was swarming with
dirt-stained greylings, shaking soil from their claws.

"By the damned Pit, they must have started digging as

soon as they arrived," said Orkam bitterly. "Was this their plan all along? How did we not see it?"

Reed shook his head. "It was too dark, too many places to hide. We torched the fields, but a lot of the outlying estates were left standing. They could have set up camp in any one of them."

"No sunlight underground either," rumbled Ferris, rubbing his square jaw. "No need to attack at night."

More greylings poured from the tunnel, chittering and capering madly with excitement. They were less than fifty yards away. Arrows pattered down among them with little effect.

Reed turned to look back towards the keep, tall and bleak against the morning sun, its red pennants still fluttering proudly from the tallest towers. He raised a hand to stop the advance.

"We'll hold them here. The collapsed barbican and fallen buildings have cut off most of the side alleys. They have no choice but to come up the main road if they want to reach the keep."

"SPEARWALL!" Ferris gave a deafening shout that made Reed's ears ring. The front rank was fifteen men wide now, and the soldiers sank to one knee with a clang of steel-shod boots and raised spears. The second and third ranks joined them with a swift precision that made Reed proud. In only a couple of days, this motley group of conscripts was beginning to rival the skill of the Old Guard.

The greylings streamed out of the tunnel and up the street, their clawed feet tapping like drops of rain on the cobbles. As they left the shadow of the ruined gatehouse, they were hit by the soft rays of sunlight filtering down through the clouds. Shrieks of discomfort rose up from the mass of bodies, but still they came, pouncing in leaps and bounds from shadow to shadow.

They were seconds away. Reed closed his eyes for a short moment, remembering his mother sewing quietly by the fireplace. His father, ruffling Reed's hair with his calloused hands. The delicious smell of roasting fish. The sweet, runny sap of the oak trees.

Then the horde of greylings crashed into the spearwall with a crunch and everything fell apart in an explosion of teeth and claws.

✍

Jelaïa forced her eyes open with a muffled whimper. She could see only darkness. For a dreadful moment, she thought she had gone blind, then she made out the vague shape of a gauntleted arm and realised Aldarin was lying on top of her, shielding her body with his. And crushing her.

"Aldarin," she tried to say, but her voice came out as a dry whisper. Dirt caked the back of her throat and lips. She tasted hot blood in her mouth.

"Aldarin," she said again. There was no reply. She pushed hard against his armoured frame. It was like trying to move a mountain. *Oh, by the Pit, I'm trapped*, she thought. What if he was dead? There was no way she could move him by herself. She would die here, smothered to death by a Knight of the Twelve. The absurdity of it all made her giggle.

"My Lady?" came a weary voice from somewhere above her and the weight on her chest and legs shifted slightly.

"Aldarin! Thank the Twelve! You are hurting me."

With a moan, Aldarin rolled off her onto his back. Jelaïa drew in a lungful of air, then winced as the movement made her ribs ache. Glancing down she saw that her hands and dress were covered in mud, a stinking black ooze mixed with clumps of straw. She blinked a few times to clear the grit from her eyes and looked groggily around at her surroundings. A plump pot-bellied pig was watching her calmly a few feet away, munching on a rotten turnip from a rusty trough. They were in a pigsty.

"By the Pit, what is that rank smell?" Aldarin was sitting up, his once pristine plate armour splattered with mud and muck. He had lost his helmet, and his tanned face, already bruised by his altercation with the threshers, was covered in dozens of new cuts and scrapes. His left eye was filled with blood. His nose was askew, the cartilage twisted unnaturally. It must have been broken again.

"Oh, Aldarin, are you all right? You look awful!"

"'Tis but some filth and a few scratches, my Lady. I have had worse than this from the training yard at the Temple." Shrugging off his gauntlets, he pinched the bridge of his nose with one hand and gave it a short, sharp twist, snapping the bone back into place with an agonising crack that made Jelaïa blanch.

"It appears my aim was correct," he continued with a weak grin, gesturing at their current surroundings. "The bales of hay and this ... offal ... must have softened our fall somewhat. I did not have much time before we jumped, but it looked like the best option." He picked some pieces of straw out of his hair.

Jelaïa could see now where they had fallen. Several bales of hay lay flattened in the muck, spilling straw out onto the ground. If Aldarin's aim had been off by just a few feet, they would have landed on hard stone instead, or one of the tiled roofs bordering the pigsty. She looked at Aldarin's wounded face and suppressed a shudder. By landing on the bales, he had saved their lives.

She glanced up. The pigsty was boxed in on all sides by tall buildings and she couldn't see the gatehouse — or what was left of it — only the curtain wall spreading out like a cliff face in both directions. Men were rushing along the ramparts towards the faint sounds of battle somewhere behind her. She felt something tugging at her dress and looked down to see the pig snuffling at the muddy fabric curiously.

"What now?" she asked, pulling the dress away from the animal who wandered off back to the trough. She spied the knight's fallen helmet nearby.

"Give me a moment," Aldarin replied tiredly, and Jelaïa realised the fall had shaken the knight more than he was leading her to believe. She watched him haul himself to his feet and sway unsteadily, catching himself on the side of the sty to stop him from losing his balance.

"Brachyura, give me strength," he murmured fervently, slipping his hands back into the articulated gauntlets. His double-bladed axe had become detached from his back when he fell and he bent to retrieve it, wincing. The haft was covered in brown mud.

"My Lady, it may not seem like much to you, but would it be possible to spare me but a small piece of cloth to clean my weapon? I am most pained to see it defiled so."

"My dear Aldarin," said Jelaïa with a smile. "Just moments ago, you jumped from a collapsing building, saving my life without a thought for your own. I believe you have earned a bit of muddy cloth from my dress." She unceremoniously tore off a length of green fabric and handed it over.

Aldarin accepted with a nod and wiped the haft clean. A thin beam of light leached through the overhanging buildings and caught the tip of the silver script engraved into the wood, making it shine.

It was a simple thing, but it somehow gave Jelaïa a renewed sense of hope, and she saw it had the same effect on Aldarin. The Knight of the Twelve seemed to stand taller, his aches and tiredness forgotten.

"Thank you, Brachyura," she heard him murmur as he sheathed the axe. He turned to her, his eyes filled with a sense of purpose.

"You asked me what we should do now, my Lady," he said. "I am forced to make the difficult choice between friendship and duty, but I know what I have to do."

"If the gate has well and truly fallen, the people of Arelium are in danger. My friend, Reed, among them. But I cannot in good conscience leave you here unattended, neither can I ask you to accompany me to the front lines, it would be far too dangerous. I have no other choice but to return you to your father. Once you are safe, I will try to re-join the others."

"But—"

"I will not be swayed, my Lady. Your father would never forgive me if I let something happen to you while you were in my care. Come, you know these streets better than I. Let us use the alleyways to avoid the main road and get back to the keep."

Jelaïa knew he was right. It was all too easy to forget

she was the Baron's daughter and heir to what was left of
Arelium. The last time she had seen her father he seemed to
be recuperating, but if ever he should fall … she would be
all that was left.

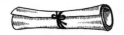

CHAPTER 20
A WAY OUT

"I've personally scoured those docks a hundred times. I've sent out the watch to perform random searches. Why, one time I even shut the whole harbour down for a day and raked through every nook and cranny for illicit goods. Never once found anything. And yet contraband still makes its way into Arelium. I don't know who it is, or how they manage it. But I'm going to find out."

ORKAM, CAPTAIN OF THE ARELIUM TOWN GUARD, 423 AT

❧

JELAÏA FOUND THAT the infirmary was much quieter than when she had left it. The Baroness greeted her with a relieved hug and explained that the more lightly wounded soldiers had been moved to the guest quarters or allowed to return to their homes.

She led them over to the fireplace where the healer still

slumbered in his comfy chair, snoring softly. Opposite him
sat Loré del Conte, a glass of wine in one hand, his legs
swathed in a fur rug. An exquisitely-wrought longsword
with an eagle's head worked into the pommel was propped
against a table within easy reach.

He tried to smile when he saw Jelaïa and Aldarin
approach but, after a quick grimace of pain, he abandoned
the idea and resorted to raising his glass in salute.

"Good day to you both," he said. His voice came out
as a throaty rasp, and he spoke with a slight lisp due to his
cut lip and shattered teeth. The suave smile and dulcet tones
would forever be a thing of the past. "You look just like
I feel. We heard the gatehouse has fallen? The enemy has
broken through?"

Jelaïa glanced over at Aldarin, who had found a space on
one of the benches lining the wall and was rubbing the mud
from his armour with a bedsheet. She took stock of her own
torn and stained dress. A few muted patches of green were
fighting a losing battle against the encroaching filth.

"We were on the gatehouse roof when it fell, my Lord.
Aldarin jumped."

Loré gave a short wheezing sound and it took Jelaïa a
moment to realise he was laughing. "By the Twelve, I would
have liked to have seen that! Listus was always telling me the
Knights of the Twelve were more bark than bite. I guess he
was wrong about that, eh?"

Jelaïa flashed him a brief smile. "I don't know how things
stand now. Aldarin insisted on bringing me straight here."

Loré sighed. "I have walked every inch of those ramparts
many, many times. I know every fissure in the stone, every
clump of moss growing on the wall. If the gatehouse has

fallen, Arelium has fallen. We can do nothing more now than wait for the end." He gently swilled his wine around his glass, watching how the thick red liquid swirled up the sides. "At least I will not have to live long as a cripple."

Loré's words cut deep. Jelaïa was not stupid; she had spent hours tending the wounded and seen her father's mangled golden armour. She knew the enemy was not to be trifled with. But she had always kept a faint glimmer of hope locked deep within her, a hope that the defenders could push the greylings back, or at least hold out until help arrived. With a shiver, she felt that small spark flicker and die, leaving her empty. The wall was breached, and they were alone.

"Jelaïa, your father has been asking for you," said the Baroness. The First Lady of Arelium looked exhausted, dark circles under her puffy eyes. "And please change before you see him, you look like you've been rolling around in the mud like a farm girl."

"Yes, that's not too far from the truth," admitted Jelaïa absently, patting at her unkempt hair. "Aldarin, if you feel up to it, would you please go to my father's chambers and tell him I'll be arriving shortly?"

"Of course, my Lady."

"Thank you. Mother, things seem to be well in hand here. It's time for you to get some rest."

"But I don't think—"

"Please, Mother. You will be no use to Listus if you are asleep on your feet."

"You are right, Jelaïa." She leant forwards and gave her daughter a peck on the cheek. "And I am proud of you. You will make a fine Baroness."

Jelaïa felt tears welling in her eyes and turned her head

to hide the wetness on her cheeks. She hurried from the infirmary and up the stairs to her bedroom. Mava had found time to lay out a selection of clothes on the bed and refill the washbasin in the corner with clean water.

More evidence that woman has some kind of magic powers, she thought, pulling what remained of her dress off over her head and throwing it to the ground with a sodden squelch. A few minutes of intense scrubbing removed the several layers of grime from her face and arms, revealing pink, clean flesh. She tried unsuccessfully to straighten out her uncooperative hair before giving up and resorting to a quick ponytail.

The bed was covered in frilly, multi-coloured dresses and elegant evening gowns. Mava was obviously still in denial about the current situation. Jelaïa threw open her dresser and selected a pair of leather riding trousers, a plain sky-blue blouse, and a dark crimson doublet.

As an afterthought, she took a slender dagger from a drawer in her bedside table and attached it to her waist with a silver-buckled belt. Pouches were woven into the belt, and these she filled with her reading glasses, a quill and ink bottle, some dried medicinal herbs, and a creased roll of paper.

Jelaïa lingered in the doorway for a moment, looking back into the room one last time, committing all she could to memory. It was ironic, in a way, that after years of trying to escape the confines of her quarters, she was now so reluctant to leave. But such is the way of things, whether it be luck, destiny, or something else, her path had been set and she had no other choice but to walk along it. With a heavy sigh, she pulled the door closed for what could be the last time, and went to see her father.

⇜

"I will not sound the retreat," thundered the Baron, his steel eyes glinting with anger. "We can hold!"

Jelaïa had arrived in the midst of an argument. Listus del Arelium was sitting up in bed, propped up by a pile of linen pillows. Praxis stood at the far end, Verona and Nidore at his side. The steward had his hands raised as if physically fending off her father's angry retorts.

"I did not say we could not hold, my Lord," he said soothingly. "Only that our losses will be high. We would do well to retreat."

"Nonsense! Another day and del Kessrin himself will be here with reinforcements. Together we'll send this filth scurrying back to the Pit."

"My Lord, the refugees are not riding horses. They are on slow-moving boats, sailing at a third of the speed. They won't reach Kessrin before this evening at the earliest, maybe even the day after if the current is slow. Then the Baron will have to muster his troops, decide on a plan of attack, and make the journey from Kessrin to Arelium. I fear there will be no aid from Lord del Kessrin for another week at least."

"I agree with the steward," came Aldarin's deep voice from the corner of the room. He was calmly sharpening the blade of his axe, working out the kinks and scratches with patient tenacity.

"I did not ask you here for your counsel, Knight of the Twelve," said the Baron testily. "Even with the gatehouse breached, we have enough men to stem the tide. We can send in the spearmen from the reserve guard and reinforce the archers on the wall."

"And if they reach the keep?" asked Praxis softly.

"Then, by the Pit, we will fight them here. We will fight them every step of the way, Praxis, with everything we have, with every able man and woman who can lift a sword or wield a bow. We will give weapons to the wounded, to the servants, to the nurses. I will make them bleed for every step they take. They will not take my lands. I will not allow it. Not while I still draw breath."

The Baron fell back into the pillows, wheezing and clutching the stump of one arm with the other. An uncomfortable silence remained, punctuated only by the rhythmic scraping of whetstone on axe.

Praxis was the first to speak. "Of course, my Lord. It shall be as you wish. And what of your daughter?" His eyes flickered to Jelaïa who had yet to move from the open doorway.

"Yes, yes, of course. I may be old, but I'm not stupid, Praxis."

"No, my Lord."

"No indeed. Jeli, approach."

Jelaïa came to stand beside the bed and took her father's remaining hand in her own. It burned, hot and feverish. She could feel the gnarled bones and wiry tendons under his tightly-stretched skin.

"I am here, Father."

"I have been talking with Praxis. We both agree that it is not safe for you here."

"But Father—"

"No. Listen to me. You are heir to Arelium. As long as you live, wherever you are, you carry our lineage with you. Farms can be rebuilt. Crops can be sown, trees can be planted.

It is the loss of life that will be the hardest thing to repair. The people will need someone to help them rebuild the Barony of Arelium. I sincerely hope that person will be me." The Baron gave a wolfish grin, deepening the wrinkles around his eyes and mouth. "But it would not be prudent for us both to stay here and, as I am in no state to travel, it is you who must go. I am sending you to Kessrin. You will be in good hands there."

"I … I suppose you are right, Father," Jelaïa found herself saying, much to her own surprise.

"I often am, my child. Now, I would not have you make the journey alone. Aldarin. You have already done much, but I would ask you one more favour. Would you escort my daughter to Kessrin? It would bring me great comfort to know you are travelling at her side."

Aldarin stared at the Baron, conflicting emotions playing unhidden across his broad features. He shook his head.

"I cannot, my Lord. Reed is still out there. He was down by the gatehouse when I saw him last. I do not know if he is still alive but, if he is, he will need my help. I cannot abandon him after all he has done for me."

The Baron leant forwards. "You are a credit to your Order, Sir Knight, as honourable and as valorous as your predecessors. But your chivalry is obstructing your logic. I have no one else I can trust with my daughter's safety. If I let her go alone, she may not survive. Who would your founder Brachyura tell you to save, a Captain of the Old Guard, or a future Baroness?"

"Please, do not ask me to do this, my Lord. Please let me go." Aldarin whispered.

"I am sorry, Sir Knight, but I must do what I can to protect my family, and this is the best way I know how."

With a distraught cry, Aldarin leapt to his feet, the metal plates of his armour grinding together in protest. He spun, axe in hand, and hammered the blade into the wall behind him, embedding the metal deep in the plaster. He let go of the handle, leaving the axe stuck there, then turned on the startled Baron, his blue eyes afire.

"By the Pit, I will do this for you, Baron! Not because it is what I want to do, but because it is what I *have* to do. We leave now. I will take your daughter as far as Kessrin, then I will return here, either to see Reed again or to bury his body."

The Baron, to his credit, did not flinch before the knight's tirade, but did not reply either. Neither man spoke, Aldarin's powerful frame dominating the crippled man.

Praxis coughed loudly. "The Barony of Arelium thanks you for your aid, Sir Knight," he said perfunctorily. "You will be well rewarded for your service. And I assure you that I will do all I can to see that Reed is here to greet you when you return."

Aldarin reached up and yanked his axe from the wall in a shower of flaking plaster. "How would you have us leave the city, my Lord?"

"I ... we hadn't got that far," said the Baron gruffly. "A rope over the wall, perhaps."

"If I may, my Lord?" Verona and Nidore had said nothing since Jelaïa had arrived, but now Verona stepped forwards with a curtsy. "I have a way to get both Aldarin and Jelaïa out to the river without alerting the greylings."

"Indeed? And what would that be, exactly?"

"Well ... my father, as you may know, was a trader — silks and fine fabrics mostly — but he did occasionally transport ... other things that needed to get quickly and safely from one town to another without attracting too much attention."

"He was a smuggler, you mean," said Praxis with a scowl.

"I think he preferred to call himself a purveyor of fine arts, but yes, I am not sure that all his dealings were fully within the bounds of the law. Be that as it may, there were times when he needed to leave Arelium without passing through the town gates. Um ..." she paused, blushing furiously.

"Yes, yes, go on girl," said the Baron impatiently. "It's not like we can punish your father for anything now, is it?"

"Yes, um, so there is a hidden trapdoor in the back of the shop that leads down to an underground tunnel. The tunnel passes under the wall. There's another trapdoor on the other side, right next to the water. We keep a little rowboat there, hidden in the reeds."

"Your father was a stupid man," said Praxis. "Anyone who found that tunnel could bypass our entire defences!"

"And that is why the trapdoors at both ends are firmly locked, and why only two people have the key. My father, of course, and ..." She removed the silver chain from around her neck and snapped open the heart-shaped locket. Nestled inside was a small iron key. She looked up at them and smiled. "And me."

The Baron and Praxis exchanged a glance, and Listus nodded almost imperceptibly.

"Very well," said the steward. "Verona, you will take them as far as the boat—"

"I will go with her," interrupted Nidore.

"Well, I suppose that—"

"I wasn't asking."

"Enough!" said the Baron. "Let the boy do what he wants. The enemy press their attack. It is time. Sufficient food for a few days' travel has been prepared for you down in the infirmary, but not much else I'm afraid. You will have to get by on what you can."

He turned to Jelaïa and gave her hand a quick squeeze. "My daughter, I am not very good at goodbyes, but do not mistake my lack of words for a lack of feelings. Your mother and I are so, so proud of you. You have become all we hoped you would be and more besides. I believe you have inherited the best of both of us. Do not let others define who you are or what you must do. One day, you will be named Baroness del Arelium, Lady of the White Wolf, and undisputed leader of thousands of men and women. Listen to your heart, trust your intuition, and you will be fine."

"I love you, Father," said Jelaïa in a choked voice, bending to kiss her father's forehead.

"As I love you, Jeli. As I love you. Praxis! Come help an old man to the window; I wish to see how the assault goes."

And Jelaïa left her father alone with Praxis, staring out at the miniature figures clustered around the ruined gatehouse down below, a small circle of crimson shapes standing firm against the encroaching blackness.

CHAPTER 21

THE LAST OF THE OLD GUARD

"We are the watchers, the protectors, the guardians of the wall. We are the light against the darkness, the burning sun against the cold of night, the mighty shield against the unknown. We pledge our lives to the defence of the wall. And we entrust our lives to the will of the Twelve."

ORLEUS YUSIFEL, CAPTAIN OF THE OLD GUARD, 404 AT

"PUSH THEM BACK!" yelled Reed, stabbing his spear into the belly of an attacking greyling. He pulled the blade out fast, slicing through the dry grey skin and spilling the creature's entrails onto the floor. It collapsed with a cry and was lost from sight as more attackers clambered over the fallen body to throw themselves at the spearwall. Reed was part of the second line, standing one step behind a row of kneeling guardsmen.

Miraculously, the wall was holding. High above them on the ramparts, archers fired their last remaining arrows down into the mass of attackers.

Another greyling bounded high over the first row of spears, aiming to land among the men behind. But Orkam was too fast. He caught the creature with the tip of his weapon and knocked it back to the ground where Ferris stamped on the thing's neck, killing it instantly.

"We are holding, Sunny!" he said loudly, wiping a streak of blood from his face with a hairy hand. "They can't get past us!"

Reed was inclined to agree, but something gave him pause. Looking further down the street, he saw that closer to the tunnel entrance several groups of greylings were not joining the attack but clustering around the blocked side alleys, biting and clawing at the fallen debris. He tapped Ferris on the arm to get his attention and pointed.

"They aren't going to try and get past us, they want to get around us! A spearwall won't survive an attack from all sides, I saw it at the Pit. We have to stop them!"

"How?"

"We are going to have to push them back, keep them bottled up nearer the entrance. I want you to repeat my orders to the men."

"Yes, Sunny."

"Ferris, what did I tell you about calling me—"

"Yes, Sunny, *Sir!*"

Reed sighed. "Better, I suppose." A greyling ducked under his spear and aimed a vicious swipe at his legs. His leather boots were thick enough to stop the claws from reaching his skin, and he kicked the creature away where it was skewered by the soldier kneeling in front of him.

"Right, listen up!" He heard Ferris echoing his words in a roar that carried all the way to the back of the formation. "We are moving the wall forwards. I want you advancing in time to '*The Country Fair*'. Second rank, as soon as Ferris starts singing, I want you to step over the kneeling men of the first rank. At the end of the first line, second rank kneels and first rank stands. Posterior ranks move up and fill any gaps. Am I clear?"

"Yes, Sir!"

"Louder!"

"YES, SIR!"

"Very well. Ferris, do your thing!"

Ferris cleared his throat theatrically and began to sing:

"I saw a girl at the country fair, prettiest I could see,"

Twenty men stepped forwards in unison, spears at the ready. The greylings skittered backwards to get away from the sharp metal tips. One or two hapless creatures were not fast enough and were cut down. The men knelt.

"Saw a girl at the country fair, her name was Marjorie."

The second rank moved, carefully stepping over the front line and setting their spears. Greylings retreated further, snarling. One took an arrow to the neck and dropped without a sound.

"Saw a girl at the country fair, but she didn't want to dance with me,

But she whisked me off for a tumble in the loft and next year we were three."

The soldiers had gained a good ten yards, inching closer

to the mouth of the tunnel and the ruined gatehouse. There had been no casualties.

"Again!" yelled Reed.

We might actually make it, he thought as he stepped over the first line, lashing out at a greyling who hadn't retreated fast enough. The greylings were in a panic now. The spear-wall continued to roll steadily forwards. They were less than twenty yards from the opening. Reed could just make out a rough, muddy slope heading down into the pitch black of the tunnel.

An earth-shattering shriek echoed up from somewhere deep underground, a high-pitched alien sound that made his ears ring. Reed had heard it once before, what seemed like a lifetime ago, up on the walls of the Pit. The same command-ing tone had stopped the assault and pulled the greylings back off the ramparts.

Something similar was happening here. The creatures disengaged the spearwall and retreated, chittering, back into the comforting darkness of the tunnel. In minutes they were gone, leaving only the dead and wounded behind them. Reed called for Ferris to halt the advance.

An eerie silence settled over the ruins. Reed could hear the men around him breathing heavily, the creak of leather boots, and the soft clinking of iron ringlets. The air stank of sweat and blood. Ferris removed his helmet and dabbed at the wetness on his forehead.

"What's going on, Sunny?" he asked warily, eyes search-ing the mouth of the tunnel. Others looked expectantly at Reed, confused. High above them, one of the archers gave the sign for all clear.

"I'm not sure." The cold, unrelenting darkness of that

opening reminded Reed of the Pit. He shuddered. He thought he could see figures moving somewhere deep in the tunnel. Something was coming.

"Spearwall!"

The men barely had time to bring their spears up before the first thresher burst out of the darkness. It was huge, well over seven feet of dark grey muscle. It held an enormous obsidian sword in both hands.

"Brace!" screamed Reed as the thresher crashed into the front line. Wooden spear shafts exploded into splinters. The heavy sword came down like a guillotine, cutting a soldier in half in a spray of gore. His shocked companions reacted quickly, stabbing at the beast, but the thing's leathery skin protected it from the sharp tips. Arrows hit its exposed back with no more strength than an insect bite. The spearwall collapsed.

Reed muttered a silent prayer to the Twelve and launched himself forwards, aiming for the thing's legs. His thrust pierced the soft flesh behind the knee joint and the thresher staggered sideways with an angry growl. Orkam darted into the gap, narrowly avoiding a sword blow to the face, and hammered his weapon through its left eye. The thresher reeled backwards with a howl of agony and dropped its sword. More spearmen moved in, exploiting the blind spot to the left, stabbing at the neck, armpits, and groin until the thing collapsed.

"Reform the line!"

Reed heard the shout from the ramparts and turned to see a dozen more threshers charge from the tunnel mouth brandishing an assortment of axes, pikes, swords, and flails.

"Spearwall!" he bellowed as the first thresher reached

him. He ducked a sweeping axe blow, but wasn't fast enough to avoid a punch to the shoulder that sent him spinning. A second blow to the back floored him. He struggled dimly to his feet, watching groggily as Ferris threw himself at another thresher, knocking the weapon from its grasp and grappling the monstrous beast to the ground.

Something hot and red spattered onto his face and he tasted the metallic tang of blood in his mouth. A soldier collapsed less than a foot away, his throat torn open.

"To me!" he tried to shout. It came out as a croak. More bodies hit the ground as the threshers tore through the front lines. The steel breastplates and helms of his men were simply not strong enough to halt the powerful blows of the attackers. Here and there, soldiers were trying unsuccessfully to reform the spearwall. Arrows buzzed like angry flies, only to be swatted away or ignored.

They were losing.

Another thresher appeared. This one had lost its breastplate and its upper torso was covered with bleeding cuts and bruises. A badly-healed scar snaked down the right side of its face, ending in a puckered whorl of tissue where its ear should have been. It carried an obsidian mace in one hand, the spiked metal ball bigger than Reed's head. With an angry roar, it sent the weapon whistling forwards with surprising speed. Reed threw himself sideways, but was not quite fast enough. The mace hammered into his shoulder with a crunch and Reed felt an explosion of agony as the bone shattered.

He fell heavily, then pulled himself to his feet with a scream. The thing advanced slowly, uttering a series of guttural barks. It sounded like it was laughing at him. He watched through a haze of pain as the thresher brought the mace up over its head for the finishing blow. Time slowed as the mace came down; he could see with dreadful clarity the bits of his own bone and muscle stuck to the metal spikes. He closed his eyes.

Ferris careened into Reed moments before the mace hit, pushing his captain out of danger. The thresher adjusted its swing and the mace took Ferris in the jaw, ripping his jaw-bone from its socket in a burst of blood and broken bone. Ferris let out a garbled cry from his ruined face before the thresher's reverse swing caught him on the side of the head and crushed his skull. He fell silently into a pool of his own blood, never to sing again.

Reed wanted to cry out, but found he could barely move. He lay on his back staring up at the curtain wall. Greylings were swarming up either side now, slaughtering the few remaining archers.

The thresher approached calmly. Its beady eyes looked down at him and Reed could see an ancient hatred burning there, a hate born of years of defeat, of hiding underground, waiting for the right time to re-emerge and exact revenge on those who had punished them.

The thresher dropped its mace and placed one booted foot on Reed's chest. It worked its mouth as if struggling to articulate something, then spoke.

"Uuu-mann," it grunted. Reed looked at it in shock. *By the Twelve,* he thought. *These things speak our language? There is so much we do not know. And now it is too late.*

"Uuu-mann. Youu. Die. Noww."

The foot pressed down slowly on his chest, building up pressure as the thresher exerted more and more of its prodigious strength. Reed howled in pain as a rib snapped. Darkness overwhelmed him; soft, warm, and inviting.

The sound of battle faded and he could hear the lulling murmur of running water. The wind rustled through the oak trees. Somewhere out on the lake, his father would be waiting for him in his hide boat. They would fish for a time, then return home for supper. There was no other place he would rather be.

He felt the ground tremble beneath his feet, a deep rumble growing louder and louder, but it was not important. The only thing that mattered was seeing his father. Reed smiled contentedly and walked down the path to meet him.

⁓

Jelaïa followed the others through the twisting back-alleys of Arelium, adjusting the leather strap of the satchel full of supplies that was chafing her shoulder. Fires had sprung up throughout the town as more and more greylings made it over the wall. The four travellers had been the last stragglers allowed out of the keep before the heavy doors had been barred shut. They were committed now.

The creaky whine of the painted sign heralded their arrival before Verona's shop. The door had been torn off its hinges, but the interior was quiet and empty.

"It's through the back. Follow me, please," said Verona, pausing to light one of the lanterns dotted around the room. She had changed back into her black leggings and night-blue riding cloak, the hood drawn up around her face. Nidore was always close by, rapier at his side, his black ash wood bow and a quiver of arrows slung over his back. He still wore the same grimy breastplate, brown leather trousers and boots he had been wearing on the wall. Jelaïa wondered if he had even slept. He looked tired, but vigilant.

A few paces behind her, Jelaïa could feel the comforting presence of Aldarin, his eyes constantly probing the path ahead from beneath the shadow of his ornate helm. The Knight of the Twelve had said little since leaving the Baron, still troubled at having to desert his friend Reed.

Verona led them behind the display counter into a small storeroom packed to the rafters with rolls of fabric and large crates.

"Nidore, Aldarin, those two crates against the far wall are empty; would you move them aside?"

The crates were hiding a small trapdoor, about three feet wide, oak reinforced with bands of iron. An intricate lock with a tiny keyhole was set into the top.

"It has been a while since I followed my father down here," said Verona with a sad smile. "I hope if he is watching us that he understands why his secret needs to be shared. In any case, let us pray that he has not changed the lock." She unclasped her locket and inserted the iron key. It turned smoothly with a comforting click. The trapdoor sprung open on oiled hinges, revealing a sturdy metal ladder descending down into the darkness.

"It looks much deeper than it is, there can't be more than eight or ten feet. Then a couple of hundred yards to reach the river bank. I'll go first." Handing the lantern to Nidore, she made her way swiftly down to the tunnel floor below.

Jelaïa followed with some trepidation. She had never

felt entirely safe in enclosed spaces. It was probably Nidore's fault. He had locked her in the castle pantry as a prank when she was a little girl and she remembered banging on the door for hours before someone had heard her and had come to let her out. It had been cold, dark, and silent save for the snuffling of a family of rats.

The tunnel was cramped and narrow. Aldarin had to remove his helm and bend his knees and, even then, his axe scraped along the earthen ceiling. They moved cautiously in single file. Jelaïa fixed her gaze on the bobbing yellow light of the lantern and concentrated on breathing slowly and regularly.

She trudged along, one foot after the other, slowly losing all perception of time. How long had they been down here? A few minutes? An hour? Mercifully, it was not long before the ground started to slope upwards and she could make out the silhouette of another trapdoor similar to the first, pale light filtering down through the cracks in the planks.

The lock on the second door opened as easily as the first and they emerged blinking into the sunlight down by the River Stahl. Jelaïa was surprised to see that they were deep in the marshlands that bordered the eastern bank, not far from the spot she came to be alone, and where Praxis often found her. Did he already know about the trapdoor? It was certainly possible; there wasn't much that went on in Arelium that escaped him. Damn the Pit, she was thinking about him again. She hadn't even had two minutes alone with him before being rushed off to Kessrin. *Focus!* she told herself, marshalling her thoughts.

There was not a greyling in sight. The reeds were so tall that they completely hid the town from view; even Aldarin admitted he could not see over the dense foliage. Sounds of distant combat were brought to them on the wind, but muffled and faint. Verona's father had chosen his spot well. They would be safe from prying eyes here.

"Just a little further," said the silk trader's daughter, pushing on through the marsh. Aldarin closed the trapdoor behind them with an oiled click. The thinning reeds soon opened out onto the river, its wide, deep confluence flowing lazily from the mountains down to the Kessrin estuary. A short wooden pier sprouted from the muddy banks out into the brackish water. At the end of the pier, a small boat bobbed at its moorings. And standing in front of the boat stood two tall, near-identical figures in matching night-blue cloaks. They were big, almost as big as Aldarin, blocking the width of the pier entirely.

"What is this?" said Aldarin with a scowl. He drew his double-bladed axe from its sheath on his back.

Verona turned and pulled back her hood. Jelaïa gasped as she saw the expression on her friend's face. Her full red lips were contorted into an ugly sneer that transformed her perfect features into something harsh and alien. Her once-kind eyes were hard and cold. She shot Jelaïa a look of pure hatred before wheeling on Aldarin.

"Why, *Sir Knight*, you surprise me? Do you not recognise your brothers?" she said in a voice full of undisguised contempt.

The men moved down the pier to join her, removing their hooded cloaks as they did so. They both had pale, aquiline faces with high cheekbones and a thin, bony nose, so alike they must have been twins. Purple veins were clearly visible under their alabaster skin and dark, greasy, shoulder-length hair.

They wore full sets of dirty plate armour, stained almost black by layers of blood and dust, the rusty interlocking joints squealing in torture as they moved their limbs. But despite the filth and rust, there was no mistaking who these men were.

Before them stood two Knights of the Twelve.

CHAPTER 22

THE BROKEN HEART OF ARELIUM

"I spend far too much time stuck in the musty corridors of the keep. Arelium is like a carefully nurtured garden, full of hidden beauty. It has been too long since I heard the larks sing in Kaevel Forest, the buzzards shriek over Jaelem, the kingfisher dive into the Stahl. It is time for this to change. It is time for me to remember the lands that carry my name."

BARON LISTUS DEL ARELIUM, 426 AT

⤙

PRAXIS STOOD BESIDE the Baron and looked down at the red-cloaked figures fighting for their lives before the ruins of the gatehouse. He saw the greylings scaling the walls from both sides and, beyond that, hundreds more still dotted about the valley floor, moving purposefully towards the town or milling around a crumbling mansion, which must be hiding the entrance to the tunnel that had collapsed the barbican and brought about the downfall of Arelium.

"What can we do, Praxis?" asked the Baron softly. Praxis tried to think of something to say, but could not find any words that would bring the old man comfort.

"Nothing, my Lord. The outer wall is lost. We have barricaded the doors to the keep and manned the inner wall with what forces we have left. It would be suicide to go out there now; we must wait for them to come to us."

"My men are dying out there. I told them the enemy would break against our walls. I lied to them. They are dying and it is my fault."

Threshers were hammering the soldiers hard now. The losses would be tremendous. It would not be long before they were overrun.

"That is not true, my Lord. In fact, it is I who am to blame. I—"

A tremor shook the room, causing the windows to rattle in their frames. A pile of scrolls fell to the floor, some rolling under the bed.

"What's that, Praxis? Another tunnel?"

"I don't think so, my Lord, it's something else, something coming from down in the valley."

The steward looked out over the burnt fields of corn, his hands going to the silver scales emblem hung around his neck. The sun was high in the sky now and he could see almost as far as the undulating green hills on the far western ridge. Something twinkled there, out where the river threaded its way through the grasslands towards Kessrin.

The distant sparkle was joined by another, then a score

more, then a hundred, pouring down into the valley like a shower of falling stars.

"Praxis, my eyeglass, quickly!" barked the Baron, and Praxis ran to fetch it from a nearby table.

The Baron peered through the eyeglass at the fast-approaching lights and his face split into a feral grin.

"Hah!" he blurted out, and handed the eyeglass to Praxis. He brought it up to his left eye and the far-off lights snapped sharply into focus. Armoured figures thundered across the plain in perfect formation, each rider astride a massive barded warhorse, their burnished silver plate shining like a hundred comets. The riders wore intricate helmets incorporating twisting horns or pincers. A banner grasped proudly in the hand of the lead horseman showed a silver axe over a round tower.

"I don't believe it, it's not possible," said Praxis breathlessly. "The Knights of the Twelve. By the Pit! They have come!"

"I'm starting to think I was a bit harsh on that Aldarin fellow," said the Baron jovially, still grinning broadly. "He may be a stubborn, arrogant, pompous brute, but he has managed to save not only my daughter's life, but also my entire Barony. Thank the Twelve he sent for help as soon as he arrived."

Praxis said nothing. As he watched through the eyeglass, the lead knight, with a series of precise gestures, sent half the riders south down the valley to the dilapidated mansion and ordered the others towards the ruined curtain wall.

The thrumming noise was deafening now, a host of iron-clad hooves churning up the burnt earth as they crashed like a steel tidal wave into the greylings attacking the wall.

The charge barely faltered; screeching greylings simply disappeared under the pounding war steeds, mauled and trampled to death as the column swept over them. With another command, the knights adopted a looser formation and drew their double-bladed axes. From his vantage point, it looked to Praxis like a sea of silver nails.

"No, no, no, this is not meant to happen, not like this," he whispered.

The first line of knights had now reached the gatehouse and they dismounted, turning their rider-less horses loose to run amok among the fleeing greylings, wreaking further havoc. The knights carefully navigated their way through the ruined maze of shattered stone and fallen beams, dispatching anything foolish enough to challenge them.

The threshers that were still engaging the remains of the Arelium town guard near the tunnel entrance turned in surprise as the knights emerged from the ruins and hit them from behind. They outnumbered the threshers three to one. Praxis knew what the Knights of the Twelve were capable of; he had seen Aldarin take down two threshers by himself. Thirty gleaming axes rose and fell. It was a massacre. He heard the Baron chuckling gleefully as the knights ground the threshers into oblivion.

"Praxis! Look at that! Have you ever seen such precision? Such skill with the blade? They are unstoppable! We will go out to meet them. No reason they should have all the glory! Then, with their help, we will rebuild Arelium! Maybe ask some of them to stay? A garrison of knights stationed here would keep our Barony safe for aeons! Come, Praxis, help me with my armour!"

"I am so, so sorry, my Lord," Praxis replied, in a strained

voice. Something strange about his tone made the Baron look at him with concern.

"What are you talking about, man? We have won!"

"No, my Lord. You have won. I have lost." And with a terrible grief-filled sigh, he turned and stabbed the Baron through the stomach with his knife.

Bright blood bubbled from the Baron's lips and he stumbled backwards, his remaining hand clutching at his stomach, his eyes wide in shock and disbelief. With a push, Praxis sent his liege lord sprawling on the bed, staining the pristine sheets with a splash of red.

"Who ... who are you?" sputtered the Baron with a wheezing gasp.

Praxis wiped his blade and sat on the corner of the bed, looking down sadly at the dying man. "I am Praxis, your steward. And I am also Praxis, Knight of the Order of Zygos, Seventh of the Twelve. This is the sign of my Order, hiding in plain sight." He held up his silver medallion for the Baron to see. "The scales represent balance, and balance we must have, in all things. This is what Aldarin will not tell you. This is why the knights have been absent from the affairs of the realm for so long. This is why you believe our numbers are dwindling. It is because we have turned on each other. Some still support the Baronies of man, others — like those of my Order — believe our time is at an end and it is time to return this land to its rightful owners."

"Ma ... madness."

"Perhaps, but it is what my founder believed, and I am sworn to follow his creed. My initial task was to sow discord between Arelium and Kessrin. Once the greylings returned, I was to ensure Arelium fell, and that its Baron and all of his progeny were wiped out. I tried to have you murdered by assassins posing as the Kessrin delegation, but that failed miserably. If I hadn't stepped in, that babbling fool Diacrosa would have revealed everything. I then thought to let you fall in battle, but Aldarin arrived too soon, or I was too slow. It matters not now."

He stood up, and drew a second dagger from his belt, a curved blade quite different from his stiletto. The emblem of Kessrin was etched into the leather hilt. Praxis studied the markings thoughtfully.

"The blame for your death must lie with Kessrin, of course. They will be the next to fall. Do you think your subjects will be stupid enough to believe you were murdered by a Kessrin assassin? It is possible, I suppose. Orkam will, of course. Loré may need some more persuading. Damn that man for his tenacity, he should have never survived those wounds."

The Baron was ashen now, his face drained of colour, the bed covered in blood. He opened his mouth feebly and murmured something Praxis couldn't hear.

"What?" he said irritably, bending close.

"My ... daughter ..."

"Oh yes, that detail was entrusted to a separate Order, that of Mithuna, Third of the Twelve. They are much more sadistic than me, I'm afraid. I do hope she will not suffer much; I have grown quite fond of both of you. Your daughter especially had such delightful banter. I will think of you often."

The Baron tried to say something more, but it was too late. He spasmed once, twice, and was still. Praxis watched dispassionately as the last spark of life left his Lord's eyes.

"Goodbye, Listus," he whispered, and cut the dead man's throat with the curved knife.

It would not be enough to convince them. Wincing, he brought the Kessrin blade to his cheek and cut a deep jagged line from below his left eye down through his immaculate beard to his chin. Fresh blood ran down his face. He gave himself another cut on the thigh and several scratches on his black leather breastplate before throwing the dagger onto the mattress near the Baron's body. After a moment's hesitation, he ripped the silver scales from his chest and hid the medallion under the bed.

Now to attract the guard. He overturned the bedside table with a crash. A lantern was dashed against the wall where it burst into pieces. Hearing heavy boots on the stairwell, he quickly grabbed a wooden chair and launched it through one of the windows, shattering the glass. Cold air rushed in, extinguishing the candles and plunging the room into darkness.

Praxis inhaled calmly and cleared his throat.

"To arms! To arms! The Baron is under attack!" he yelled as loudly as he could, adding a touch of panic to his voice.

Moments later, two armed guards exploded into the room, weapons drawn.

"Out the window!" cried Praxis, clutching at his wounded face.

One man rushed over to the window, the other stared in shock at the bloody bedclothes.

"He's gone," said the first guard. "How fares the Baron?" The second man shook his head.

"Come!" said Praxis. "We can do nothing more for him now. Have you heard the news? The Knights of the Twelve have arrived! They are fighting for us down by the gatehouse, fighting to save Arelium! Fighting to save our wounded men! I for one will not let them fight alone. Will you join me?"

"Aye, my Lord," said the first guardsman, and the second nodded briefly, still looking at the disfigured corpse. Praxis was surprised to see tears on the man's face. He grasped him firmly by the shoulder. "He was my liege lord, too, soldier. We will avenge him. But for now, we fight!"

Praxis ran from the room and down the stairs like a man possessed. He raced through the infirmary, scattering nurses and patients before him, and burst out into the courtyard.

"Unbar the gates! The Knights of the Twelve are here! For Arelium!"

"For Arelium!" came the reply and the gates were thrown open. Praxis led the charge down the street, smoke from the rampant fires rustling his cloak. He needed to act fast. His time was now. The moment had come to put to good use all the tricks and subterfuge he had learnt at the temple of Zygos. The first rule of his Order was simple: balance is obtained through control. And to achieve that, he must be seen as a saviour.

He arrived at the site of the skirmish just in time. Only one thresher remained, battered and bleeding, its scarred face missing an ear. It was fending off three armoured knights with a spiked mace.

"He is mine!" yelled Praxis, brushing past the attackers and throwing himself at the thresher with reckless abandon. Ducking a jab to the face, he feinted left before spinning to the right, lashing out with his dagger and opening a deep cut across the thing's bicep. The wounded thresher turned to meet him, but Praxis was faster, dodging round to his enemy's exposed back. With a cry, he ripped through the hard skin and buried his blade deep in the thing's innards.

"For Arelium!" he shouted, drawing the dagger free in a splash of dark ichor. The thresher crashed to the ground amid the cheers of the Baron's men. *My men,* he corrected himself. *Soon they will be mine.*

He raised the gory weapon high above his head as if saluting the sun and bathed in the roar of victory. *This is what they will remember,* he thought. *They will remember the knights, they will remember the Baron, but above all they will remember me, standing here, reclaiming their lands and lives.*

"Help the wounded!" he ordered, turning to greet the knights. Their leader had removed his helm to reveal the wrinkled, tanned face of a man in his late sixties, his forehead and cheeks covered in scars. He was bald, with a long white drooping moustache that fell nearly as far as his neck.

"Well met, steward of Arelium!" he intoned in a solemn voice, bowing stiffly. "Your call for aid has been answered. We have purged the creatures from this town."

Praxis returned the bow, lowering his face to hide his disdain. "And Arelium thanks you, Sir Knight, for all you have done. Without you, we would have surely been lost. Let us send the stragglers back to the Pit and burn the corpses of the fallen until not one of them remains to blight our fair valley."

The knight seemed pleased with this flowery response. He nodded curtly and walked briskly back to his men to organise the cleansing of the battlefield.

If only they knew what their honour and faith have brought upon them, thought Praxis. The hypocrisy of it all sickened him.

"My Lord Praxis!" a voice called out.

"Yes, soldier?"

"We've found him! We've found the captain!"

And behind him on a stretcher lay the shattered body of Merad Reed, last of the Old Guard.

CHAPTER 23

TWISTED TRUTHS

"History is such a strange and malleable thing. What is believed by all to be an indisputable fact can be changed in an instant with the stroke of a pen. Think about it. When the unstoppable river of time pulls our compeers into its icy waters, the only records of what we did here will be those found in books and scrolls. Things we can control."

MITHUNA, THIRD OF THE TWELVE, 123 AT

◆

"VERONA, WHAT HAVE you done?" Aldarin whispered. The two pale-skinned knights stood unmoving on the pier, arms crossed. Nidore took a step forwards and one of the twins dropped his hand to the pommel of his sword with a shake of his head.

"Tell them, Aldarin," said Verona, her voice void of all

emotion. "Tell them who we are. Tell them of your greatest shame, and your greatest secret."

Aldarin shifted uneasily. Jelaïa lay her hand on his arm and forced him to look into her eyes.

"You can trust me, Sir Knight. What you say here will be said in confidence and not repeated. Who are these men who wear armour so similar to your own, and yet are so different?"

Aldarin's stoic features collapsed into a grimace of terrible anguish. "They were once my brothers," he said quietly, "my comrades and my friends. The Twelve Orders stood together and fought together, protecting the legacy of our founders. Each facet of the Twelve complemented the other, the confluence of talents and ideas somehow greater than the sum of its parts."

"Then, roughly sixty years ago, we were betrayed. Brother fought brother. A great schism divided our Orders and for years we were locked in a brutal struggle for survival. Only the temple elders know the cause and they are forbidden to speak of it. All I know is that some of us fought to maintain the Council and the Baronies of men whereas others, like the Order of Mithuna" — he gestured to one of the black-plated knights who sneered back at him — "wanted to undo all we had built here. After a time, we prevailed. The dissenting Orders fled their temples and we tore them down brick by brick. But the cost was high, years of attrition took their toll on our numbers; we became unprotected and weak. And in our hubris, we decided to hide this weakness from the Council. It is, as you say, Verona, our greatest shame, but also our greatest mistake as we have let you regroup and reconsolidate. We should have eradicated the traitors when we had the chance."

With a metallic shriek, the twins drew their swords almost simultaneously and would have thrown themselves at Aldarin if Verona had not stopped them with a raised hand.

"Is that really what you were told?" she said incredulously. "Then you know nothing. Nothing of import in any case. Your elders hide the truth from you as your founder did. If only you knew what Brachyura really did, and why he disappeared ... you would throw down your axe and beg me on your knees for forgiveness. Traitors? You do not even know the meaning of the word. I pity you, Aldarin, I pity your ignorance and blind faith in the liars and cheats you look to for guidance each time you invoke the names of the Twelve."

One of the knights bent forwards and whispered something in her ear.

"Of course, we are wasting time. Forgive me the small indulgence of watching this reject squirm in discomfort. We need to leave. Aldarin, I thank you and your friends for saving me. I am *so* glad you found the attack on the silk caravan convincing; it took me days of hard work to set that up. Oh, and thank you for getting me close to the Baron and his daughter." She gave Jelaïa a mocking curtsy. "I could not have managed it so quickly without your trust in me. Jelaïa, my dearest, I would ask you to come with us. It is time to end the cursed line of del Arelium." She stretched out her hand and smiled encouragingly. Jelaïa backed away.

"Come to me, girl. I promise you will not be harmed. We do not need to kill you, only make sure you do not return here ever again. We can take you far away from here, or kill you and leave you to rot. The choice is yours."

"I cannot allow that to happen," said Aldarin tiredly. Jelaïa saw he was supporting himself with his axe, leaning on it with both hands to take the strain off his legs and feet. *He is hurt more than I thought.*

"Sir Knight," she heard herself say. "You have done what my father asked you to do. I am out of the city. Your obligation to me and my family ends here. I give you leave to return to Arelium. Perhaps Reed is still alive and waiting for you."

"I cannot do that, my Lady."

"Please, Aldarin. They will kill you. Please leave me. Why won't you go?" She could feel herself start to cry.

"Because it is wrong," replied Aldarin simply. "And it is not what I was taught. The Knights of Mithuna are duplicitous schemers, twisting and contorting the truth to fit their hidden agenda. I do not believe anything Verona says and neither should you. They will take you a few miles downstream and slit your throat."

"Verona," came a plaintive tone. Nidore was looking at her with a confused expression, wringing his hands anxiously. "Is it true? Are you lying to us?"

Verona suddenly seemed to remember him and smiled widely, although the smile never reached her eyes. It was only a mask, to be worn when needed then discarded. She moved to his side and grasped his hand in her own.

"Of course not, Nidore. Look into my eyes. Feel the warmth of my hand in yours. Does it seem unreal to you?"

"Nidore—" began Aldarin warningly.

"Quiet, Sir Knight," Verona shot back. "I have let you say your piece. Now it is my turn. Nidore, you know how I feel about you. I have felt it ever since we met. There is something between us, something deeper than all this. You will stay with me, won't you? I will need your strength and compassion in the days to come. Please, Nidore. Please?"

It was not sincere. Far from it. Anyone could see that. Jelaïa would have laughed in her face. But then she saw how Nidore gazed upon Verona with a deep, boundless affection, and it hit her that he was well and truly lost.

"Of course, Verona. Of course you can count on me, now and always," he said thickly, pulling her close.

"Don't do this, Nidore," Jelaïa implored. The noble wheeled on her in fury. "You *dare* come to me now? You ungrateful wretch of a girl. My family gave *everything* to yours. Power, protection, wealth, and even friendship. Without us you would be beggars in the streets, living off scraps and the generosity of others."

He spat at her feet and Jelaïa recoiled in shock.

"We sacrificed everything for you. My father would give his life for yours. And in return we were mocked, pushed aside, forgotten. I despise you, Jelaïa. To think I envied you once, desired you even. But you really are a spoiled brat, hiding behind your father's coat-tails. There is but one person here who truly understands me, and I will stay with her as long as she will have me."

"Enough," said Aldarin sternly. "I do not believe you are thinking straight, Nidore, but it matters little. I will not let you leave with the future Baroness."

"Then we will take her," Nidore snarled.

"Hush, hush, my dear," soothed Verona. "My brothers have been waiting for a long time to cross blades with a Knight of Brachyura, even a tired and wounded old fool like this one. We should not deny them this pleasure. We will wait for them down by the boat." She stepped aside and her muscular companions prowled menacingly forwards like wolves closing in on a wounded stag.

"Behind me, my Lady," growled Aldarin. He slipped into a defensive battle stance, feet firmly planted in the muddy earth of the riverbank, his axe held protectively across his body to block incoming blows. His eyes flickered from left to right, taking the measure of his two opponents.

The left knight attacked first, moving much faster than Jelaïa thought possible for someone wearing heavy plate. Aldarin deflected the blow easily, but was too slow to stop the second knight whose blade skittered off his right pauldron. The twins leapt back out of range and circled him slowly, looking for an opening.

Again they attacked, this time hitting him from the front and rear simultaneously. Aldarin batted the first sword aside and side-stepped the second, the blade coming close enough to graze the front of his helmet.

One of the twins laughed mockingly and favoured him with a thin-lipped smile. "You are worn out, brother, and you are slow. We will enjoy cutting you to pieces."

The macabre dance continued, and it soon became clear that the twin was right. Aldarin was reacting too slowly, his big axe too large for his tired hands. The knights were playing with him now, darting in and out for a quick jab before Aldarin could counterattack.

A vicious slash to his tibia pushed him down on one knee. A punishing kick to the face sent the helmet spinning from his head. Aldarin leant heavily on his axe and tried to rise, but a backhanded punch knocked him to the ground.

"So, this is what you have become in the last ten years," said the twin, his voice dripping with disdain. "While we were hiding away in the dark, fighting to survive, you grew fat and complacent."

Aldarin struggled to reply. The twin smiled again and bashed him in the mouth with the pommel of his blade.

"It is time to finish this ... brother," he said raising his sword.

"No, please!" screamed Jelaïa and threw herself across Aldarin, her hands raised in supplication.

The twin did not stop and she was hit by an excruciating pain in her left hand as the blade passed clean through the centre of her palm and punched into Aldarin's shoulder, just below his gorget.

She felt the warmth of his blood as it mingled with her own, running along her arm and into the torn flesh of her palm. A white-hot flare of light exploded behind her eye sockets as she was assailed by a myriad of jumbled images, dozens of memories that were not her own, burrowing into her brain like splinters of broken glass.

A young olive-skinned boy curled into a ball on the floor of a dirty wooden hut, an older man standing over him with a bloody birch rod.

The boy, in his teens, sitting beside an elderly woman, her face covered in pustules. Holding her hand. His blue eyes filled with tears.

A meeting in a village square. Two knights in shining silver armour flanking a stern-faced lady with flowing red hair, her left hand cut and bleeding. The boy is brought before her. One of the knights pricks the boy's fingers with a dagger. The lady takes his hand in her own. She cries out in agony.

The boy is a young man now, halfway up a sheer cliff face, fingers digging into a hairline crack no deeper than his nail. Storm clouds gather overhead. The man is pelted by hailstones and lashed by stinging winds. He grits his teeth and ignores the burning fire in the muscles of his arms and legs, pulling himself closer to the summit, inch by laborious inch.

A temple, built into the same cliff face, a marvel of inter-twining stone columns and open balconies looking out over the ocean. In one of the courtyards two men wrestle, their oiled bodies covered in sweat. One slams his elbow into his opponent's nose, snapping the bone with a crack.

A blacksmith's forge, deep underground, the fire pit carved into the rock. The man is older now, his once handsome face marred by several scars and a broken nose. The heat and steam from the forge batter his shirtless body. He is lost in concentra-tion, eyes fixed on the red-hot square of metal on the anvil before him. The hammer rises and falls and the metal takes the shape of a curved butterfly axe-head.

Faster and faster the memories came, each one a pin-prick of pain, so many she thought her head would burst.

Jelaïa screamed. Her eyes were on fire. She could see nothing except bright blue flames. It was too much to hold on to, the heat threatened to overwhelm her. She knew that if she gave in, it would consume her from the inside out.

"Let it go," came a ragged whisper from somewhere near her feet. *Aldarin.* "Let it go, my Lady."

Her vision cleared for an instant and she could make out one of the twins standing over her, his eyes wide and fearful. His brother stood a few paces behind, sword on the ground, hands clasped over his ears.

She couldn't hold on any longer. Raising her hands, she let the pent-up energy burst out of her tortured body with a piercing shriek. Blue-white flames exploded from her fin-gertips, engulfing the fallen Knights of the Twelve. Black armour liquefied. Skin and bone melted like wax. The closest knight was dead in an instant, the flesh seared from his body as the wall of fire rolled over him and crashed into his twin, setting his hair alight. He had time to cry out once in agony before the molten metal of his gorget burned through his throat and neck. He collapsed soundlessly.

The wall of flame dissipated as it reached the pier, charring the first two wooden struts and sending up great clouds of steam where it hit the water. It left behind a blackened trail of burnt reeds and two smouldering bodies.

Jelaïa stood up slowly, her head spinning. She felt a tingling in her left hand and looked down to see the wound in her palm had been burned shut, leaving a wide puckered scar of pink skin.

I just killed two people, she thought. The stench of scorched flesh hit her nostrils. She tasted bile in the back of her throat.

"You did well, my Lady," said Aldarin. He had pulled himself up onto his knees and was staring at her intently.

"Wha—" Jelaïa croaked. She cleared her throat and tried again. "What happened?"

"I will explain. But first we must deal with them."

Verona and Nidore stood at the end of the pier, untouched by the flames. The young nobleman was standing in front of Verona, shielding her body with his own, not unlike Aldarin and Jelaïa moments before. His bow was raised and nocked, the drawstring quivering from the strain.

"No closer," he said.

Jelaïa could hear the tremor in his voice. *He's afraid of me*. She flexed her fingers. The burning sensation was gone, but what would happen if she touched Aldarin again?

"We cannot let them go, my Lady," said the tall knight.

Blood oozed from his wounded neck and shoulder, and his left arm hung limply at his side, but his cold blue eyes were clear. "Verona knows what you are now. They cannot let you live. If you let them leave, they will return with others. They will track you down, wherever you go."

Jelaïa looked at the charred remains of the fallen knights. Not far behind her, above the reeds, Arelium burned. She shook her head sorrowfully.

"Enough. I have seen enough. I have watched the fields of Arelium burn, my people flee their homes in fear. I have assisted in bloody suturing and amputations. I have seen my father lose his arm. Bodies of brave men crushed, limbs twisted and broken. Farmers and traders cut down defending their lands. And I could do nothing."

"My Lady—"

"This is for me to decide, Aldarin." She brushed the ash and soot from her face, and called out to Nidore in a clear voice.

"You may go, Nidore. Take Verona and leave. You are no longer welcome in Arelium. I declare you exiled. Return here on pain of death." Nidore said nothing, only lowered his bow and grabbed Verona's hand. He turned east, aiming for the Morlakian border. The last thing Jelaïa saw was Verona looking thoughtfully at her, a strange smile on her lips. Then they were swallowed by the reeds and lost from sight.

"Aldarin?" Jelaïa asked, exhausted.

"Yes, my Lady?"

"I think it's about time you told me what in the Pit is going on."

CHAPTER 24
NEW BEGINNINGS

"Come here, Jeli, come sit on my knee. Let me tell you what my father told me. A Barony is like a human body, he always said. And to be a good Baron, you must not be the brain, for you will have advisors and aides to offer you counsel. Nor must you be the arms or legs, for you will have subjects and vassals to work and protect your land. No, to be a good Baron, you must be the beating heart. The organ that regulates all others, the centre through which the blood of the Barony flows, and without which everything would fall apart."

BARON LISTUS DEL ARELIUM, 413 AT

᪥

PRAXIS TRIED TO hide his irritation as the healer prattled on about the Baron's murder. He stood with Orkam and the pudgy doctor in the late Lord's chambers, looking down at his bloodless corpse. Listus had not been touched, his lifeless eyes rolled back in their sockets, the sheets and mattress forever coloured a crimson red.

"So, you say the assassin was hidden behind one of the curtains, yes?" the healer continued, squinting at the corner of the room over his half-moon spectacles. "He waited until it was just the two of you before revealing himself and, um, stabbing the Baron in the stomach?" He waved a hand towards the floor near the broken window where a dark, sticky mark could be clearly seen on the varnished wood.

"Yes, yes. I've told you all this twice already," snapped Praxis impatiently. The left side of his face hurt like the Pit. The self-inflicted wound was already puffy and inflamed. *Why was I so quick to cut my face?* he thought bitterly. *An injured arm would have been quite sufficient.*

The healer was looking at him expectantly and Praxis realised he had been asked a question. He forced himself to smile. "I'm sorry, healer. This whole ordeal has been quite difficult for me. What were you saying?"

"He was stabbed in the stomach, then you wrestled for the dagger. He cut your face, slit the Baron's, um, throat and dived out the window, yes?"

"I seem to remember it happening like that."

"Hmmm. Most interesting." The healer picked up the Kessrin dagger from where it lay on the bed and held it at arm's length as if loath to get too close.

Praxis exhaled with a long, slow breath. They were wasting time. He needed to consolidate power here as quickly as possible, and that meant ridding himself of the Knights of Brachyura.

"Please do elaborate, healer," he said, marvelling at the calmness of his own voice.

"Well, there are two things that I cannot explain, my Lord Steward."

Orkam had been listening silently, his face expression-less, but now he moved closer, thick eyebrows drawn close together in concentration.

"The first," the healer continued, "is the nature of the wounds themselves. As you can see, the Kessrin style of weaponry is very different from our own. We prefer straight, traditional blades. The blade of this dagger is curved, almost like a tusk. The curved blade makes cutting and slicing easier, but stabbing more difficult, as the blade must be thrust at a slight angle if the attacker wishes the tip to enter the body first." He demonstrated by moving his arm in a half-circular movement rather than in a straight stab.

"The entry wound made by a curved blade clearly differs from that made by a straight one. I would have to study the body more closely, but my preliminary hypothesis is that the wound and the blade don't match up."

"Fascinating," said Praxis through clenched teeth. "And where is all this knowledge gleaned from?"

"Oh, I have worked in several Baronies, my Lord. I have seen many injuries over the last twenty years. Even here in Arelium, we get the odd stab wound during a bar fight, or some other disagreement between visiting Kessrin."

"What was the second thing?" asked Orkam gruffly. Praxis could see the man was exhausted. He had come straight from the infirmary where Reed was still in a deep coma. The healer had not been optimistic about his chances.

"Ah, yes! The second discrepancy, as it were, is the second wound. You see, when a throat is cut, whether the victim is standing or sitting, there is what is known as arterial spray.

The carotid is severed and the pressure causes the blood to spurt from the wound. Now, if the Baron was standing by the window, why is there no spray?" He pointed to the wall behind them.

By the Pit, I have been careless! thought Praxis. *It was not meant to happen this way. Arelium should have fallen to the greylings. This bumbling excuse for a man should be dead. All these years of careful planning lost in an instant because my thrice-accursed brother knights arrived far too quickly. Damn Aldarin for summoning them here!*

"Both are good points," he heard Orkam say. "What is your opinion, Praxis?"

I must give myself time to correct this.

"I agree, something doesn't add up. Maybe I am remembering it wrong? I have not slept for a couple of days; my mind may be a bit addled." He favoured them with one of his disarming smiles that he had spent many years perfecting.

"Of course, of course," said the healer hurriedly. "I meant no offence, my Lord. If you would permit it, I will call the orderlies to move the Baron to the undercroft and have him washed and dressed in clean clothes. His wife has asked to see him, and I would like for it to be as painless as possible."

"An excellent idea," said Praxis with some relief. "Please do so. Orkam, would you accompany me to the library on the second floor? Loré and the Baroness are waiting for us there. I thought it would be the best place for some peace and quiet to discuss the future of the Barony."

Orkam nodded and, with a last glance at the dead Baron, he followed Praxis along narrow, meandering corridors to the small room that served as the Baron's library.

They entered to find Lord del Conte and the Baroness conversing in hushed tones across a circular table positioned in the centre of the room. The table was littered with books and scrolls while hundreds more filled the shelves bolted into the stone walls, some rising as high as the ceiling. On the far side, opposite the door, an immense framed map showed the Barony of Arelium and the three bordering Baronies of Kessrin, Morlak, and Da'arra. There were no windows. The only light came from a single lantern perched on a pile of books sitting on the table.

Praxis knew the old Baron loved this place; it was where he came to escape the stress and responsibilities of the outside world. It was fitting that it would be here that all his hard work would be undone.

"Lord del Conte. My Lady," he said, bowing smoothly. Orkam growled something polite behind him. The Baroness raised her head to reveal a gaunt face, her eyes red and raw from weeping.

"My dear Praxis, come join us," she said in a quavering voice. "I would speak to the last man who saw my husband alive."

"Of course, my Lady." Praxis drew up a chair. He had spent many hours throughout his tenure as steward discussing (or maybe arguing) the logistics of running the fiefdom with the Baroness. She was gifted, thoughtful, and shrewd, much more so than her late husband. He would have to tread carefully here.

Her hand traced the puckered wound on his cheek. "My poor man! That must hurt terribly. I heard you were with him at the very end. Did he die well? Did he have any last words?"

Praxis looked her in the eye. "His last thoughts were of his daughter," he said truthfully. "He asked me to keep her safe."

The Baroness's expression became hard and grim. "And what of my husband's murderer?"

"He has not yet been caught," Praxis replied, once more twisting the truth.

"I will find him, Praxis. I will devote every waking hour to tracking him down. I will not rest until he is on his knees before me, and I will force him to tell me who made him do this. And then, when I am finished, I will cut his throat myself with his own dagger." There was no hesitation in her voice, no thought behind her words, only the cold monotone of anger and grief.

"Of course, my Lady. And you are not alone. We are with you on this, until the very end." He glanced at the other two men present, who nodded swiftly in agreement.

The Baroness seemed to relax. She smiled sadly and patted his hand. "My dear Praxis, I fear I will need you now more than ever."

"Indeed, my Lady. In fact, I have brought you all here for that very same reason." He paused, gathering his thoughts. His plan hinged on these next few moments; he must choose his words judiciously.

"The enemy has struck us a great blow this day. He has taken from us the White Wolf, the one we all turned to for guidance. Listus embodied the heart and soul of Arelium and he cannot be replaced."

The others were silent, save for a small sob from the Baroness.

"Why did they perpetrate this odious act? The answer

is obvious: they hope to send us spiralling into despair and disarray, to create panic and discord among the loyal men and women of the Barony. They believe that without the Baron we are weak and helpless."

He let his words sink in. Orkam was as expressionless as always, but something smouldered deep within his eyes. Loré del Conte was listening keenly, his ruined lips pulled tight.

"We must show them that we are not divided. That we stand together. So much has been lost. The nobles have been decimated, their families have fled these lands. We four are all who are left of the Baron's inner council. It is for us to decide who will lead us now."

He licked his lips. "For me, there is no discussion needed. If we follow the chain of succession, the Baroness must succeed her husband and take his place as ruler of Arelium. We will—"

"No," said the Baroness sharply.

"My Lady?"

"Look at me, Praxis, I am not meant to rule. I am a bookkeeper, a clerk, nothing more. You are right, we must not appear weak or divided. And it is for that very reason I cannot rule in my husband's place. I will continue to balance the books and serve the Barony in my own way, but I will not sit in his chair."

One down, two to go.

"Who, then, should take the Baron's place?" he asked innocently.

Orkam was silent.

"I would put forth a name," came the ragged voice of Loré del Conte. He coughed, and dabbed at his lips with a handkerchief before continuing. "I believe that if the Baroness relinquishes her right to rule, the next in line is her daughter, Jelaïa del Arelium."

"Is she ready?" asked Praxis, and his heart did a somersault. *So close now.*

"I believe so. These last harrowing days have changed her more than anything else over recent years. She has always been intelligent, curious, and well-mannered, but lacking in self-assurance. The woman I saw in the infirmary was decisive and determined. And she would not be alone; the four of us would remain by her side to guide and advise her." Del Conte sat back with a grimace. Speaking for so long clearly caused him some discomfort. He removed a glass phial from his silk waistcoat and downed its contents, shuddering at the bitter taste.

"A herbal concoction prepared by the healer," he said when he saw Praxis looking at him. "It dulls the pain somewhat. Though I will never be able to ride a horse or fire a bow again." He tapped his bandaged left eye.

"Let us hope you will never need to," said Praxis with a smile. "I second the motion."

"As do I," agreed the Baroness softly and Praxis could see her eyes were filled with tears.

"Very well. Jelaïa del Arelium will succeed Listus del Arelium. I will have the necessary documents drawn up within the hour. Of course, we will have to wait until she returns from Kessrin to make it official. Some sort of ceremony, perhaps? The refugees will be returning to destroyed homes and burnt fields. Others will learn of the deaths of their husbands and sons. A public investiture will give them some hope for the future of the Barony."

"Even if we send word to Kessrin immediately, it may take some time for Jelaïa to return," said Orkam. "We cannot wait that long to begin rebuilding. Who will manage the current affairs of the Barony in her absence?"

"Maybe between the four of us ..." began Praxis.

"No, that would not work. I am a soldier, not a politician."

"And I am not yet ready," said Loré hoarsely.

The Baroness looked at Praxis fondly. "You have been a staunch supporter of my husband since you arrived, steward. And you have been invaluable in shaping the trade policies that have made Arelium the strong, independent state it is today. You fought to save the Baron's life on the wall, and led the counterattack that ended the threat to our town. I think my daughter would agree that you are the best person to govern the Barony in her absence."

"I am honoured, my Lady," Praxis replied, inclining his head respectfully. "I will not disappoint you." He could feel his heart pounding in his chest like the thunder of a thousand galloping horses. He had done it. Arelium was his.

"Until Jelaïa returns, of course," interjected Orkam.

"Of course, I wish for nothing more. Let us have the papers inked and sealed immediately. I will retain the title of steward and relinquish governing rights once Lady del Arelium returns from Kessrin."

And she never will return, he thought. *Verona will make sure of that. And if for some reason she fails, our allies in Kessrin will ensure Jelaïa never sees the walls of Arelium again.*

The others nodded and with that, Praxis, Knight of Zygos, Seventh of the Twelve, became ruler of Arelium.

CHAPTER 25
THE BLOOD THAT BINDS

"I know you disagree with me, Mother. You believe the Old Guard to be a dying relic from another age. But I know now that this is what I want to do. I cannot stay here, spending my days fishing. I need to feel that I am doing some good in the world. I need to make a difference. I am sorry, Mother, but my decision is made. I am leaving tomorrow."

MERAD REED, OLD GUARD, 404 AT

⁓

"I AGREE, YOU ARE owed an explanation," said Aldarin. "But it would not be wise to linger here. I must still honour the oath made to your father and take you to Kessrin."

He tried to raise his left arm and winced in pain.

"I am not able to row. We will have to let the current carry us."

He retrieved his helmet. One of the horns was gone and the left cheek-guard was cracked nearly in half. Shaking his head, he tucked his helm under one arm and limped down the pier to the rowboat.

A cormorant cried out mournfully as it banked low over the river, looking for fish. Somewhere in the valley, a faint rumbling could be heard, like thunder from an approaching storm. The reeds whispered quietly in the wind.

Jelaïa joined him and together they untied the knotted rope attaching the boat to its mooring at the end of the pier. A push from one of the oars sent the craft bobbing out into the middle of the river. It caught the current and started to drift sluggishly downstream.

Aldarin settled down at the stern and began the same old ritual of removing his armour, stacking the pieces neatly in front of him. He cursed softly as his hands slipped on the intricate clasps of his breastplate, and Jelaïa went to help him, careful not to rock the boat. Together they managed to undo the last of the leather straps.

The rear portion of the curtain wall came into view, and behind it the keep, partially obscured by smoke from the fires still burning throughout Arelium. They were too far to get a glimpse of the keep's occupants but even so, Jelaïa imagined her father looking down at them from his chambers high above. She would not be seeing him again for a long time. Thank the Twelve they had parted on good terms. The river bore them swiftly away from the walled town, and Arelium was soon lost from sight.

"The Twelve always had a connection," said Aldarin suddenly. "It was told they moved in such perfect synchrony that it was as if they could read each other's minds. And to a certain extent, that was true. They shared a higher conscious-ness, an understanding that went beyond feeling. It was in their blood. And it is in ours."

He flinched as he felt a twinge of pain from his shoulder. "You see, Jelaïa, we are not simply followers of the Twelve, but their descendants. The Twelve were among us for over a hundred years, producing much progeny. The temples were built as a means to train us, but also to contain us, to limit the dilution of the bloodline. In the early days, procreation was strictly monitored. If we wished to have children, the only choice was to find a partner among the other members of our Order. There was no other way to make sure that the blood of our founders would survive untainted from genera-tion to generation.

"After the betrayal of our brothers and the terrible war of attrition that followed, it quickly became clear that con-trolled growth was no longer feasible. We had lost too many of our number, our Order was but a shadow of its former self. The initiates were allowed to leave the temple, to search further and further afield. Most returned. Some did not, but we had neither the time nor the numbers to find out what befell them."

Jelaïa nodded in understanding. "When our blood mixed, I saw flashes, memories. I think they were your own … I saw a teenage boy and a woman grasping hands in a village square. So, you were not born in the temple? Your parents were not part of the Order?"

"No, they were not. The Twelve used the temples to house all their known descendants, but there would always be those who slipped through the cracks. Illegitimate chil-dren. Extramarital affairs. Infants hidden from the Twelve in fear or shame. Scattered throughout the nine Baronies are hundreds of men and women bearing the mark of the Twelve. I am one of them. As are you.

"The temples knew this, of course. To try and counter this anomaly, every ten years they send delegations to the Baronies for what is known as the Scrying. Our most powerful priestesses travel from village to village, mixing their blood with that of the young children. The stronger the bond, the stronger the reaction.

"For some, it is only a slight tingling sensation when the bloody palms are clasped. For others, a painful shock from fingers to shoulder. And for a select few, the strongest of them all, the link between priestess and child is not only physical but psychic; a melding of thoughts and memories that ebb and flow as the two minds mingle."

Jelaïa shivered despite the warmth of the morning sun. "So that is what happened to us. Unpleasant memories for the most part. Memories and pain."

"Indeed, the link between the two of us was exceedingly strong, stronger even than on the day of my Scrying. I cannot explain it. My mother was of the Order, my father a butcher. Brachyura's inheritance is a part of me. But you? The daughter of the Baron of Arelium? Your bloodline is well-known and can be traced back hundreds of years. You must have seen scrolls in your father's library detailing your family tree."

"I have," Jelaïa replied. "There is something my father is hiding from us. Or my mother." She massaged her throbbing temples with her knuckles. "We will need to discuss all this with them directly when I return."

She settled back against the stern of the boat, buoyed by

the rhythmic bobbing of the current. They were nearing the edge of the valley, the scorched earth and burnt fields slowly giving way to low hills and grasslands.

"So, we shared memories. That I can understand. But it's not just memories, is it? Where did those pulsing flames come from? I could feel them building up inside me, pushing against the constraints of my body until I had no other choice but to let them out or burst. Have you ever seen anything like it?"

"Once or twice. When a link is strong, it creates a massive discharge of energy. The most powerful of our Order can harness this energy and shape it to their will. It takes—" he coughed and averted his gaze. "It takes an extremely close bond, or an incredible force of will to do what you did back there."

Jelaïa laid a tentative hand on his arm. "Aldarin, you have saved my life many times today. You saved my father. You have done everything he asked of you, even if it meant abandoning others. I admire and respect you. And I am forever in your debt. I do not know what the future has in store for us, but I can think of no one better to have by my side."

"Thank you, my Lady," said the tall knight, and Jelaïa saw with surprise that he was blushing. She suppressed a smile and gave his arm a squeeze.

"So, what now?"

"The river will carry us as far as Kessrin. It sits on the cusp of the estuary, looking out over the sea. I will take you to see the Baron, as your father asked of me. Derello is his name. Derello del Kessrin. The refugees will have already arrived; he should be well appraised of the situation here. In fact, he may be mustering troops himself. After we meet him … it will be up to you and the Baron to decide what to do." Aldarin frowned. "Traditionally, when one of my Order discovers someone who has the blood of the Twelve, we must bring them back to the temple for further instruction. I would not force you to do this, but—"

"I will go," said Jelaïa immediately. Something was gnawing at her deep beneath the aching muscles and exhaustion, a hunger to feel that burning sensation course through her body once more.

"Very well," said Aldarin. "My temple is a few days ride from Kessrin. We will petition the Baron for leave to go there."

"And what about Nidore and Verona?"

"They will need time to rally and regroup. Verona will return to her Order and report on her failure. That will not be pleasant for her. But I meant what I said. All Knights of the Twelve, whatever their differences, are bound by the oaths they swear. It is one of the great pillars of our creed. If Verona pledged to end your life, she will not stop until either her oath is fulfilled … or she is dead. It is our way."

He took up one of the oars and guided the boat through a series of small rocks, carefully avoiding their jagged edges.

"It will be more difficult for her now. She has lost the element of surprise. Not only that, but she has seen what you can do."

"Aldarin, I have no real idea how I managed to kill those two knights; it just happened."

"Perhaps, my Lady, but she does not know this. She knows nothing about the level of control you have over this power. It will make her overly cautious, and give us some time to prepare."

"I … I did not want any of this, Aldarin," said Jelaïa in a quiet voice. The pain in her head was getting worse, the throbbing more insistent. The world around her seemed too bright, hurting her eyes. She blinked against the glare, sending two tears running down her cheeks. Verona, Nidore, the Knights of the Twelve, hidden family secrets. It was too much.

"Rest, my Lady," said Aldarin gently. "I will navigate the dangers of the river and bring us ashore when the light begins to fade."

"I don't know if I can sleep …"

"Listen to my voice." He cleared his throat and began to sing in a slow baritone.

> *"It was the time of man's great plight,*
> *The world was trapped in endless night,*
> *From caverns deep and tunnels black,*
> *The hordes of darkness pushed men back.*
>
> *They saw their wives and children die,*
> *Their fallen ashes filled the sky,*
> *They gathered for a final stand,*
> *As lightning scarred the ruined land."*

The soft, sorrowful song wrapped around Jelaïa like a warm winter cloak, smothering her doubts and fears. She closed her eyes, and let the ripples of the River Stahl rock her to sleep.

꘏

Reed could see the fish thrashing about in the water a few feet away, pulling hard against the hook stuck in its mouth. The fishing rod bent under the strain; the sinewy wire pulled taut as the fish fought to break free. Reed loosened the reel and let the fish run for a minute or two, before slowly reeling it in. With a grunt of effort, he flicked the end of the line out of the water and into the boat. The fish flapped aimlessly, its gills opening and closing in panic. Then it was still.

"A fine catch!" came a boisterous voice from behind him. His father clapped him on the shoulder, hard enough to send the boat rocking. "A big fat redbreast! We'll eat well tonight. Put it in the bucket with the others."

Reed removed the hook and slipped the fish into the hide bucket at the boat's prow, trying to avoid looking into the creature's glazed eyes. A cool breeze sent small waves undulating across the lake, and rustled the leaves of the ancient oak trees on the far shore. The sun was dipping low over the horizon, lengthening the shadows.

"Time to head back," said Reed's father. He took the wooden pole in his calloused hands and effortlessly steered the punt back to dry land. He jumped lithely out of the boat, his heavy boots landing in the sod with an earthy thump.

"Come on, Son," he said impatiently. Swinging the two fishing rods over one broad shoulder, the bucket of fish in his other hand, he started back up the path to Jaelem and the wattle hut they called home. Reed made to follow, but only managed a few steps before he bent over, wracked with pain.

"I can't breathe," he tried to say. It came out as a muffled sob. He coughed and tasted the tang of blood in his mouth.

"Father …" The older man didn't hear him, his long strides taking him further and further away. Reed struggled to his feet and stumbled after him, trying to ignore the burning sensation in his chest. He passed through the stockade into the village. He was finding it hard to breathe, the air leaving his lungs in short, explosive bursts.

With a final cry of effort, he pushed open the door of the hut and staggered inside. His mother sat on a stool by the fire pit, stirring the contents of a steaming pot hanging over the dancing flames. Her husband was crouched next to her, gutting the first of the silvery fish with a filleting knife. They both looked up in surprise as he entered, coughing.

"Merad, my boy, whatever is the matter?" his mother asked, her brow creased with worry. "You look awful!"

Reed was too exhausted to reply. He took a few laborious steps forwards and collapsed next to her.

"Do not worry, my child. You are here now. You will be safe with me." Reed felt his mother's cool hand on his brow. The cold spread from his forehead down through his upper body like a cascade of icy water, quenching the burning fire in his chest and invigorating his tired limbs. He laughed out loud as his strength returned to him.

"What's so funny?" said his father suspiciously, one hand stuck in the fish's innards. "Are you playing tricks on us, boy?"

"No, Father, just a bit tired, that's all."

"Aye, well we still need your help so you're not off the hook yet. And speaking of hooks, add some more wood to the fire there, then come help me clean these fish."

The three of them set about preparing the evening meal, and soon the hut was filled with the tantalising smell of fish stew and vegetables. Little was said, but it was enough for Reed to simply spend time with the two people he loved more than anything.

The stew tasted as good as it smelled. Reed drained the last few drops from his pewter bowl and started industriously wiping the sides with a crust of bread. His father was checking the fishing tackle for nicks and scratches, while his mother was hunched close to the fire repairing one of his old tunics.

"How long will you be staying with us, Merad?" she asked suddenly. She had put her sewing down and was fixing him with her soft green eyes. Reed felt a sudden chill. The flames flickered madly, casting deep shadows on the wall of the hut. To Reed it seemed as if the shadows took form: a crumbling stone wall, a ruined gatehouse, a tall, muscled monster with a thick neck and beady yellow eyes. He blinked and the strange shapes disappeared.

"I don't know, Mother," he heard himself say.

"Do you not want to go back?"

"Back?"

"Yes, back to Arelium, back to your friends."

The fire roared and the images returned. A tanned man with a double-bladed axe and piercing blue eyes. A bald guard captain with a boxer's face and a permanent scowl. A young woman with long black hair, voluptuous lips, and a night-blue riding cloak. A man, naked, tied to a stake, his belly cut open, weeping tears of blood.

"I ... I don't know," he repeated. His chest was beginning to hurt again. "I think I would rather stay here. There is nothing for me back there, only pain."

"I see," his mother said. She seemed disappointed.

"And what of those who gave their lives to save yours, my boy?" interjected his father quietly. "What about them, will you not honour their sacrifice?"

An off-key, muffled tune entered his head. '*I saw a girl at the country fair …*' He had a flash of a ruddy-faced man in red livery throwing himself at a grey-skinned beast only to be tossed aside, his skull caved in.

"Ferris …" he whispered. The pain in his chest was unbearable. He closed his eyes and clenched his fists, willing for it to subside. "I don't think I can, it's too hard, much too hard."

A hand tousled his hair. He looked up to see his father smiling down at him, eyes twinkling. "The easiest way is rarely the best way, Son. It is through times of hardship and strife that we learn who we really are. And you stood firm when others would have faltered. You brought people together when others would have driven them apart. I am proud of you, Merad."

"Father …"

"Go on, lad. We'll be here waiting for you when the time is right."

Agony exploded in his chest and he cried out, a terrible drawn-out scream of grief, pain, and loss.

And opened his eyes.

EPILOGUE
THE PIT

"You know what we have to do. And you know why we have to leave. All of this is our fault."

BRACHYURA, FOURTH OF THE TWELVE, 123 AT

❧

THE PIT WAS silent.

The greylings that had been spawned from its depths would not return here. Scattered by the Knights of Brachyura, they would flee to the caves and forests of Arelium to hide and heal.

The bodies of the Old Guard lay where they had fallen, mutilated by the enemy, picked apart by the carrion birds that still circled overhead. More towers had collapsed into the darkness, and a huge section of the eastern wall had given way, leaving a ragged hole of fallen masonry.

Close to the eastern barracks, a group of bodies was

clustered around a tattered gold and crimson standard fluttering in the breeze. The final stand of the Old Guard. They
had acquitted themselves well, holding the enemy back for
over two hours before falling to overwhelming numbers. The
last to die was Captain Yusifel, his officer's sabre buried deep
in a thresher's belly, a faint smile on his lips.

The sun was rising timidly over the plains and the first
rays of questing sunlight hit the embroidered red and golden
thread. For an instant, the standard burst to life, its former
glory restored in the soft light of dawn.

Something moved at the edge of the Pit, a dark, monstrous shape. One massive, dirt-stained hand appeared,
scrabbling for purchase. A second hand followed the first,
latching on to a piece of ruined wall. With a grunt of effort,
the figure pulled itself up and over the edge of the Pit and lay
panting on the hard earth. It was naked, its huge muscular
body covered in scars. Its masculine features were completely
hairless, the dark skin of its face and head clean and smooth.

The thing stood up and took in its surroundings. It was
almost human in appearance, but for the eyes. There was no
iris, no whiteness, no colour, only two pitch-black globes of
darkness as bottomless as the Pit itself. Something flickered
deep within those eyes, a great and ancient intelligence.

Disappointment creased its prodigious brow. It strode
over to one of the fallen towers and ran a hand over a piece
of cracked stone, frowning.

A dozen great strides took the creature from the edge
of the Pit to the sorry remains of the Old Guard, heaped
around their banner. The thing crouched down beside
the fallen body of Captain Yusifel and carefully closed the

corpse's open eyes. It stayed there a moment, head bowed in silence.

Rising to its feet, it took down the standard and wrapped it around its burly frame like a cloak.

"I have been absent too long," it said in a deep, cavernous voice that seemed to shake the earth itself. "There is much to be done."

And pulling his makeshift cloak close to his body, Brachyura, Fourth of the Twelve, turned his back on the Pit and began the long journey towards the rising sun and new beginnings.

End of Book One

APPENDIX

A BRIEF TIMELINE OF EVENTS

The calendar used throughout the nine Baronies is intrinsically linked to the Twelve, with the year of their first appearance among the scattered tribes termed 'The Arrival of the Twelve' (AT). The events described here take place in the year 426 AT.

❧

-58 AT	A series of natural disasters, later known as the Calamity, wreaks havoc on the land and its inhabitants
00 AT	The first appearance of the Twelve among the human tribes
13 AT	An innumerable host of greylings is defeated in the Battle of the Northern Plains
14 AT	The Twelve separate, dispersing to aid the

	surviving tribes and eliminate the remaining greylings
33 AT	The Old Guard is established, sworn to defend the Pits
35 AT	The Council of Baronies is created by the Twelve, who gradually concede rulership of the nine provinces to the tribal leaders
41 AT	The first founding of the great temples of the Twelve, and their Orders
122 AT	The battle of Hellin Pass
123 AT	The last recorded appearance of one of the Twelve
365 AT	Birth of Listus del Arelium
370 AT	Birth of Loré del Conte
386 AT	Birth of Merad Reed
404 AT	Merad Reed joins the Old Guard
404 AT	Birth of Nidore del Conte
405 AT	Birth of Jelaïa del Arelium
416 AT	Praxis begins his tenure as steward to Baron Listus
418 AT	Auguste Fernshaw is elected Mayor of Jaelem
426 AT	Greylings appear in great numbers at the Southern Pit

Printed in Great Britain
by Amazon